Valley of Murder

A Bekbourg County Novel

by Sherrie Rutherford

VENCIN Publishing

Venice, Florida

Bekbourg County Novels

Valley of Murder

Pathos of Murder

Bookends of Murder

This book is a work of fiction. Names, characters, places, events, incidents, business entities, and organizations are the product of the author's imagination or are used fictitiously. Any resemblance to actual places, organizations, business entities, events, incidents, or persons, living or dead, is entirely coincidental.

ISBN: 978-1-7345992-2-0

Library of Congress Control Number: 2020919540

VenCin Publishing

Venice, Florida

This book is dedicated to Kelsie

Acknowledgments

To Larry, my love, who walks alongside me and whose commitment in the Bekbourg County series has been an inspiration. His ever-present patience and belief in me are pillars to my writing and have made the Bekbourg County novels come to life.

To Gary Steinhilber and Pat Goetz for their support and ever-ready willingness to share their time as readers.

To family and friends for the outpouring of support and enthusiasm for the Bekbourg County mysteries.

To Clarissa Thomasson, my editor, for her guidance.

To Cross Ink, Corp., for cover design.

To all the people who read my novels.

Valley of Murder

A Bekbourg County Novel

By Sherrie Rutherford

Chapter 1

Sean Neumann was enjoying his morning coffee and reading the newspaper. When Cheryl Seton, his fiancé, walked in, Buddy, their Lab, jumped up from beside Sean and scampered over to welcome his mistress and get a hug and head pat. Cheryl walked up behind Sean, put her arms around his neck and kissed his cheek. "Anything worth reading in that paper?"

"Yeah. Some pretty good articles. The editorial is darn good. I might want to stop by and tell that beautiful editor what a great job she's doing."

Cheryl giggled and planted another kiss on his cheek before pouring coffee and refreshing his. She sat down across from him, smiling. "Well, while you're doing that, I might just pay that sexy new sheriff a visit."

Sean laid down the paper, laughing. "Who would have thought—a sheriff and a news lady?"

Cheryl had been an investigative reporter for a respected newspaper, the *Cleveland Presenter*, when a murder of five family members drew her back to Bekbourg, the small town she grew up in, to investigate. She also used her time to clear her grandfather's name in a twenty-year-old murder. During those investigations, she and Sean had met. As deputy, he was investigating a drug operation as well as the murder case. Cheryl and Sean became engaged, and she continued working for the Cleveland newspaper, commuting between Bekbourg located in southeast Ohio, and Cleveland. A golden opportunity arose when the owners of the *Bekbourg Tribune* decided to retire and sell the newspaper. Cheryl had recently become the new owner.

The evening before, Cheryl and Sean had attended an election-night celebration for his victory as Sheriff of Bekbourg County. She asked, "How was your run this morning?"

"It was fine. I've got a route down where I can get my five miles that includes some hills, so it's a good work-out. Oh, I'm going to the high school gym after work this evening to work on the machines with Coach."

"Do you think he'll continue to do that once he retires?"

"I hope so." Sean took a sip of coffee. "I was just reading about the election results. People around the county are waking up to new leadership. The hold that Randall and Jeff Thompson had with that one-party system is gone."

"Thank goodness. The Reform Party candidates were certainly happy last night—a sweep. Bri is the new city mayor, and she has two new city council members to serve along with her, Boone Carter and Sally Chambers. Although he squeaked by, Noel defeated Riley Barns for County Commissioner. After what happened with Pauline Kaufmann, it was a foregone conclusion that Jason Worley would become the new County Treasurer."

"I guess since no one was running against me, there was no mystery about who the new sheriff would be," Sean deadpanned.

Cheryl's laughter filled the room. "Sweetie, even if they had, you would have won hands-down. Solver of murders and drug operations—and on top of that, people still think of you as the celebrity quarterback who won the state high school championship."

Sean had returned to Bekbourg after serving twenty years in the Marines where he was an investigator for a special crime unit. His military career ended when he sustained grievous injuries in a fatal explosion that killed his team member and best friend, Clint Neely. Pain from shrapnel imbedded in his body was a frequent intruder, but the hellish nightmares had subsided. His exercise regimen helped alleviate the stiffness his body still suffered. After his retirement from the military two years ago, he returned to his roots to heal. His best friend from high school, Mike Adams, the sheriff, offered him a job as deputy. Sean became interim sheriff when Mike resigned under a cloud and after nearly perishing from gunshot wounds received in an ambush.

Sean smiled, "So, what have you got on your agenda today?"

She stood, poured more coffee and unwrapped a package of scones that Bri had baked at her B&B. "Mmm. The cinnamon scones are my favorite—so scrumptious. I sure hope Bri keeps baking now that she's mayor. Anyway, to answer your question, I thank my lucky stars every day that Milton is here. He is handling the day-to-day stories and working with the reporters. That has freed me up to start drilling down on the business side of things. This morning, I have meetings with some of our advertisers. We are fortunate that the business community is supportive of our newspaper. This afternoon, I'm meeting with Drew, our CPA, to discuss where we stand on our short-term and long-term assets and liabilities."

"Listen to you," Sean grinned. "You sound just like a CEO."

Her eyes sparkled. "It's been a steep learning curve. Every day, I learn more. Sometimes, the more I learn, the more I feel I don't know, but I'm starting to feel comfortable. I owe all that to Milton." Milton Grant had been a well-known reporter around Cleveland until a heart attack forced him to slow down. During his last few years at the *Cleveland Presenter*, he assisted its reporters with his wealth of experience and contacts. He mentored Cheryl during her early years at the newspaper, during which time they developed a special father-daughter bond. When she mentioned her interest in buying the *Tribune*, he told her of his plans to retire from the *Cleveland Presenter* and offered to relocate and assist her where needed.

As she set the scone down in front of Sean, he said, "I knew it wouldn't take long for you to learn the business side, honey. Once you set your mind to something, you give it your all."

Cheryl smiled, "Well, the fact that Mattie and Seth, the previous owners, were willing to work with me has certainly made the transition easier. During my spare time, which hasn't been much, I'm going through the archived files. You wouldn't believe how many boxes there are. Fortunately, there is an inventory for a large portion, but that is mostly by year. The really old records are in bad shape and have not been catalogued. To do a good job for the town, I need to know the history. I've also got some ideas for new columns for the newspaper. It's just going to take time." She took a bite. "So, what does your day look like?"

"I've been talking with all the deputies and staff, reviewing everyone and their abilities. Now that I have officially been elected sheriff, I want to move forward with reorganizing the department the way I want it. There's no need to wait until I am sworn in. I'm going to make some personnel changes. Some people may not like it, but I need to do it my way. I've already brought in two new deputies. One is Arlo Lopez, who I hired on a permanent basis when another deputy took a job in a nearby city. The other one is Sydney Johnson. I hired Syd on a temporary basis a few months ago. She was fresh out of the academy, and she is going to be a good officer. I am going to let Kyle Ramsey go and hire her on a permanent basis to fill the slot left by Kyle. I'm hoping that Mack Harris will retire. That would be best, because I'm making a change involving him. He's talked about retiring, but I don't know what he is going to do."

"Are you thinking about letting him go?"

"No, I don't want to force him out. He was Mike's assistant. He's been with the department longer than anyone. My plan is to name Alex Ogle as my assistant, which will be a demotion for Mack."

"The good news is that you've been the interim sheriff for a while, so you know what you want to do."

He sipped his coffee. "That's true. By the way, I'm also having lunch with Mike today."

Cheryl started gathering their dishes. "You'll like catching up with him. I'm glad he and Geri put off moving to Montana. We need to get together with them for dinner real soon. With all the hoopla last night at the election-night party, I didn't get much of a chance to talk to Geri. Well, Sweetie, I better finish getting ready."

"I'll take Buddy for another quick walk," Sean said as he was getting Buddy's leash. Buddy heard the word, "walk," and was prancing in place waging his thick tail when Sean got to the door.

Dealing with personnel matters was one of Sean's least favorite things. He figured it best to get it done, so he set up the meetings first thing.

Mack Harris had been with the department for over thirty years. He joined the department after his return from four years in the Army. Sean never understood why Mike had appointed him as his assistant. Maybe there wasn't a better candidate at the time. Certainly, neither Kyle Ramsey nor Ben Clark would have been in the running. Mack's reports and performance were mediocre at best, and initiative was lacking.

"Mack, I guess you know when there is a new sheriff, there is some reshuffling. I wanted to talk to you about it. I know it's none of my business, but I've heard you've been talking about retirement."

"I've been thinking about it, and I'm eligible, but it's not something I'm able to do at this time. I need to keep working to build up my pension further. I don't want to be a rent-a-cop."

"Will you be eligible for social security?" asked Sean. Mack's lined face and silver-streaked hair hinted at his age in contrast to his physically-fit body.

"Yeah, but not for a few more years. My wife didn't work enough to qualify."

"I understand, Mack, but there are going to be changes with the force. You've been the assistant sheriff, but I have to change that. Alex is going to be the assistant sheriff. You will be a deputy. I know you will take a hit in your pay, but unfortunately, that's the way I have to do it."

Mack's placid demeanor revealed nothing as he responded, "I wish you would reconsider that.

I've got more experience than all the other deputies combined."

"My decision is made, Mack."

Mack looked out the window and finally returned to look at Sean. "I know you've been relying on Alex a lot, but I didn't see this coming. Anyhow, you're the sheriff. If that's what you want, that's the way it will be, but I can't retire."

"I'm glad you are still going to be a member of my department. We'll talk down the road once I get all this in place."

Relieved there wasn't more pushback, Sean watched Mack leave his office.

Sean's next meeting was with Kyle Ramsey, who had started about twenty-six years ago—about two years before Mike Adams, the previous sheriff. Kyle and Ben Clark had hired on about the same time. Sean remembered Ben and Kyle patrolling together before he joined the Marines. Ben was a corrupt deputy and had been killed while attempting to kill Sean and Cheryl. Not only was Kyle tainted with his association with Ben, his performance was subpar. Sean had a small number of deputies, and they were spread thin enough with their duties. He could no longer afford to have them cover for Kyle.

"Hi, Kyle. Have a seat." Everything about Kyle was quiet—his voice, walk and movements. Even when he sat down in the chair, it didn't squeak.

"Sure, Sheriff."

"You know, whenever a new sheriff takes office, there are changes. He or she needs to organize the department the way they think it will work best."

Although Kyle didn't comment, he started chewing on his cuticle.

"Kyle, I'm going to get to the point. You patrolled with Ben Clark for years. You've admitted that you suspected Ben of illicit things but never reported them. I suspect that if we go back through the files, we will find specific instances of actions by Ben that should have been reported by you but weren't. I can't have my officers looking the other way when things happen that shouldn't. I'm prepared to let you resign, and if you do, I've received authorization to offer you a severance. But if you won't resign, your service with the department will be terminated."

"You're firing me if I don't resign?"

"That's correct. You are no longer needed in the department. Your inactions over the years make it impossible for you to continue to work here."

Looking at Sean's desk, Kyle sat for a minute. "I don't think that's fair. I couldn't help what Ben did. Besides, it wasn't on me to do anything 'bout it. Seems to me it was the sheriff's job to say somethin' to Ben. I never heard that Mike said anythin' to him 'til he fired him for hittin' Earlene. He never asked me anythin' 'bout Ben."

"The fact remains, Kyle, you and Ben patrolled together. You were with him when he did a lot of his dirty work. I remember the night that the Burkhardt house burned over twenty years ago when Ben was harassing me. You went along with him and pulled your gun on me. I don't believe for one second that you didn't know that Ben was crossing the line time and time again over the years. You never reported him. That's unacceptable, and like I said, I won't have deputies in my department who don't follow the law."

Kyle looked at his hands for a while and then said, "Well, I don't see how's I have much of a choice. I don't want to be fired."

"Okay, Kyle." Sean handed him the papers. "You will need to sign this. It is your resignation, and in exchange, it spells out your severance terms and your severance payment, which will give you time to look for something else."

Kyle paused, looking lost as he took the papers. His hand trembled as he picked up the pen, "Where do I sign?"

After scribbling his name, he laid down the pen and didn't meet Sean's eyes. Sean said, "I need your badge and gun, Kyle."

Those words dragged Kyle from his stupor. He stood and removed his badge and unbuckled his holster belt. He laid them on Sean's desk and turned and left.

Sean leaned back in his chair thinking how Kyle should probably have never been hired into the department. He realized that it was sometimes hard to find qualified officers in small counties. There had been turnover in the short time that Sean had been with the department. The lure of higher pay by the larger Ohio cites was a draw for officers from the smaller jurisdictions. Except for Mack, Sean's deputies were young. Darrell Logan was next in seniority, and he had just turned thirty. Despite their youthfulness, Sean was proud of his team. Alex, his assistant, was green around the ears, but he was smart, had good instinct, and was a dedicated professional. Sean had recently hired Arlo Lopez to replace a deputy who took a position in Cincinnati. His experience in the military gave him the maturity and skills that were needed. Sydney Johnson was a recent graduate from the state police academy—at the top of her class—who was resourceful and had the makings of a good law enforcement officer. With the exception of Mack, Sean was pleased with his department.

Chapter 2

Mike Adams pulled into the parking lot and smiled at the old sign sitting on top of the front entrance—"Frau's Diner" painted in faded black letters with a picture of an iron skillet—which brought back fond memories. Frau's had been serving country dishes for breakfast, lunch and dinner along with German choices since it opened in the late 1940's. How many times had he slipped a coin in the old jukebox when he and Geri were dating? Matt and Miranda, their children, had enjoyed coming here as young children and still as teenagers. Although Bekbourg had more dining options today, teenagers still frequented Frau's and listened to tunes playing from the same jukebox while sitting in the timeless plastic-covered seats on tarnished stainless-steel bar stools and chair frames. Even the laminate tabletops were unchanged.

Another reason for his cheerfulness was having lunch with his best friend, Sean. Throughout his life, he had loved Sean like a brother. They were inseparable growing up, and their combination on the football teams from Youth Football through high school was dreaded by the opposing teams. All the years that Sean was serving in the military, Mike felt a void knowing that Sean had moved on. His spirits were buoyed when Sean returned to

Bekbourg, and even though their relationship was strained before Mike retired, Mike's admiration for Sean never wavered. Of course, Geri and his children were the most important people in his life, but Sean was his best friend and would always be tucked into that special place in his heart.

A couple of men walking out of the front door tugged Mike's attention. He was surprised to see Zeke Pinkston and a younger man. *What are they doing over here?*

When Mike got out of his truck, Zeke spotted him. Zeke said something to the younger man, who continued toward the driver's side of the pickup truck. Zeke ambled over to Mike. "Well, Sheriff. It's been a while."

"Zeke. I guess you know that I'm no longer the sheriff here."

"Yeah, I know'd it. I guess it's hard to break some habits. How you been?"

"Fine, Zeke. I'm a little surprised to see you in town."

"Well, I had some business to attend to. Also, I still have family here. Suzy and that baby."

"Mmm. Well, I'm meeting someone inside."

"Say, I'm glad I saw you. Saved me tryin' to find you. You know, Sheriff, we still got some business 'tween us."

Mike paused. "I don't know what you mean, Zeke."

"You should. My boys are dead, Sheriff. That's not somethin' I take lightly."

Mike wasn't going to cower. He laughed. "You're not threatening me are you, Zeke?"

Zeke's laid-back appearance vanished. "Call it what you want, Sheriff. You know'd this business don't stop with us."

"What the hell is that supposed to mean?"

"You know'd damn well what it means."

Mike's 6'5" physique took on more proportion as his expression turned to granite. "Hear me on this, Zeke. Don't you *ever* threaten my family or me again and don't think I am going to forget this conversation. Now, I'm late."

Zeke scowled as Mike walked away.

Zeke lived in the next county over, Tapsaw County. Several years ago, his two sons, Tony and Ray Pinkston, and a nephew had moved from Tapsaw to Bekbourg and expanded their illegal drug activities from a marijuana business into selling meth. What they didn't realize was that a cartel was operating a nationwide drug ring, and Bekbourg was one of its processing and distribution operations. The cartel did not want federal or state authorities sniffing around, and the Pinkston operation became a source of angst for the cartel. In a move to quell possible federal and state attention to the area, the Pinkston drug operation came to a violent end. Five of Zeke's relatives were killed, including his two sons and nephew along with Zeke's grandson and daughter-in-law. The only survivors were his granddaughter, Suzy Pinkston, who was working night-shift, and her infant daughter, whom the killers spared. Mike Adams had been the sheriff at the time and close friends with a county commissioner, who along with one of Mike's deputies, were responsible for the deaths.

Zeke harbored deep resentment against Mike who he felt was involved even though Mike had nothing to do with it. Zeke's streak for vengeance ran deep, and in his twisted way of thinking, he cast a wide net in deciding when the score was settled.

Mike and Zeke had a couple of run-ins after the Pinkston murders, and Mike knew of Zeke's anger. As he entered Frau's, Mike figured he was caught in Zeke's vindictive net, and that wasn't something to take lightly. There was no way in hell he was going to let Zeke threaten his family.

When Zeke got in the truck and slammed the door, his twenty-four year old son, Rocky, asked, "What happened, Pap?"

Zeke fumed, "You know'd what happened. He blew me off."

Looking where Mike had entered Frau's, Rocky sneered, "That SOB. I'd like to knock that smirk right after his face." Rocky looked posed to open the door.

"Easy, Son. This isn't the time or place. We'll take care of matters in due time."

"Hell, we've waited long enough. It's time to set things straight."

"Look, Son. We've been waiting to get this property matter settled and get Suzy back home. These things take time. I delivered the message. Now he'll be thinkin' 'bout it. We'll handle things on our terms. I want to drive by and see Suzy, and then we'll drive over to Koot's and put down our other marker."

Mike saw Sean waiting at a table. "Hey, Mike," Sean said as they shook hands and sat down.

Sean's coffee cup was half full. "Sorry I'm running late. I had a meeting that ran longer than I thought it would."

"That's okay. Anita said the special is a burger."

"Well, that suits me."

About that time, Anita came up and took their orders and poured coffee. After talking about the election party the night before, Sean inquired, "So, Geri told Cheryl that you're busy with something."

Mike took a drink. "Yeah, and it's good. That's what I wanted to talk to you about. You know that Geri really likes working for Mary's foundation. It was me that was pushing to move. I wanted a change. We would be closer to the kids, but they have their own lives. Matt is really serious about a girl now," Mike grinned. "Geri's hoping that she's going to hear wedding bells." They both laughed. "Anyway, a few weeks ago, C.P. approached me about an opportunity, and well, that's what I'm doing. That's where I was before I met you here. We were talking about the progress I've already made."

This surprised Sean. "What is it you're doing?"

C.P. Traylor had grown up in Bekbourg but left decades ago. During his time away, he had risen to the executive ranks in a major railroad company and then took a high level position in a federal agency. Having accomplished his objectives in Washington, D.C., he had recently returned to Bekbourg with other plans.

"C.P. doesn't want it to get out, but I know he won't mind me telling you." Anita brought their lunches. Mike continued, "C.P. doesn't want this to become common knowledge because he's not sure he's going to go through with it. That's why he hired me. You know that old spur line that runs up toward Lake Peatmont?"

"Sure. That's the route I run every morning—up the road there. The tracks aren't always visible from the road."

"That's right. It's been abandoned for years and is about twenty-five miles long," Mike grinned. "I know this because of my work. It's as much as a quarter of a mile off the road in some places. The track runs along the creek. Anyway, C.P. is thinking about buying that spur line."

"Really? What's he planning to do with it?"

"Sean, again, don't mention any of this, but you know C.P. is a wheeler-dealer. I think he's got big plans around here. I don't know what they are, but I got that feeling when I talked to him about this job. Part of what he wants to do is turn that spur line into a scenic railroad for tourists. It may be a few years off, but it would be great for the town if it works out. It runs up near the lake and state park. If the state moves forward with the lodge and meeting facilities, it could bring tourists into town, and people in town would have easy transportation to get there. It fits right into what people have been working toward on growing the tourism business here."

"Wow! That would be something. So, what's your part in all this?"

"C.P. flew over the area but couldn't tell much about the track's condition with the overgrowth of trees and everything. He walked the part near the downtown, about a half-mile, which he thought looked pretty good. He wants me to walk the entire length of the line and give him a report on the condition of the track to see if it's worth messing with. I'm taking pictures from different angles and recording my observations. There are specific things I'm supposed to be looking for. I asked him why he wanted to hire me to do this, and he said that since I was a policeman, I was used to closely documenting things."

Mike was grinning. Sean laughed, "That makes sense to me." They laughed some more.

"It's a good time of the year to be doing this with the leaves off the trees. Once I complete my analysis, if he thinks it's worth pursuing, he'll hire an engineering firm to go in and do a real feasibility and cost study."

"Mike, this is great. How far along are you?"

"I've already done about five miles. It's a slow go, but I enjoy doing it." Mike smiled and shook his head. "When I told Geri about it, the first thing she brought up was the 'Ghost of Mader Valley.'"

Sean arched his eyebrows. "That's right. I had forgotten that. Is that still a thing around here?"

"Oh, sure is. Teenagers especially like to go up there and camp out and scare each other. Around Halloween, it's really a draw. A couple of times, it got out of hand with kids getting drunk, but for the most part, it's just something harmless for them to do."

Sean remembered their past, "Yeah, I remember we all went up there during our junior year. Couldn't go around Halloween because of football."

"That's right. Say, I guess you're going to Coach's retirement party Saturday night?" Mike asked Sean.

"Wouldn't miss it. You're going, aren't you?"

"Yes. It's a big thing. He's an institution around here. Won those state championships and sent many players into the college ranks."

Sean smiled, "Yep. He is really going to be missed. How do you think Buster Collins will do as the new coach?"

Mike frowned, "You know, Sean, he's been Coach Jackson's assistant the longest. That's probably why the School Board gave him the job, but between you and me, I'm just not sure he's up to the task."

"Mmm. I wondered. I've lost touch being gone from here so long. I hope he turns out to be good. I'd hate to see the program go downhill. It's got such a storied history." Sean changed the subject. "You'll never believe who was in here before you got here."

"Let me guess. Zeke Pinkston."

"So you saw him?"

"Yep. Did he say anything to you?" Mike asked.

"Not really. He came up to the table with—I guess it was a son who was with him. He just spoke and left. Why? Did he talk to you?"

"Yeah, he saw me and came over. You know his type, Sean. Can't let go of things. He said something about us still having business."

"What did he mean by that?" Sean frowned.

"I guess for some crazy reason, he blames me for his family being killed."

"That's asinine, Mike. Ben and Jeff were responsible for their deaths. I drove over and told Zeke that Ben and Jeff had killed them and that they were dead. There's no reason for him to be holding a grudge against you."

"Well, I think he does, but I don't know what he wants. He seems to be spending a lot of time in Bekbourg. I saw him and his son pass by the other day when I was putting something in my truck on Mader Road. It'd be interesting to know what business they had up there."

Sean asked, "Did he say what he was doing here?"

"Said he had some business and also mentioned wanting to see Suzy and her baby."

"Mmm." Sean wondered what Zeke was up to. It wasn't like him to be hanging around Bekbourg.

Rose Waters had just finished giving her two-year-old great granddaughter, Tootsie Pinkston, a snack when she heard someone knocking on the front door. She pulled back the edge of the curtain before opening the door. *What in tarnation is he doing here?* The last person she wanted to see was her deceased daughter's father-in-law, Zeke Pinkston. She opened the door to face Zeke through the locked screen door.

"Didn't expect to see you, Zeke. What are you doin' here?" *Probably nothing good,* she thought to herself. She harbored hard feelings toward Zeke. She knew he wasn't directly responsible for the deaths of her daughter and grandson, but she couldn't absolve him either.

Zeke's overalls stretched tight around his broad mid-section. Dark bristly eyebrows and a wide misshaped nose failed to divert from his calculating, dark chocolate-colored eyes. Rose knew Zeke could change his stripes depending on who he was talking to. He could wear friendly about as well as anyone, but beneath that façade was a ruthless man who bided his time until he got what he wanted.

"I was in town and stopped by to see my great grandbaby and also talk to Suzy 'bout somethin'."

"Well, Suzy ain't here. She's working day-shift now at the hospital, and I keep the baby."

"Well then, maybe I'll just spend a little time with the baby and talk to Suzy another time."

"No. You ain't going to see the baby now. You don't just stop by here like this. If you want to see her, you need to first get Suzy's permission, and I've not heard that she gave it."

"Well now, Rose, there's no reason for you to be so ornery. I don't think Suzy would mind that I see my great granddaughter for a few minutes.

After all, I've come all this way. I also got these papers I need to give Suzy."

For the first time, Rose noticed him holding a large envelope. She also glimpsed Rocky leaning against a pickup truck looking their way.

"Well, I ain't openin' the door. You can just put those papers on the table there on the porch, Zeke. I suggest you leave me be. I ain't goin' to let you see the baby without Suzy tellin' me it's okay."

"I'm disappointed, Rose. There ain't no reason for there to be hard feelin's between us. After all, we both lost our kids. Those that killed them are dead, but there's some others that need to pay for what happen'd to our kin. I want you to know'd that I ain't forgot."

"I don't know what you're talkin' about, Zeke, but you best be on your way."

"Too bad you feel that way, Rose. I'm entitled to see that baby, and I'm goin' to. I already told Suzy that she and little Tootsie need to move over with us. I'll get her a trailer for them to live in. They're family. They need to be over with me."

He dropped the envelope on the table and uttered over his shoulder as he shuffled away, "Be sure Suzy sees those papers."

Eddie Thompson lounged at his usual corner table in Koot's thinking, *What am I going to do with this joint?* His brother, Randall Thompson, had followed in their father's footsteps and controlled the law and political forces around Bekbourg until his death almost two years ago. Eddie's grandfather, a bootlegger, had controlled the area's liquor supply during prohibition. He opened Koot's to maintain his control when Ohio legalized liquor. Times changed, but Koot's remained in operation. The family enterprise eventually passed to Randall, but long before that, Eddie had left Bekbourg. Now, nearly forty years later and after the death of his brother Randall, he had returned to claim the family properties. This old bar for sure wasn't much to look at, but a fairly stable clientele of bikers and local rednecks still quenched their thirsts here.

Business was slow during early afternoons, and he was enjoying his beer when he saw the door swing open. Eddie focused on the old man whose overalls stretched over his girth. He wasn't a tall man, and he waddled as though plagued by hip problems. Despite his decrepit condition, he had purpose as he approached the bar. The bartender too had watched the old man and waited to see his intent. The man spoke, and as Clay continued to wipe the glasses, he nodded in Eddie's direction.

Eddie watched as the man neared. When he made it to Eddie's table, he asked, "Mind if I sit down here?"

Eddie stared at him, "Sure. Sit down. What's your business?"

"So, you're Eddie Thompson, Randall's brother?"

"Yep. The devil's own."

The old man looked around, "See you've done pretty good for yourself since he's gone."

Eddie took a drink from his beer, "If you call this rat trap good, I guess I have."

"That makes you Jeff Thompson's uncle." When Eddie didn't reply, Zeke continued, "Well, we've got some unfinished business."

Eddie narrowed his eyes. He knew the code. "Stop right there. Don't give me any of that shit. I've been gone from here a long time. Didn't know a thing about it. What's your name anyway?"

"Zeke Pinkston."

Eddie gave no indication of recognition, even though he knew what had happened between the Pinkstons and Jeff, Eddie's nephew.

"Not the way I see it," Zeke persisted.

"I owe you nothing, old man. Both of us lost over this. Your boys knew the rules when they invaded our county."

Zeke was not used to anyone standing up to him.

"Well, there's a reckoning to be had here. I just wanted to tell you that this business ain't finished. Us Pinkstons take care of our own."

Eddie was not going to back down one bit. "Don't think you can come over here like this, Pinkston. It works both ways. You've lost a lot, and I've lost a lot."

"All I can tell you, Thompson, is to watch your back."

Eddie's eyes hardened. If Zeke thought that Eddie would quake at his threats, Eddie's next words proved that Eddie knew a lot more than he let on and that he wasn't to be taken lightly. "You know, you're a lot more vulnerable than me. I know about you. You've got a young son that I assume you want to take over your business. Just keep that in mind. I can take care of myself. I'm quite familiar with hunting. In Colorado, it's a way of life. Also, I got a lot of friends in militia groups, so if you want to start a war, Pinkston, I'll finish it for you."

They sized up each other, neither flinching. Eddie watched as Pinkston rose from the table and shuffled through the door. Clay walked over, "Everything okay, Boss?"

Looking toward where Zeke had exited, Eddie quipped, "Yep."

Zeke's twenty-four-year old son, Rocky Pinkston, was waiting in the truck for him.

"Let's go," Zeke instructed as he closed the door.

"What happened, Pap?"

"I put down the marker, Son—just like I did with that sheriff. Now I need to think 'bout things."

"What was your impression of the man?"

Zeke looked out the front window. "We damn sure don't want to underestimate him."

"Well, if you want me to take care of him, I will."

"I'll take care of things if need be, Son. I have to think 'bout this. Our business here ain't over, but I've got to think, and I don't want you takin' things into your hands like you tend to do. You hear me?" Zeke looked at Rocky to see that he was paying attention. "I know'd how you like to take things into your own hands. Hell, you nearly killed that kid in high school. If Elmer hadn't been the sheriff and handled things, you might have ended up in the pen."

"I ain't afraid to shoot the SOB, and no one would find out." Rocky muttered as he turned the ignition.

Zeke slapped his hand on the dashboard, "I mean it, Rocky. That man's not to be fooled with unless I say. You got that?" Zeke demanded. "I don't give a damn that you're a crack shot!"

"Pap, you taught me that we take care of our own."

Zeke roared. "I know'd what I taught you, but I got to think this through. I done lost enough kin. I want your word on this, Rocky." Zeke paused, then continued with introspection, "Besides, sometimes men like Eddie Thompson can be useful. One thing I learned was that he's not out for revenge for his brother and nephew's deaths. That could be a startin' point for a partnership down the road."

Rocky glanced at Zeke wondering what he had in mind.

Chapter 3

"Hey Boss," Kim Connor cheerfully greeted Sean. The first time Sean walked into the precinct and saw Kim, he recognized her value to the department. She knew most everyone in the county and had a talent with people. Many times when people called, she would ask about their kids, grandkids, parents, or other relations. She efficiently and competently handled the department's administrative matters. Another valued trait was her upbeat and positive attitude, which lifted the morale around the place.

"Hi, Kim. Anything I should know about?" Sean was returning from a vandalism call at the high school.

"Well, Irma Ritter called. She was driving by John Pawley's place. They both live in the upper end of Mader Valley before you come to the end where Poplar Road crosses. Mr. Pawley's place is on the left, and Mrs. Ritter's place is just past his. There's a hill between, which is on Mr. Pawley's property. It's a good thing they can't see each other from their places." He was accustomed to Kim's drawn-out way of telling things. Sean patiently listened, because on more than one occasion, a pertinent kernel was mixed in with her narrative. "Mr. Pawley owns about twenty acres, and Irma probably owns five acres. With it being as cold as it is, I'm a little surprised John wasn't freezing his you-know-whats off." Sean's eyebrow arched, *I bet this is a doozy.*

"As Irma drove by, she saw John walking around the front perimeter of his property with army boots, a belt with bullets all around it, and a toboggan. He also had a gun strapped on his shoulder. Thing is, that's all he had on. She said he was 'naked as a jaybird.' Her two young granddaughters saw him. She said she couldn't stop them from talking about what they saw. I asked her what kind of gun. She said it was a huge one, but she didn't get a good look, because she was trying not to run off the road. It's not the first time she's called in. She may not have called it in this time except her grandkids were in the car. She said it wasn't everyday someone saw something like that."

Sean agreed, "No, I guess not. Anything I should know about him before I pay him a visit?"

Kim chuckled, "I guess with a story like that, you'd wonder about the man. He's a little strange, but I wouldn't be too concerned, Chief, about going over there. He's more bark than bite."

"Okay, that's good to know." Sean looked around to make sure no one could overhear. "Say, Kim. Now that I'm officially the sheriff, there's going to be some changes. I hope that you're planning to stay on."

Merriment danced in her eyes. "You bet. I love it here. I'm thankful every day that I walk through that door."

"Good to hear. I feel the same way about you working here. Well, I'd better go and talk to Pawley. I don't want someone wrecking seeing all that."

Kim's laughter followed him through the door.

Sean drove up a gravel drive. The welded wire fence resembled a truncated prison barrier as it paralleled the road and sharply turned, stretching towards the back of the property. The old wood farm house had seen better days. Located in the front yard was a cinder-block well house and garden beds dispensed by the autumn season. A weathered rainwater storage tank blighted the house's back corner with galvanized gutters extending from piping along the roof's edge. Beyond the cistern a rickety chicken coop hinted at a food source. Firewood was stacked on the front porch and under a tin-covered frame held up by log posts. Smoke puffed from the stone chimney.

A large beast came barreling around the corner of the house barking ferociously, stopped only by the fence as it lunged toward the cruiser. The large mastiff galloped back and forth along the fence near Sean's cruiser, its bark hitting bass octaves. *This is going to be interesting. I sure hope Kim was right.*

Sean got out of the cruiser and stood, surveying the house. A man appeared from around the corner where the dog had emerged. Despite the chill in the air, he was shirtless. He still had on his holster and gun, and resting on one shoulder was an M16 and on the other, an axe. Sean suspected the M16 was the "huge" gun earlier seen by Irma Ritter. Beneath his toboggan, long hair was pulled back in a ponytail. A long, scraggly beard obscured most of his facial features. Sean was relieved that he now wore pants.

As he walked toward Sean, Pawley yelled a command, and the dog immediately stopped barking and sat but never took his eyes off Sean.

"Mr. Pawley, I'm Sean Neumann. I'm the sheriff in Bekbourg County." Sean observed the mountain man. His eyes were clear and alert.

"Hi, Sheriff. I've heard about you. I've even heard about your state championship."

"Unfortunately, Mr. Pawley, that's not what I'm here to talk to you about."

"What can I do for you, Sheriff?"

The dog still hadn't taken his eyes off Sean, and drool was dripping from its massive jaws.

"We received a phone call this morning, a complaint that accuses you of indecent exposure. The person who called this in would normally have just ignored it, but she had her young granddaughters with her when she passed your place today. I'm sure you know what I'm talking about."

"Yes, Sheriff, I do, but it's my right to walk around my property any way I see fit. I have the right to patrol the perimeter any time I want. If people drive by, they don't have to look. It's my property."

"Well, Mr. Pawley, that's not exactly the way the law reads. If you would like for me to cite you and drag you into court, I can do that, but if we can come to an understanding, maybe we can avoid this in the future."

"That nosey old biddy. She comes by here all the time. I didn't know she had anyone in the car with her. I'm sure not going to stop patrolling my property just because she drives by here."

"Well, Mr. Pawley, that's not what I wanted to hear from you."

"I know, Sheriff, and I don't want to get in trouble with the law. The next time I hear her clunker coming, I'll hide behind a bush. Of course, she always slows down when she drives by—must be something she's interested in seeing. If she looks hard enough, she might still see me behind the bush."

"Another thing, Mr. Pawley. What about that gun you were carrying. She said it was a huge gun and that scared her more than anything else she saw."

"Well, haven't you ever heard about the Second Amendment, Sheriff? I legally own this gun. It's my right to patrol my property like I did when I was on sentry duty."

"Well, an M16 rifle is a little bit of an overkill here in Bekbourg County—even if it is legal. You shouldn't be scaring little kids and old ladies."

"That was never my intent, Sheriff. Like I said, the next time I hear that old rattle trap coming by, I'll hide behind a bush."

"Mr. Pawley, I hope you don't catch pneumonia, but if you do, just call 911, and we'll be out here to pick you up."

"Mighty kind of you, Sheriff. Oh, by the way, I heard you served in the Gulf."

"Yeah, I put in twenty years with the Marines."

"Next time, you can call me 'John.'"

Sean looked at him, "Well, I guess you can call me 'Sean' the next time we meet."

"Thank you, Sheriff. Semper Fi."

Chapter 4

Recently released from prison, Cooper Townsend was tired of living with his mother, but without an income, he couldn't move out. He had applied for jobs, but so far, nothing had come through. The managers he talked to were humoring him until they could get him out of their offices. One owner even told him not to ever "show his ass" again at his place of business. He was now sitting in the manager's office at the box department store, Shopper's Pavilion, interviewing for a stocking position. The manager hadn't called him in for an interview, but Cooper didn't want to wait until a rejection letter arrived in the mailbox.

"Mr. Townsend, I'm sorry, but we don't have a position for you. I wish I could help, but I can't. Now, I have something else that I need to do, so if you'll excuse me."

"It's because I served time, isn't it? I never had any record before that, and I never should have been convicted. I was framed. You see from my application, I worked four years at Koot's. No problems."

"I'm sorry, Mr. Townsend, but I really must ask that you leave. I have a busy schedule, and like I said, we don't have a position for you."

Cooper pushed his long, lanky body out of the chair with a huff and walked out. After he was gone, the manager's assistant walked in. "I'm sorry about that. He wouldn't take 'no' for an answer. I didn't know what to do. He said he wanted to talk to you about a job, and I just didn't know whether to alert security or what."

"I know it caught you off guard. I don't think he'll be back. I made clear that we're not interested in hiring him. I'm going to tell security about him. If he comes back to the offices again, we need to have him escorted out. No way would I hire him. Rumor has it he was skimming off the Thompsons when he worked at their bar. Not only does that show he's not trustworthy, it shows he's stupid."

Cooper was cussing a streak when he got to his truck. He nearly tore the door off its hinges as he slung it open. He slammed both hands hard on the steering week—hard enough to hear it creak under the force. "Damnit! This shit ain't right. That damn lawyer. Too bad he's dead. Hell, even the Thompsons are dead. They know I wasn't guilty. That damn sheriff, he ain't done shit for me in clearing my record. Ain't nobody goin' to hire me with a record. He's got to get off his ass and do somethin'. He owes me. Hell, they all do."

Having been a bartender at Knucklepin's for years, Percy knew all the regulars, so when Kyle sat down at the bar, Percy asked, "How's it going, Deputy?"

"Can't call me 'deputy' no more," he sulked.

"Huh? What do you mean?"

"I quit. Say, give me two boilermakers." He'd taken a liking to the beer and shot of whiskey, which had been Ben's favored drink.

When Percy sat the drinks in front of Kyle, he asked, "How come you quit? Did something happen?"

"Naw. Just don't think Sean wanted me there no more. So, I quit."

Another customer motioned for a refill, so Percy moved on. Kyle brooded. He couldn't have stopped Ben. Ben was going to do what he wanted to. It wasn't his place anyhow. It was the sheriff's place. *Had Sheriff Adams done his job, I wouldn't be in this fix. Ben would have been fired, and I would still have my job.*

Brooke sat down beside him. "Hi, Sugar. Sorry I'm late. Momma called me as I was getting in the car. She asked me to run by the drive-through and get her something to eat. I dropped it off."

She noticed Kyle seemed well into his drinking, which surprised her. Although they hadn't been dating that long, she didn't know him to drink a lot.

"Say, Sugar. Let's get a table and order some wings. I'm hungry, and I bet you are."

"If you want to."

She held his hand and noticed he was unsteady. The waitress came up, and Brooke ordered a soft drink and some chicken wings. Kyle ordered another boilermaker.

"You doing, okay, Babe?" She was concerned.

"Might as well tell you. I ain't no longer a deputy," he slurred.

"Huh?"

"I resigned."

Brooke's eyes widened. "How come?"

The waitress brought their order. Brooke took a bite, but Kyle opted for another sip. He put the glass down. "I didn't fit in that SOB's new department." By now, Kyle's eyes were glassy, and some of his words were slurring more. "Ben was right."

She didn't know who Ben was, but she didn't ask. Instead, "What was he right about, Sugar?"

"That Mike was weak. That he let that SOB just walk in and take over."

"You mean the old sheriff?"

"Yep." Kyle took another drink, and she picked up another wing. "Mike didn't have a backbone, you see. When Sean started as a deputy, he rolled over Mike. Took over and pushed Ben off some cases. I know'd Ben did wrong by Erlene, but even she said he was upset 'bout what Sean did to get him pushed off the cases."

Kyle finished off the drink and motioned for the waitress to bring him a beer.

"You ought to try the wings. They're good tonight," Brooke encouraged.

While he waited for the beer, he ate one. Brooke was having a difficult time following Kyle. She wasn't familiar with the events. She had recently moved back to Bekbourg and met him when he came into the Shopper's Pavilion, the large box store in Bekbourg. He came through her line. He was wearing his uniform, and they talked while she rang up his order. He stopped by a couple more times and went through her line before he asked if she wanted to meet sometime for something to eat.

He took a long slurp from the beer. She had decided that he was in no condition to drive home. "So, this Mike let the new sheriff named Sean call the shots?"

"About ever' thing. Even caused Ben to get fired. Ben could be tough, but he'd nev'r done what he did if he'd not been pushed to it."

"What'd he do?"

"He shot Mike and was goin' to kill Sean, but he got shot instead. Too bad Ben didn't take care of 'em both when he had his chance."

Brooke put down her soft drink. "Sug, you don't mean that."

Kyle looked at her, his head tilting. "Yep, ev'r word."

"Hey, Ma Maw. I'm home," Suzy yelled as she walked in the back door. Tootsie came toddling through the house, squealing with delight, "Mommy home, Mommy home." Suzy swept her up in a big hug, "Hi, Baby Doll."

Rose was right behind Tootsie. "Hi, honey. How was your day?"

"Fine. One of the girls was off sick today, so we all had to share her workload, but it was fine."

Suzy Pinkston was on the cleaning staff at the local hospital. She and Tootsie had been living with her parents, Tony and Ruby Pinkston, and brother, Aaron, when they were killed one night while she was working night shift. Thankfully, the killers didn't harm little Tootsie, who was seven months old at the time. She and Tootsie then moved in with Rose, her maternal grandmother. During her pregnancy with Tootsie, Suzy had broken off her relationship with Tootsie's father, Pete Vance, because she was afraid that her dad might kill him. Once her parents died, she and Pete renewed their relationship and were now engaged. He wanted to be able to make a life for them, so he joined the Army to get training. He had two more years to serve, and then they were going to get married. They weren't sure yet if he was going to stay in the military or if he was going to move back to Bekbourg. Either way, they would be together as a family.

"How was Tootsie today?"

"Oh, she was just as sweet as ever. She and I played with her dolls and watched some videos."

Suzy was surprised. "You didn't go on your walk to the park today?" Rose walked over to the kitchen sink and picked up some dishes. "Did something happen, Ma Maw?"

"Well, I might as well tell you. Your grandpa stopped by."

"Whaaat?" Suzy shrieked, startling Tootsie. Suzy tried to calm her despite her alarm. "Shhhh, Baby. It's okay." She sat down with Tootsie on her lap and started rocking back and forth. Tootsie calmed and snuggled into the warmth of her mother's embrace.

"Yeah. Zeke wanted to see you and Tootsie. I told him you were at work, and that I wasn't going to let him see the baby without your permission. He also left some papers on the porch. I wouldn't let him in the house."

"What's in the papers?"

"He didn't say, and I didn't open 'em. I'll bring them in here." As she was carrying them into the kitchen, she added, "That's why I didn't take the baby to the park today. I was afraid he might still be hangin' around. That younger son of his was drivin' their truck."

Reaching for Tootsie, Rose said, "Tootsie, Baby. Let me put you in your chair. Dinner's ready."

While Rose was getting Tootsie settled, Suzy opened the envelope. She didn't know what it all meant, but she frowned. Rose knew something was up. "What's it about, Suzy?"

"It looks like Grandpa is making a claim on Momma and Daddy's property?"

"What? That ain't right. That property belongs to you with both of 'em dead and Aaron dead too."

When Tony and Ruby Pinkston, and Suzy's brother, were murdered nearly two years ago, Suzy was the heir to their hundred acres in Bekbourg County where they lived. Since Tony and his brothers had operated an illegal drug operation on the property, the property had been tied up as the federal government decided on claims to the property. When the federal government dropped any claim to the property, Suzy thought she would be the rightful owner through the inheritance laws.

Suzy laid the papers in her lap and sighed. “What am I goin’ to do, Ma Maw? I don’t have any money to hire a lawyer. If Pete decides he doesn’t want to make a career in the Army, we were planning on farming that land.”

Tootsie sensed the tension and started to fuss. Rose turned to put some food out for her while Suzy got up to sooth her. Rose knew that Suzy was upset. “Don’t fret ’bout this, Baby Doll. I’m goin’ to call Cheryl. She was over here last week for a visit, and we caught up. She bought the *Tribune*. She’ll know what we should do.”

Chapter 5

It was Loretta Harris's day to host the weekly bridge game. Being married to a deputy, Mack Harris, gave her a sense of gravitas that she relished crowing about, especially since he was the longest-serving lawman in Bekbourg. She was convinced that the women liked when it was her turn to host, and she thought she knew the reasons. They admired, maybe envied, the way she had her house decorated, and she always used her good china to serve them coffee and desserts.

Last week, June had surprised them with an "English tea" theme for their bridge game, which didn't sit well because she thought June was again trying to upstage her. Although she played along with the other women in praising June's efforts, she thought she could have done better. After all, June used her everyday coffee cups for the occasion and granular sugar. Loretta knew she could top that. Because she didn't want the women to know where she bought the cups, she drove to Columbus and bought four china cups and saucers and a matching creamer and sugar bowl. Because she wanted everything to match, she purchased matching dessert plates to serve the lemon squares that her friends just loved. While she was at it, she thought that she might as well buy a new dress for the occasion, and *Oh, wouldn't it be the perfect touch if she wore one of those little hats she had seen English women wear on the old TV shows when they drank tea?* She just had to have those sugar cubes she had also seen on TV served with afternoon tea, so she stopped by a grocery store in Columbus. The ladies would be impressed. She didn't think the Shopper's Pavilion carried them. *Sugar cubes would be so much classier than what June served.*

She hoped that neither June nor any of the other ladies made it a habit to have themes at their bridge games. For some reason, Mack had not been putting money into their banking account like he used to. It was running low. She had used a credit card for these purchases. But, if June or anyone pulled that theme stunt again, she already had ideas for Valentine's Day and St. Patrick's Day. *Oh! I've got a great idea—how about a Kentucky Derby party around the first of May? Ha! I'll surprise everyone with a Derby hat. June would never do something like that.*

That afternoon, she preened as the women showered her with compliments, assuring them that it "was nothing at all," and she thought "a fascinator would be something fun and the perfect touch."

The bright sun and the warm November day led Cheryl and Rose to sit on the front porch watching Tootsie play on her play set.

"Rose, what would prompt Zeke to do this now?"

"Well, the only thing I can figure is that he somehow found out about the Feds. Last week, Suzy got a letter from the judge that the Feds had dropped all claims to the property that Tony and Ruby owned. You know, that's where Tony and his brother, Ray, and their cousin, Victor, were makin' meth and growing marijuana. I guess they just didn't want it for some reason or didn't have a claim. I don't know. I just know that with the Feds not confiscatin' it, Suzy, being the only heir, was to get it. Now, Zeke is claimin' he should get it. Suzy ain't got no money for a lawyer. I've got a little, but not near enough to help."

"Do you know why Zeke wants the property? I thought he owned a big place over in Tapsaw County."

"He does. You probably know this, but he left Bekbourg when he was young and moved over there. His brother, Earl, ended up with the family property here. When Earl and his wife, Ruth, could no longer take care of the place, they decided to sell so they could move into town. That was about six years ago. Earl asked Zeke if he wanted to buy it. Zeke didn't want it, but Tony did. Tony and Ruby bought it and moved there. They lived there for 'bout four years before they were murdered. Cheryl, I don't have a good feelin' about this. Zeke's not a good man. It's going to be hard on Suzy. But there's something else that's got me worried."

"What's that?" Rose was a feisty woman. Cheryl thought it would take a lot for Rose to admit she was worried about something.

"I don't know if Zeke really wants the property or if he's got something else in mind. See, he's been calling here and talking to Suzy. He wants her and the baby to move over there. He's offered to get her a trailer where she and little Tootsie can live. Suzy told him several times that she doesn't want to do that. She and Pete are going to get married when he finishes up his service. She likes working at the hospital. They're making plans. From what Suzy told me, Zeke don't want no part of hearing that. He's controlling. He wants her and the baby over there. I think maybe he is trying to pull this stunt on the property to try and force her to move over there."

"Well, the first thing Suzy needs to do is to get an attorney to help her. My good friend, Annalee Carter's, husband is an attorney. I'll talk with him and see what he has to say. I'll get back to you, but Rose, try not to worry about this. It'll work out."

The following afternoon, Cheryl met with Boone Carter and explained the situation. "Boone, I hate this is happening to them. They have had so much to deal with, and the thing is, they don't have money to hire an attorney. Do you have any thoughts on what Suzy can do?"

"Business really picked up for us over the last year, so we hired a young attorney to help out.

I've been impressed with her, and this case will be a good one for her to work on. I'll oversee her work, of course."

"But I still don't know if Suzy can afford her."

Boone was reassuring. "Don't worry about that, Cheryl. We will work with Suzy. We do pro bono work for some cases. Have Suzy call me. We'll set up a time, and she can bring in the papers that Mr. Pinkston brought her. It the meantime, the attorney that will be assisting on this is Morgan Ramirez. I'll ask Morgan to go to the courthouse and check on what's happening with the property and the probate."

Chapter 6

Chester Paul Traylor, nicknamed C.P., was born in the early 40's in Bekbourg, Ohio. He played football on the Schriever High School team. Out of high school, he started work on the MV&O Railroad in Bekbourg, and after a year, he transferred to Cincinnati where he could continue working for the railroad while attending college. Given that he was a part-time college student, he was drafted and assigned to the U. S. Army Railroad Corp. He was stationed in Fort Eustis in Virginia and served two years, gaining wide experience in the operation of a railroad and discovered he liked running things and was good at it. After completing his military service, he worked part-time as a yard clerk with the railroad while completing his college degree.

In the mid 60's, C.P. was promoted to yard master in Cincinnati. A year later, he joined a trainee program. Because most of the manager ranks at the railroad were older, the railroad executives recognized the need to start recruiting younger people for management positions. The top brass started taking note of C.P.'s abilities. He was on the fast track, moving to different cities and learning the entire rail system and about the industry itself. When the MV&O merged with another railroad to form the OMVX Railroad

Corporation, he was selected to lead the merger team. It was during this time he earned a reputation of being a hard-nosed manager who identified redundancies, inefficient practices, and ways to reduce costs. Once the merger was finalized, he was promoted to an executive position within the newly merged company to head the merger implementation. During this time, he streamlined and closed redundant rail lines and operations. Facilities were closed in many cities and towns, and jobs were cut. It was not easy to merge railroads, but C.P. was relentless. In the end, the leadership praised his accomplishments in maximizing synergies and squeezing out excess costs.

From early on, C.P.'s objective was to become the Chief Executive Officer. With the CEO approaching retirement, it was C.P.'s time if it was going to happen. However, when C.P. realized that OMVX's Board of Directors intended to move in a different direction, C.P. put out feelers about other opportunities. A colleague was a cabinet secretary and offered C.P. a high-ranking position with the Department of Transportation in Washington, D.C. His friend's objective was to deregulate and implement competitive policies, and C.P.'s expertise was invaluable in trying to restructure railroad regulations as well as bringing new ideas to other transportation-related industries. After a while, C.P. decided that he didn't particularly care for bureaucracy and wanted to get back into the railroad industry. He knew that the WVB&C lease was nearing its expiration, and he thought the OMVX would likely exercise its right to terminate the lease. So, he returned to Bekbourg with the next phase of his professional life planned.

Since recently relocating to his home town, C.P. had embraced Bekbourg and become active in the community. One of his goals was to support Mary Zimmstein in her foundation, Bekbourg Gives, founded to support domestic violence victims, drug prevention programs, and those suffering from drug addictions. Dusty Shaw had worked for the OMVX railroad going on thirty years. During his early life, he battled a drug addiction but had been clean for many years. His significant other, Carla Huber, was an elementary school teacher. Together, they worked with addicts and ran meetings at a local church for people fighting addictions. Because their program was a beneficiary of Mary's foundation, C.P. wanted to meet with them and discuss their program. He knew that Sean was friends with Dusty and Carla and asked him to arrange a dinner.

Dusty and Carla already had a table at Frau's when C.P. and Sean joined them. Sean introduced C.P. After they were seated, Dusty said, "It's liver and onions night."

Dusty was one of the colorful characters that Sean and his grandpa had exchanged stories about. Right out of high school, Sean's grandpa got him a job on the railroad, but after two years Sean decided to join the Marines. His grandpa used to say that "Dusty would talk to a brick wall if no one was around." Dusty was the type who couldn't sit still, so his upper body was always bobbing from his foot bouncing up and down.

"Just so you know, this is on me tonight," C.P. said.

"You know I remember when you were superintendent in Cincinnati," Dusty said. "I had just hired in. Everyone told me you were good to work under."

"That's good to hear. I tried to be fair to everyone in the terminal."

Anita, the waitress, took a liver and onions order from everyone.

"You started up here in Bekbourg as a clerk, didn't you?" asked Dusty.

"Yes, things were a lot different back then. We had to check each car manually and compare them to the serial numbers on the bills."

"You know it's been a while since we had to carry the bills with us. It's done by computer now, but you would know that, wouldn't you?"

"Yes, I was there. I was part of the change. The industry underwent a rapid change in those days. With the advent of technology, equipment and processes were modernized."

Anita delivered their food. After everyone was set, C.P. said, "Carla, Dusty and I could talk all night about the railroad, but let's talk about the good work that you and Dusty have been doing with your program. Mary is grateful for the service you provide here in Bekbourg to those suffering addictions and is glad her foundation can support you. I believe in the work that she is doing and wanted to meet you both and understand more about your program."

Carla smiled, "Dusty and I appreciate the support of Mary's foundation. Before she created the foundation, people mostly heard about our meetings through word of mouth. Since we started receiving funds from her, we've been able to print and distribute brochures and even run notices in the *Tribune*. Word is getting around, and we've seen an increase in the attendance. These problems have been simmering under the surface for so long. Money from Mary's foundation is making a difference."

Over dinner, they discussed Dusty and Carla's program. C.P. asked Dusty, "Do you plan to continue doing this work now that you work out of Cincinnati? Will you have time?"

Dusty looked surprised. When C.P. saw Dusty's surprise, he volunteered, "I still have my connections with the railroad."

"Well, it's interesting you would ask me that. We just got a notice offering us a buyout, all the men on the Ohio Division here. It sounds like they are getting ready to shut the whole operation down. There are only two or three trains a week that come through anyway, and those don't have much business to speak of."

C.P. nodded. "Yes, I know that."

"So, I'm thinking seriously of taking this payoff, but I still have too many years before I'm old enough to get my pension."

"Yeah, I see what you mean, but you never know, Dusty. This payoff may close one door, but other doors might open. You have a good life here in Bekbourg, and you're very important to a lot of people. I know how overwhelming railroad life can be."

They heard Chaw's mouthing before he and Mule Head got to the table. Chaw was a conductor nearing retirement. Everyone called him "Chaw," because he was always chewing tobacco. Mule Head had been injured on the job a few years ago and retired on disability. Chaw was a little tipsy in his celebratory mood. He zeroed in on Dusty, "Hey, Dusty, have I told you I'm getting a bonus to retire?"

Dusty shook his head, "Yeah, Chaw, you've mentioned it a few times."

Chaw suddenly noticed that others were sitting at the table, "Oh, hi, Sean, Carla."

Mule Head spoke, "Hi. How're you all doing?" Tilting his head toward Chaw, "You know, some guys can fall in a pile of shit and come out smelling like a rose."

They all laughed.

Sean spoke, "Chaw, Mule Head, I want you to meet somebody. This is C.P. Traylor."

Chaw squinted, "Hell, I know you. I remember when you were just a punk kid starting here in the yard. You messed up my bills and delayed my train."

"I only did that once. I just got them out of order," C.P. easily replied.

Chaw huffed, "That proves one damn thing, that's the kind of people they make into big shots on the railroad." Laughter erupted from everyone.

"Why don't you join us?" C.P. offered. "It's on me, so order dinner if you want to. The liver and onions are good."

Chaw and Mule Head scooted over a table and they arranged the chairs, and Anita came over and took their orders.

"I'm happy to see you're back in town," Chaw said, "but it's kind of sad what's happening to the railroad. We think they're going to shut down our railroad. It's been around since the 1840's."

"Why do you say that?" asked C.P.

"It's obvious. Hardly any business anymore, but I'm checking out."

C.P. looked at Chaw but didn't comment.

Dusty was absently tapping his spoon on the table, "I think you're right, Chaw. That's why I'm considering the payoff. I just don't see me living in Cincinnati."

C.P. wanted to get to know these railroaders so he opened a topic that he knew they would enjoy. "You know, I had a lot of good times back in my early days on the railroad. There were a lot of characters in those days."

On a roll, Chaw hooted, "Oh hell yeah! Do you remember old Miles Turpin?"

C.P. nodded as the name registered, "Sure, yeah. I remember him. I worked with him a lot."

"You remember that story about him and his wife?" Chaw asked.

Mule Head snorted, "Hell, there were a lot of stories about them. Which one are you talking about?"

"The one about the bridge."

C.P. was enjoying the banter. He knew these railroaders were the heart and soul of the operations. It was hard work, and much of it done in unfavorable weather conditions.

Dusty chuckled, "Mule Head, they had heads harder than yours."

"That's the damn truth," Chaw grinned. "I never knew anyone quite like them." He looked at C.P. "See, they lived up in a hollow, and a creek ran through the front of their property. An old rickety bridge made of logs crossed that creek on their driveway down near the road. Right after you crossed over the bridge there was a dog-leg curve, so you couldn't see around the turn.

"One morning, Miles' wife was running late to work. She was driving like a bat out of hell coming down that drive. Miles was comin' home from workin' the night shift, because the train was late getting in. The sun was just starting to come up, so neither of them had their headlights on. She had just bought a new Chevy Impala, and Miles had a new Ford pickup." Chaw and Mule Head were laughing.

"Miles was coming across that bridge. There weren't any rails, of course. He saw her come flying around that curve and forgot he was on the bridge and swerved right off the side. About a two-foot drop. She couldn't stop in time and plowed right into his truck as it was going off the side. They got in a screamin' match—each blamin' the other. Glad they didn't have guns with them. They might have shot each other."

Everyone at the table was laughing and shaking their heads. C.P. said, "That's some story. I never heard that one, but I remember Miles."

"Does everyone know about Skeeter McIntosh's land boat?" asked Mule Head.

Both Dusty and Chaw started laughing. Chaw said, "C.P., you probably remember him. He was a yard master. He had a'73 Sedan DeVille Cadillac. He gave that darn thing ten coats of paint. He loved that car. There's no way in hell he'd get rid of it. That's where he lived when his old lady kicked him out of the house."

The railroaders were on a roll. Bursts of laughter from their table sometimes drew looks from customers.

"Everyone remember Banana Nose?" asked Mule Head.

Chaw chimed in. "He retired before you started, Sean. Did your grandpa ever mention him?"

"He might have. Who was he?"

"He was a brakeman."

"How did he get that nickname?"

They were chuckling. "It's because of all the damn bananas he ate. Every day, he'd bring an entire bunch of bananas and eat the whole blasted bunch. Every day! That's why the men called him 'Banana Nose.'"

"C.P., was that your nickname on the railroad?" Dusty asked.

"Yes, at least that's what everyone called me to my face." They all hooted.

"It stuck, even away from the railroad."

Dusty was curious, "What was your nickname, Sean?"

"Well, like C.P., everyone just called me by my initials, S.N."

Chaw spoke up, "Yeah, initials were often used for nicknames 'cause they were used on the time slips. Only some of us more illustrious men got special nicknames."

"Yeah, and there were lots of those," Dusty snorted.

Chaw huffed, "Jules Leroux was an exception. Everybody just calls him 'Jules.'"

"Why doesn't he have a nickname?" Sean asked.

Dusty piped up, "That's 'cause the men couldn't agree on one. For a while, they called him 'Lefty' because he was left-handed. Rolled off the tongue when you said, 'Lefty Leroux,' but then other men thought 'Red' was better because of his red hair. Because he was always using disinfectant in the engine cab, 'Skunk' stuck for a while." Dusty was holding up his fingers as he counted each name. "Since he struts around always acting like a lady's man, 'Peacock' attached for a while, but it didn't roll off the tongue very well. After a while, everyone settled on 'Jules.' One of those few times the men couldn't agree on a nickname. Actually, with him being a Frenchman, I always thought that 'Jules' was just as good as anything."

They all were laughing, enjoying the good time.

Chapter 7

Sean was working on a report when Kim buzzed him. "Sheriff, Cooper Townsend would like to talk to you."

Sean thought, *now what?* "Tell him I'll be out in a minute."

Cooper was slouched in one of the chairs with his arms crossed over his chest when Sean walked into the waiting area. "Cooper, what can I do for you?"

Cooper sat up straight as he said, "I need to talk to you."

"Okay, let's go into the conference room."

After they sat, Sean asked, "What's on your mind?"

Cooper blurted out, "You ain't done what you told me you'd do. You ain't cleared my name. I can't get a job being an ex-con. That's what's on my mind."

"First, Cooper, I never told you that I could clear your record. I told you I would look into it, and I did. Ben Clark was the arresting officer, and he is dead, so I cannot ask him. The Thompsons are dead, so I can't ask them if they framed you."

Cooper interrupted, "Well, you could have asked that drunk of a lawyer I had, but he's dead, too."

"Look, Cooper. I did ask him. He told me that when he was representing you, he asked you who framed you and you wouldn't tell him. His hands were tied on the defense. You had your chance to help yourself when he was representing you, and you didn't do it. You're not helping yourself by blaming other people, Cooper. There's not anything else I can do without more evidence. If you really want to do something about this, you need to hire yourself a lawyer. I looked at the files, and there's not anything I can do about this."

"That's the problem, I was set up."

"Well, unfortunately, Cooper, even if you were set up, Ben is dead, Randall and Jeff Thompson are dead, and there is nothing we can do about that."

"Well, Mike's not dead. He knows the truth. He was part of the set up. I heard what he said at the trial. It was all lies."

"Listen, Cooper, Mike doesn't lie. What he said at the trial was in the evidence. I am getting tired of you coming in here and accusing everyone. You're hardly sin-free over this with your history of skimming at Koot's."

"You can't prove that, and that's not why I went to jail. I went to jail on the drug charge, and Mike could clear my name if he would just tell the truth. I used to believe in you, Sheriff—that you could be trusted, but I believe you're part of the set up. I don't think you've looked at this at all."

"Cooper, I'm fed up with your attitude. I don't like people being set up, but frankly, you brought all this on yourself. There is nothing I can do. There is nothing Mike can do. If you have nothing further, there's the door."

"Well, Sheriff Adams is still alive. He knows the truth." Cooper lunged out of the chair, knocking it backward. "You don't want to help me. You're just like Sheriff Adams was, sitting on his ass while a deputy set me up." He stormed out. As he passed by Kim, he uttered, "this ain't over."

Since passing the Bar, Morgan Ramirez's career as an attorney had consisted mostly of legal research, drafting legal memos, working on discovery matters, drafting and revising pleadings and filing documents with the courts. On occasion, she accompanied a senior attorney to a meeting with a client, but in those meetings, her role had been to take notes and manage the files in the event the lead attorney needed something. Since graduating law school two years ago, she had worked for a large law firm in Columbus. With its several partners and associates, she figured it would be a few years before she got any hands-on experience in presenting çases in courtroom settings and negotiating on behalf of her clients to settle litigation.

She heard that a law firm in Bekbourg was looking for a young associate. There were three partners and two paralegals. She applied, and Boone Carter, the managing partner, offered her the job as junior attorney. She had been with the firm about six months when Boone asked her to represent Suzy Pinkston.

She was excited that Boone was going to let her take the lead on Suzy's case. Suzy would be her first official client. She and Boone discussed the case, and together, they outlined the steps and research that were needed. Morgan located all the articles she could find about the Pinkston murders that had happened nearly two years ago. Tony Pinkston and his wife, Ruby, lived on about a hundred acres that they bought from Tony's uncle and his wife. They moved from Tapsaw County to the property with Suzy and her younger brother, Aaron, four years before the murders occurred.

At the far end of the property, Tony's brother, Ray, and their cousin, Victor Shultz, moved into a mobile home. Meth labs were set up behind Tony and Ruby's house and behind the mobile home that Ray and Victor occupied. They also grew marijuana around the property. They were all murdered one night while Suzy was at work. She found the bodies and rescued Tootsie from her parents' bedroom.

Since that time, the property had been tied up in legal wrangling. Recently, the federal government decided not to pursue confiscation of the property, and Suzy had been notified by the court. Zeke hired an attorney, Hiram Tysdale, to monitor the case, and when he learned of the government's decision, he filed a claim that the property rightfully belonged to Zeke rather than Suzy.

At the courthouse, Morgan found the property records. She made a copy of the pleading filed by Zeke's attorney, Hiram. After her research, she made an appointment for Suzy to stop by the office on her way home from the hospital. Suzy was nervous, because she had never met with an attorney and was unsure about the overall situation with her grandfather trying to take her property. "Ms. Pinkston, Boone Carter is a great attorney. He will be listed as co-counsel, so you are in excellent hands. Try not to worry," Morgan assured her.

Suzy took an instant liking to Morgan and felt reassured. Morgan was short and a little on the heavy side with bouncy, shoulder-length hair. She was a talker, and energy bubbled around her. Files on the table in front of Morgan were organized and tabbed. Suzy felt she cared and she seemed to know what she was doing.

"Let me tell you what I've learned. Your parents didn't have a will. As their sole living child, the property should pass to you. Your grandfather, Zeke Pinkston, is claiming that he loaned money to your father to purchase the property. That's what's in the papers that his attorney filed. What's interesting is that there isn't any documentation other than a hand-written piece of paper signed only by your grandfather stating that he loaned your dad the money. I didn't find any liens on the property between Zeke and your parents. Do you know anything about how your parents paid for the property? Do you know if your grandfather gave or loaned them money?"

"No," Suzy shook her head. "I never heard them talk about it at all."

"Your father and mother purchased the property from your great uncle and his wife, Earl and Ruth Pinkston. We need to talk to them to see what they know about the payment. We're also going to have to seek documents through discovery and depose your grandfather."

Suzy frowned, "What for, and what's that?"

"A deposition is where I will ask him questions under oath in the presence of his attorney. A court reporter will transcribe everything that is said. His attorney will probably want to depose you. The purpose of depositions is to get information to prepare for the hearing."

Suzy's eyes widened, "But I don't know anything. Do I have to do that?"

"Yes, if they request it. It is all part of the discovery process where each side has the right to find out the facts about their case. I will be with you. If you don't know, you just tell him that. We will discuss all the questions we think he will ask ahead of time. This is a simple case from that standpoint, so I really don't think he will ask you a lot of questions. There may be others he will depose, but that doesn't involve you. You don't have to be present. This is routine."

"Why do you need to ask Grandpa questions?"

"Mostly to see what bank records he has. We have to see if there is any evidence of him loaning your parents the money."

Suzy wasn't sure she liked that idea. She couldn't imagine her grandfather taking kindly to that. "Is that necessary? I don't think my grandpa will like that happening to him."

"Like I said, this is a standard thing that happens in these types of cases. I'm certain that his attorney would have told him to expect this. In order to be able to get to the bottom of things and adequately represent you, we need to do this."

Suzy bit her lower lip. She still didn't think he would like it. "Do I have to be there when you depose him?"

"Not unless you want to."

Suzy's shoulders sank in relief. "Good."

"Do you have any of your parents' records on the property or bank records?"

"Mmm. No. I left all of Momma and Daddy's things at the house. I haven't been through anything."

"Well, we need to see if we can find their records."

"The government put locks on all the doors and boarded up the windows. I don't know how we can get into the house to look for any files they might have."

"Oh. Let me check into that and see how we can get a key."

"Even if I had a key, I wouldn't know what to look for. Also, I don't like being in the house. They let me in that one time with them being with me to get my clothes and Tootsie's things. I've not been back since."

"I can help if you want me to. We can go through things together."

"I'd really like that. My Ma Maw can keep Tootsie. I can do it on my day off."

"Okay, but we also need to talk to your great uncle. What do you know about him?"

"I don't know him very well. I met him at the funeral, but my Ma Maw knows him better. Maybe we all three can go see him."

"That will work. Just let me know when you want to do that."

Suzy asked, "Do you think my grandpa can take the property from me?"

"I really can't answer that until we have all the facts."

"What do you know about his attorney?"

"I asked Boone Carter, my supervising attorney, what he knew about Mr. Pinkston's attorney. His name is Hiram Tysdale. He's been around a long time. He handles cases in the counties around here, but his office is in Tapsaw County. He's a competent attorney, but Boone cautioned me to be on my toes around him. Don't worry about him. I will be working closely with Boone, and he is so, so smart.

"Another thing. Your grandfather gave you a courtesy copy of the filing they made at the courthouse. I picked up the service copy as your attorney. We'll handle getting an answer filed."

Rose arranged for Morgan and Suzy to meet with Earl and Ruth Pinkston. When they arrived, Ruth warmly greeted them and invited them to enjoy freshly baked chocolate chip cookies. She was so happy to see Tootsie, but Tootsie was shy and wanted to be held by Suzy. Earl was sitting by the fireplace with a blanket over his lap. He attempted a smile at the little girl. He had a gray pallor and looked like skin pasted over a skeletal frame. Suzy was surprised at how much his health had declined since her parents' funeral.

Suzy introduced Morgan, who then explained why they were there. "Mr. and Mrs. Pinkston, have you been paid in full for the property that Tony and Ruby purchased from you?"

Earl nodded yes, and Ruth said, "Yes, we got all our money. Earl told Tony when he said he wanted the property that he could pay him over time if he wanted to. Tony paid us half, and then a year later, paid the rest."

"Do you know if he had to take out a loan, or if he had the money, or if he borrowed it from someone?"

Ruth wasn't sure so she looked toward Earl. His voice was weak as he spoke. "Nev'r seemed money was a problem." He coughed and took a drink of coffee. "I didn't know his money situation, so I offered to let 'em pay ov'r time." Earl coughed again. His breathing was labored. "He just said okay. That he'd pay me the rest a year later, and he did."

"Mr. Pinkston, do you know if Zeke was involved in any way with coming up with the money for Tony and Ruby to purchase your property?"

"No, don't know 'bout that. I nev'r talked to Zeke 'cept the one time when I called him and told him Ruth and I wanted to sell and see if he wanted to buy it. Zeke, bein' my brother, I thought I should ask him. It was the old home place. Our grandpa got it from his pappy. Ruth and I didn't have no kids, so I called Zeke. It was Tony that called me back and said he wanted to buy it."

"Do you talk to Zeke very often?"

"No, we nev'r talked much. Last time I talked to him was at the funeral of Tony and everyone. My advice for what it's worth is to fight fire with fire. That's what he understands."

They all thanked Earl and Ruth for their time. Ruth walked out on the porch as they were leaving and told them to visit any time. "Rose, when you are keeping the baby, bring her over. I'll help you with her. Suzy, we're your family. We want to see more of you all. Don't forget that. Earl's not like Zeke."

Later that evening after Suzy had put Tootsie to bed, Rose said, "You know, I've never been around them much, but I think Earl and Ruth are good people. Earl's not well. Ruth might need some help. If you don't mind, I might take Tootsie there some and see if I can help. If nothin' else, she might just like the company."

"That's fine with me, Ma Maw. They seem like nice people."

Chapter 8

Loretta poured milk over the cereal and sat it in front of Mack, who was sipping coffee and reading the paper. Her reddish tinted hair looked like a haphazard-mowed yard—parts flattened and parts standing straight out. She topped off her coffee and sat down at the table. "Why haven't you put money in the checking account? There's not much left."

Mack continued to read the paper. "I don't have any to put in. Don't get paid until next Friday."

"What do you mean you don't have any to put in?" she squawked.

"What I just said, Loretta. There isn't any to put in."

"Well, me and the bridge club are going to Atlantic City for our annual get-away. I need some money," she protested.

"I don't have any. Don't get paid until next Friday."

"I'll just have to use the credit cards then."

"They're 'bout maxed out. You better check before you go to make sure you don't go over the limit. You might get embarrassed in front of your friends if your cards get rejected." Mack turned a page and continued to peruse the paper.

"What have you been doing with the money, Mack?"

"I ain't been doin' nothing. You're the one who's the spender. But, you better cut back on that because it's going to be even less."

Alarmed, she shrieked, "What'd you mean, even less? What have you done with all our money? Where's it at?"

He laid the paper on the table and looked at her. "I was demoted on my job, Loretta. If you want to keep living like you're the queen of Sheba, you need to get a job. I'm tapped out."

"What about that consulting job you had? It paid good money."

"It fell through over a year ago."

"What? You never told me that. What happened?"

"Bunch of changes, and they no longer needed my services."

"I swear, Mack. Now this! Is it that new sheriff that demoted you?"

"Yeah." He took a sip of coffee and picked back up the paper.

"You haven't worked for him long. How could he do that?"

"Look. It's his department. He can do whatever he wants. Kyle's gone."

"He got fired?"

"I don't know, but he's gone."

Raising her voice, "I swear. You should have listened to me. I tried to get you to run for sheriff. You've been there longer than anybody. That new sheriff had just moved to town."

"Once Mike recommended Sean to be the interim sheriff, it was a done deal with the powers-that-be. If I'd run against Sean, Loretta, he would have fired me if he got elected. I wouldn't have stood a chance against the big ex-Marine football hero."

Loretta was getting angrier. "You didn't even try to run against him. He'd been gone all that time. People aren't going to remember about his football. You've been here all these years as Mike's assistant. If you had a backbone, you would have run and won. You'd be sheriff and making more money, not less!" She picked up his cereal bowl and dumped the uneaten contents in the garbage. Pointing her finger at him with sparks shooting from her eyes. "You better hear me, Mack. I'm not getting a job. You need to find another job. I don't care if you have to work two or three jobs!" She stormed out of the kitchen. He finished reading the paper and drinking the coffee.

Mike was heading into Frau's to meet with C.P. when he heard someone yelling at him. He turned and saw Cooper rushing toward him. "Hey, Sheriff Adams, I need to talk to you."

Mike waited. Cooper was breathing hard, having dashed to catch Mike before he entered the restaurant. "Hey. I've been tryin' to find you. Glad I finally did."

"What do you want, Cooper?"

"I've been tryin' to get a job, but no one will hire me 'cause I'm an ex-con. I need my name cleared. That damn deputy put those drugs in my car or either those Thompsons did and had him find 'em. Either way, they were in cahoots and framed me. I was innocent. I need for you to vouch for me. Tell the judge it was a mistake and get him to clear my record. You were the sheriff then. He'll listen to you."

"Cooper, I can't tell the judge that. I don't have any evidence that what you're saying is true. How would I know any of that? Besides, I'm not the sheriff any more. I can't investigate it. I don't see how I can help you."

That wasn't what Cooper wanted to hear. "You were the damn sheriff when it happened. Ben Clark was your deputy." Cooper was getting worked up. "You and that new sheriff are in cahoots yourselves. He says he can't help me 'cause he wasn't the sheriff when it happened, and you say you can't help me 'cause you're not the sheriff now. What'd them Thompsons do—bribe you both against me?"

"Cooper, just listen to yourself for a minute. What you're saying doesn't add up. You brought this on by skimming off the Thompsons. If they set you up or had Ben do it, it was because of what you did to their business. But, you wouldn't cooperate before your trial and tell me or your lawyer any of this. Had we known then, we might, and I say, 'might,' have been able to investigate and get to the bottom of it, but you didn't. Now, I've got to go."

Mike started to walk away, and Cooper shouted, "Go on then. You and that new sheriff are gonna get what's comin' to you."

Mike spun around. "Cooper, you listen to me. Don't you ever threaten me or Sheriff Neumann again!" The steel in Mike's voice caused Cooper to take a step back. He remained silent as Mike turned to walk into Frau's.

During their lunch, Mike told C.P. about his findings and gave him his written report and the pictures. He had evaluated about half of the track. C.P. was pleased with Mike's findings and progress. Mike thought, if the weather stayed good, he could wrap up before Christmas. After Mike and C.P. finished their lunch meeting, Mike decided to stop by and talk to Sean.

"Hi, Mike," Sean said as there were seated in his office. It seemed odd, he and Mike in reversed seats. This was the first time that Mike had visited Sean in the office since he'd retired "How are things going?"

"Real good. I'm making progress on evaluating that old spur line. I told C.P. after this is over if he has other things he wants me to do, I'd like to talk to him."

"That's good to hear. That was some retirement party for Coach the other night."

Mike smiled. "It sure was. All those players showing up and all the citizens around town. You could tell he enjoyed every minute of it."

"You're right. People sure have a lot of great memories of the football during his tenure here. I sure do. All those times you and I spent practicing our passing plays, and then the games we played. I never could have asked for a better wide receiver than you. You were like an extension of my arm being there to catch the ball and then carrying two or three defenders along as you ran toward the goal line."

Mike laughed. "We made a great team. You had that golden arm. Remember. The *Tribune* coined us the 'Schriever Shock Wave.'"

Sean started laughing. "Oh, yeah. I remember that. They wrote that I shocked the opponents with my throws and you waved goodbye as you sprinted toward the goal line." They both enjoyed the memories.

Mike grinned, "Well, we did go out in a blaze of glory winning that state title."

Sean nodded, "Yep, we sure did."

"I see you still have that picture of me and you in our uniforms before the championship game," he said nodding to a shelf beside Sean's desk.

Sean smiled. "Geri told me to keep it when she came to get your things. I like it there, but I told her if you ever wanted it back, just to let me know."

"You keep it, Sean. It looks good sitting there."

They both chuckled.

Mike said, "There was something I wanted to mention to you." He told him about the run-in with Cooper outside of Frau's. "Sean, Cooper is a hard one to read. He always struck me as a whiner and loud mouth, but you never know. Just don't take anything for granted with him."

"Thanks, Mike. He came and saw me, and we had basically the same conversation. I'll say the same to you: keep your eyes out for him."

Mike grinned and nodded.

"Say, there's something I've been meaning to ask you. I got called up to John Pawley's place the other day."

Mike chuckled. "Don't tell me. He was butt naked except for a long-gun walking the perimeter of his property."

Sean smiled. "So, you know about him?"

"Oh, sure."

"What can you tell me about him?"

"Pawley lives by himself. Lives off the grid. He grew up around here. That's the old home place where he lives. He's a Vietnam vet. Ever since he came back here, he's been a loner. He hardly ever comes to town. He doesn't speak to anyone except what's necessary to do his business. Most people don't know him—only know of him, and a few people who have never seen him wonder if he's a myth. Some people around here are scared of him. Others think he's an eccentric old mountain man. Some think he's crazy. I don't think there is a reason to be wary of him, but he does march to the tune of a different drummer. He's not a nutcase though. He actually is a health fanatic. He really believes that walking around naked in the elements is good for his health. Helps him stay acclimated to the environment."

"How does strapping a M16 over his shoulder fit into being a health nut?"

As a laugh escaped, Mike shook his head. "Well, you got me on that one. All I can say is that he likes his guns. Probably has an arsenal. Maybe that comes from being in the war. I never had any complaints of him doing anything violent. Like I said, he rarely comes to town. Except for Irma Ritter, most people never lay eyes on him. But according to her, she sees more than she wants." Mike grinned. "But I question that." They both laughed.

Rose was pushing Tootsie's stroller on the sidewalk but slowed when she saw Zeke's truck sitting in front of her house. *What is he doing here again?* She spied him just as he started down the steps. When he reached the walk, he glanced and saw her. She couldn't get to her house without passing him, and he was lumbering toward her. She turned the stroller around so she stood between him and the baby.

As he approached, he looked triumphant, "Well now. Seems I'm goin' to get to see my great grandchild."

Rose stiffened her back, "What are you doin' back here again? I told you that you had to get Suzy's permission, and that ain't happened."

"Now, Rose, there ain't no harm in me seein' my own flesh 'n blood."

Rose tensed up as he made a move to walk around the stroller. Rose pushed it so she stayed between it and him. Tootsie started crying. She was concerned that he might leave with the baby if she couldn't keep him away from her.

"See what you done, Zeke. You've upset the baby." Zeke was scowling as he stood close to Rose.

Cheryl had told Sean about Rose calling her about Zeke's claim of ownership to the property and Boone's willingness to represent Suzy. So, as he drove by and saw what looked like a stand-off, he pulled his cruiser over and got out. Zeke looked up and saw him, and Rose followed Zeke's eyes.

Sean walked up. "Afternoon, Rose. Zeke. Everything okay here?" The baby was squalling.

When neither said anything, Sean said, "Rose, that baby sounds unhappy. Why don't you take her home?"

Rose started talking to Tootsie trying to calm her as she turned the stroller, giving wide berth from Zeke, who was watching her moving toward her house.

"Zeke, you need to get in your truck and leave."

Anger flared from Zeke's eyes, "This ain't no business of yours, Sheriff."

"Yeah, it is, Zeke. Rose and Suzy have a right to their privacy. From what I just witnessed, it doesn't look like you are respecting that."

"Ain't nobody stops me from seein' my kin. You overstepped where you shouldn't."

Sean returned the steel look, "You're not goin' to come here and threaten Rose or Suzy or the baby, Zeke. The next time I hear of you doing so, I'll arrest you. Now, if you don't want to visit our jail here, you need to get in your truck and head back over to Tapsaw County."

If steam was capable of erupting from Zeke's ears, it would have. "You're goin' to regret this, Sheriff," he said as he turned to leave.

Chapter 9

Noel Fischner owned the outfitter's shop on Main Street at the end of the downtown area. Across from his shop stood a large, long-abandoned cigar box factory constructed in the 1890's in the Richardsonian Romanesque architectural style. Konrad Schumacher had founded the company and also built a mansion nearby in the same style. The cigar box manufacturing company closed in the late 1950's, and since that time, the building had remained vacant. Because it was constructed in the finest workmanship and materials at the time, the passage of time had been kind.

In the 1960's, the owner, a grandson of Schumacher, donated the factory to an order of nuns who ran the local elementary school with classes through the eighth grade. They planned to relocate the school into the larger building and add grades going through high school. However, they were unable to raise the necessary funds, and the building remained boarded.

Noel wanted to buy the factory and approached the nuns about three years earlier with an offer, but they weren't interested. Admittedly, it was a low-ball offer, but he thought the nuns might want someone to take it off their hands. He had planned to sweeten the offer—though not by much—now that the election was over. His thinking was that now that he was a county commissioner, they might like transacting business with someone of his importance.

When he parked in the small lot beside his business, he saw two familiar trucks sitting in front of the old factory across the street—one belonged to his brother, Cole, and the other to Otis Mueller. His brother was now running their father's construction company, and Otis owned an architecture firm. He couldn't figure out why they would be there. Other than himself, he wasn't aware that anyone had shown interest in the factory.

Curiosity propelled him to cross the street. The door was unlocked, so he entered. He overheard Otis tell Cole, "That should do it," as they were walking toward the entryway. Cole and Otis were surprised to see Noel standing there. Otis greeted Noel and looked at Cole, "I'll talk to you soon."

After Otis left, Cole asked, "What are you doing here?"

"I saw your trucks out front and wondered what you were doing here."

"I'm not free to talk about this, Noel, and in the future, I suggest you not trespass."

"I wasn't trespassing in this stone heap," Noel snapped. "I have as much right to be here as you do." Just as he said that, he realized that might not be the case. *What were Cole and Otis doing here?* "Did something happen here? Surely, no one bought this place?"

"Like I said—it's not my place to tell you anything. I need to leave. Let's go so I can lock up."

As he walked across the street, Noel worked himself into a state thinking someone may have bought it out from under him. He couldn't imagine who, and he hadn't seen anyone over there. He decided to check the records at the property department in the county building.

When he walked in, Kathy Isaac smiled, "Hello, Mr. Fischner. What can I do for our new Commissioner-Elect?"

He was in a snit and brusquely asked, "What's going on at the old Schumacher place? Did someone buy it?"

Her cheerfulness faded. "Yes, it finally sold," her tone professional.

"Who bought it?"

"I don't remember the exact name, Sir, but I will look. If you want to have a seat, I'll go check."

Noel wandered over and sat down. He absently picked up one of the Bekbourg brochures on area outdoor activities and was thumbing through it. He stopped and looked at the advertisement for his shop. He fumed at the idea that someone may have purchased the Schumacher place, but what really got under his skin was that his brother was somehow involved.

Kathy's voice interrupted his musings. "Sir, I have the purchasers."

As he stood and walked toward the counter, he asked, "Who bought it?"

"Livingstone Trust."

"Who is that?" He was impatient.

"I have no idea, Sir. I've never heard of them."

"When did they buy it?"

She looked at the sheet of paper. "Two months ago. They bought all the property, not just the old factory."

"All what property?"

"There's the old mansion that Mr. Schumacher built on Oak Street, which is in the vicinity of the factory."

Noel remembered seeing the mansion but had not made the connection between the two. "I thought someone lived there?"

"After Mr. Schumacher donated the factory and house to the nuns, they moved into the house and lived there for many years. Sadly, the size of their order dwindled to be only about six or seven. It became too expensive for them to maintain that big old house, so they boarded it up and moved back into the house they had lived in before they moved into the mansion."

"What was the purchase price?"

When she told him, he couldn't believe someone had paid almost triple what he had offered nearly three years ago.

Noel dismissively slapped his hand on the counter and turned and left. Kathy didn't know him very well but thought to herself, *I sure hope he's not always like that.*

Chapter 10

During Bekbourg's early history, the old road leading north out of town through Mader Valley was used mainly by farmers. It had never become a major thoroughfare. Eventually, it was paved but was barely wide enough for two cars to pass. Random pull-offs allowed sufficient parking for hunters and people wanting to fish along the creek. Running northward, the old spur line was located to the right side running parallel along the creek. As the railroad track meandered through the valley, its distance from the road varied to as much as a quarter of a mile away. Very little traffic drove on this road, because the main highway was a much quicker route, and the area was sparsely populated. Bikers and runners used this road even though it was curvy and hilly. The few occupied homes were old, some in better shape than others. A splattering of old abandoned farmhouses dotted the area. Farming could still be found, but much of the area was overgrown and wooded.

Sean parked his truck in one of the larger pull-over spots about a half-mile north of town and took off for his morning run. It was drizzling rain, but the cool air felt good. Thanksgiving was approaching, and the seasonal air had finally arrived. He liked this run through Mader Valley. He didn't know if there had ever been a formal name for the valley. After the murder of a man named Mader in the mid 1890's, Mader Valley stuck. Although the road's official name was Frank Road after one of the original large landowners in the area, people called it Mader Road and even referred to the creek as Mader Creek.

Sean usually ran five miles, but today, he pushed it and went for six. Except for a bicyclist passing him going north, he didn't see any other exercise enthusiasts this morning. By the time he returned to his truck, he was perspiring and breathing hard. He was thinking about getting home and walking Buddy and drinking coffee with Cheryl. She had come into his life when he least expected it, and frankly, when he was at a low point and didn't want any entanglements. His world had been turned upside down with the explosion that took his close friend and cost Sean his career. The injuries he sustained precluded him from continuing in the special investigative criminal unit.

After retiring from the Marines, he drifted to Key West where he withdrew from everything but alcohol. Even that didn't bring solace because of the physical pain from his injuries, the hellish nightmares, and the despair of being adrift. Through fortune, a former colleague recognized him and contacted Sean's former commanding officer who convinced Sean to return to Bekbourg to recuperate. His parents and Coach Jackson helped him turn the corner, but then Mike offered him the deputy position—a lifeline—a job doing something he loved.

He wasn't sure how long he would stay in Bekbourg, but it gave him something meaningful to do. But then, the Pinkston murders happened, which brought Cheryl to Bekbourg to investigate not only those murders, but a murder twenty years prior for which her grandfather had pleaded guilty. From first sight, he was attracted to the newspaper reporter from Cleveland. She was tough but with a soft edge. She wasn't scared off by the junk he was carrying around. When he feared she might be killed during a tense standoff, he knew he loved and needed her in his life.

The truck door tended to stick. Just as Sean bent to give the extra jerk on the door, he heard a bullet whiz by, *just* missing his head. *What the hell!* Having been shot at before, he instinctively dove to the ground and plunged under his truck. Three rapid-fire shots just barely missed him as he sought refuge.

When the shooting stopped, Sean waited, because he wasn't sure if there was a second shooter positioned on the other side of his truck. His gun and phone were in the truck. He listened to see if anyone was approaching. He felt the front tire start to deflate, so he eased himself out on the passenger side. He cautiously stood, looking all around. He heard an engine roar to life, but he couldn't see a vehicle. *Damnit!* He couldn't pursue the shooter because the tire was flat. He retrieved his gun and phone from the truck and called for back-up and called his friend, Harold Greene, head of the state police for the region.

Sean walked across the road and started up the wooded hill. It was hard to know exactly where the shooter had been. He heard the siren in the distance screaming closer and then the cruiser arriving below, so he walked back.

Arlo was the first to arrive, "What happened, Sheriff? Are you okay?"

"I'm fine, Arlo. The shooter took four shots at me. I heard a vehicle start soon after the shooting stopped. The gunfire came from that direction," he said pointing up the hill across the road. "We're going to need to see if we can locate any evidence." About that time, a state police car came roaring up and then Alex. Sean wanted the state police to take the lead in looking for evidence, because he didn't have enough deputies to spare.

Others arrived, and soon Harold Greene pulled up. Sean walked over to where he was getting out of his cruiser. "Hi, Sean. What can you tell me about it?"

"Someone took four shots at me." Sean explained what had happened.

"It wasn't random, Harold. I've been running this route every morning for several months. I should know better—to mix it up, but I got complacent. If someone had watched for any length of time, they would know this was my routine."

"Any idea who this could be? Have you received any threats?"

"No threats. I can think of some people who are unhappy with me but not enough to kill me."

"You think it could be Dante Gomez or someone from the cartel?"

"Well, I can't rule that out, but frankly, if they wanted me dead, I wouldn't be standing here right now."

"Yeah, that's a good point, but I'm going to contact Lucky and see what he can tell us about the cartel." Lucky Brennan worked for the FBI in Columbus.

"I'll call Boze, and see if they have any information." Russ Bozeman, nicknamed Boze, was with the DEA, and he and Sean had worked together on some cases over the years. Boze had asked for Sean's assistance almost two years ago in the DEA's investigation into suspected cartel activities in Bekbourg.

"We need to search for casings and bullets and where the shooter might have been positioned as well as where he was parked," Harold said. "I can organize that if you want me to."

"That works. Arlo knows the area around here. He might be able to help." Sean pointed him out.

"You sure no one comes to mind?" ask Harold.

"I recently had a run-in with Zeke Pinkston."

"Pinkston?" asked Harold.

"Yeah. Tony's father. Zeke Pinkston has been here in Bekbourg a lot recently. Mike told me he saw him and his son driving up this way the other day. I saw him trying to bully Rose Waters into seeing Suzy's child when they were out for a walk. I don't know what other business he might have here. Tapsaw County's out of my jurisdiction."

"That's okay, Sean. I have jurisdiction over there. I'll talk to Pinkston and see what he has to say about where he was this morning."

"A son drives around with him sometimes. You might check on where he was."

"Okay.

"There's also a man named Cooper Townsend who isn't happy about me not clearing his name on a prior conviction. I'll talk to him. If I think of anyone else, I'll let you know."

"Okay. We take it seriously when a sheriff's life is threatened." Harold saw Cheryl charging up the road. He nodded in her direction, "I'll get started. She looks determined."

Sean turned to see Cheryl, who started running when she saw him. She was the first to arrive from the *Bekbourg Tribune*, not for the story, but to make sure Sean was okay. She ran into his arms with tears in her eyes. "Oh, God, Sweetie, I heard and was so scared." She had her face buried in his neck. He was trying to calm her.

"I'm fine, honey." He kept holding her until she pulled back. Even though she was tall, she had to look up to gaze upon his handsome face chiseled with maturity.

"Sean, I was afraid something bad had happened to you."

He smiled. "I'm fine—as you can see. Let me get back to work here, and I promise to give you an exclusive."

The creases in her forehead disappeared and a smile lit her face. She knew he was fine if he was teasing. "Go on, then, but I do expect a full accounting for my readers."

He chuckled as she turned to leave.

Later in the afternoon, Harold caught up with Sean. "Sean, we think we know the shooter's movements. By the way, your deputy, Arlo Lopez, was a big help."

Sean was glad to hear that. Arlo grew up in Bekbourg, and after graduating from high school, he joined the military. Arlo was a rugged outdoorsman who had spent much of his teenage years hunting, fishing and camping.

Harold continued, "He knows the area. He knew about a place about a quarter-of-a-mile on the left side of the road before where you were parked that was used years ago by a farmer who would pull off the road and go tend his fields. It's a sharp turn and is only about a hundred feet off the road. Looks like teenagers know about it. There's discarded condoms and beer cans and liquor bottles strewn around. When hunting season is going on, a hunter might pull in there. Ronnie Vin took tire impressions, but she's not sure she can get much.

"Anyway, we think the shooter parked his vehicle there and walked a short distance up the incline to a rock formation. He could see your truck from there, and it was a good place for a shooting perch. It's a long distance, Sean. From the perch to where your truck was, I estimate about three-hundred yards. It had to have been a high-powered hunting rifle. We're combing the area looking for casings and evidence, but so far, we've not found anything."

Throughout the day, people stopped by the newspaper or called to check on Sean. With Cheryl's time tied up with those inquiries, Milton covered the attempt on Sean's life. It would be headline news in the morning's edition.

When Sean arrived home that evening, Kye Davis was visiting with Cheryl. "Oh dear, Sean. I have been so distressed since I heard the news. How can such an awful thing happen? Do you have any ideas who might be behind it?"

Kye lived next door in the duplex and was their landlord and close friend. Cheryl liked to tease her that she was a grandparent to Buddy, their Lab. Kye loved Buddy and would care for him when Sean and Cheryl were not home.

Sean sat down beside Kye, who was rubbing Buddy's neck. He could see the worry in her eyes. She had recently been through a lot of stress, and he didn't want her agonizing about him. He assured her, "Kye, I'm really fine. I don't want you to worry about this. It's not the first time someone shot at me, and I've survived a lot worst. I'll be more diligent, and we will find who did this."

She returned his smile. “Okay, Sean, but you know me. I never stop fretting about my former students no matter how big and tough they are.” Kye was a retired high school English teacher who had taught half the students in the county. She was loved and respected throughout the area.

About that time, Geri and Mike arrived. After getting past Buddy, who insisted on getting a pat, Geri rushed to give both Sean and Cheryl hugs. “Oh, I just can’t believe all this. Sean, are you sure you are okay?” concern emitting from Geri’s eyes.

Mike had nearly died almost two years ago from gunshot wounds received in an ambush. Sean hoped this incident didn’t resurrect those horrific memories for either Geri or Mike. He tried to ease her concern as he had done with Kye.

Cheryl suggested, “Geri, would you like to help me get food set out? Earlier, Bri and Max brought over several dishes. We have enough food to feed an army, which is a good thing. Several people have called and said they were stopping by.”

“Count me in, Dear,” said Kye. “I may be old, but I’m surely capable of helping out.”

Cheryl and Geri laughed as they all three headed toward the kitchen. Buddy pranced into the kitchen hoping for a sneaked snack.

Mike peered into Sean’s eyes, “Are you sure you’re okay, buddy?”

“Yeah, but it was a close call. Someone was shooting at me.”

“Do you think it’s that drug cartel you shut down?”

"Harold asked me the same thing. I really don't think so. I think if it was them, I'd be dead."

"Any idea who it might be?"

"Not really, but Cooper's on the list. Also Zeke."

"Yeah. Say, I don't want to alarm you, but if they shot at you there, any concern they might shoot around here?"

Sean grimaced, "I've had that on my mind. Buddy is a good watch dog, but if someone shoots at the duplex, Cheryl and Kye could be in danger."

"Well, let me know if I can help. I could hang out here and keep watch if you want me to. I would have come up and helped this afternoon, but I didn't know about it until I got home. My phone doesn't pick up a signal in the valley."

"Thanks, Mike. I might take you up on that. Let me see how things go."

"What do you know about the shooter?"

"Given the distance, it had to have been a high-powered hunting rifle. We haven't found any casings. They have bullet fragments from the door and a tire, but I'm not sure they can learn much from those. I couldn't chase after him because the tire was flat. Good thing he didn't hit both tires; I might have been pinned under the truck. Harold called me this afternoon. They think they know where the shooter was perched. There is a rock formation on the side of the hill. They think he was there and then hauled ass to his vehicle. My new deputy, Arlo Lopez, is familiar with the area. He took Harold's people to where they think the shooter's vehicle was parked. Unfortunately,

Ronnie's not sure how helpful the tire impressions are going to be. Forensics got some partials, but more than a couple of different vehicles had been there, and leaves and rock covered some of the area."

"Damnit, Sean. Someone put some planning into all of that."

"Yeah, I know."

Knocking on the door interrupted their conversation. Buddy came barreling though to greet the newcomers. Danny and Sally Chambers, friends from high school, arrived to check on Sean followed by Milton and Martha. Sean's parents arrived soon thereafter.

When Martha saw Kye, she laid a book on the end table, "Kye, here's the book we discussed."

"Oh, thank you, Dear. I am just finishing one. I'm looking forward to reading it."

Cheryl glanced at the book. "What's that?"

Martha spoke up, "Milton recently finished reading it. He said it was about the third time he's read it over the years. So, I decided to read it, and it now is up there with my other favorites."

"She mentioned it to me, and I told her I'd like to read it," Kye said.

"It's been around a long time," Milton offered. "It's about a war vet who returns home from war and the contrast through his eyes of our country before he left and after he returned from his service. When it was first published, it was on the best seller list for over a year."

Cheryl picked up the book, "I'm not familiar with the author. G. Keb."

"I've tried to find other books by him, but I believe it's his only book," Milton said as he drank some iced tea.

"Mmm. I'm going to get a copy and read it. You've raised my curiosity."

Everyone had left except for Kye, who was preparing to walk to her side of the duplex. Sean returned from walking Buddy. He asked if he could speak with both of them. Kye sat down. Cheryl and Kye both looked at Sean with curious expressions. Buddy plopped down beside Sean as he sat down.

"I don't want to scare you, but whoever took those shots at me may try again. The first attempt was in a secluded area where the likelihood of them being spotted was minimal. That's why I don't think they would try to shoot around here, but it's important that you be alert. If you see something that is out of place or doesn't look right, act. If someone does start shooting at the duplex, get down. Until we find who is behind this, keep the blinds closed and the doors locked."

Kye was the first to speak, "Don't worry about me, Sean. I'll keep watch. I'm not afraid."

"Sweetheart, don't worry about us. We are worried about you. Kye is ready to give you her teacher's lecture on being prepared."

Cheryl and Kye shared a conspiratorial grin.

Sean shook his head. "Okay, I get the message. Just be careful."

Kye said, "We will Sean. You be careful, too. We also have Buddy who will be on guard."

"Okay, Kye. Let me walk you home. I'll be your body guard tonight."

Cheryl and Kye laughed. "Best offer I've had all night," she said as she stood.

Cooper lived with his mother in a trailer that had seen better days. An older model pickup with rusted wheel wells, dents, and faded paint was sitting in the gravel driveway. Sean had to knock several times on the door before Cooper answered. His appearance was of having been roused from bed—his hair flattened against his head, and his eyes were red. He looked to have slept in the white stained t-shirt, and his jeans were snapped but not zipped.

"What the hell are you doin' here at this hour?"

"It's after nine o'clock, Cooper. This is Deputy Ogle. We'd like to talk to you."

"Let me get a coat and shoes," he groused. A couple of minutes later, Cooper stepped out on the small porch. "What's this 'bout?"

"I've never seen that pickup, Cooper. Who does that belong to?"

"It's mine."

"Where were you yesterday morning, Cooper?"

"Huh?"

"Where were you yesterday morning about seven o'clock?"

Cooper was getting agitated, "What the hell? I was here. Sleeping!"

"Was anyone here with you? Your mother?"

"She's havin' to help her sister in Chillicothe. She's real sick. What's goin' on?"

"Did you know someone took some shots at me yesterday?"

His eyes flashed alarm. "No, I don't know that, but if you're here to accuse me, I damn sure didn't do it."

Sean asked a few more questions, but Cooper didn't have much to say. As they were driving away, Sean asked Alex to have Syd check with the people who lived around the area to see if they had seen Cooper or his truck yesterday morning. Alex asked, "Do you think he did it, Chief?"

"I know he's upset at me for not clearing his record. With a hot-head like that, it's hard to say."

Chapter 11

Dusty and Mule Head were enjoying Frau's biscuits and gravy special. Dusty said, "I don't know if I can take this working out of Cincinnati much longer. I'm already taking off a lot. I'm working only twice a week, but with that, I'm gone two days for each work day with the driving between here and there. They are pretty good about letting me take off, but that won't last once spring gets here and business picks up. They won't leave me alone then. I'll have to about live down there, because by the time I get back here, I'd have to drive back."

"Well, what about the payoff?"

"I can't really take a payoff. I'm not eligible yet to get a pension."

They looked up when Chaw walked up to the table. Mule Head asked, "What are you doing here, Chaw? I thought you were on your last run."

Chaw sat when Anita poured him a cup of coffee. "Hell, I haven't worked in two weeks. I don't know if I'll get back on another run or not. I've turned in my retirement papers, and they said they'd be finalized before Christmas."

"Did you get enough time in to qualify for vacation next year?" inquired Dusty.

"Hell, yeah. I had that or I'd be working. Get five weeks paid vacation next year."

Mule Head huffed, "And you guys are complaining."

Chaw looked over when the front door opened, "Well, well. Look what the dog drug in."

Dusty and Mule Head turned to see just as Jules spotted them and started over.

"Sit down, Frenchy. Have some breakfast," said Chaw.

Mule Head asked, "How come you're not working, Jules?"

"At last, my lovely Renee doesn't like me being gone so much, so I'm thinking about taking the payoff."

He sat down. Anita poured him coffee and laid out his silverware. The three others watched as he took his napkin and wiped his silverware. Dusty glanced at the other two, but they continued watching with interest Jules's precision in cleaning and setting his utensils. Once his silverware was cleaned to his satisfaction, Jules tucked his napkin into his shirt collar.

Dusty said, "The payoff would be good for you old guys, but I can't retire right now. I've got several more years to work."

After Anita took orders from Chaw and Jules, "Did you read about Sean being shot at yesterday?" asked Mule Head.

Everyone perked up at this topic, glad to move on from the glum subject of the railroad.

"Yeah, what do you make of that?" Chaw piped up as he looked at the men.

"Probably that damn cartel coming back to get him," offered Mule Head. "You know how those guys are. They never forget."

Chaw shrugged, "Yeah, could be them, but I just wonder about those Pinkstons. Little bit of hillbilly justice. Lost five family members at the hands of the sheriff's department, and they never forget either."

"Maybe it was some hunters," Mule Head suggested after drinking coffee.

The other three looked like he was from Mars. "Four shots at a human standing at a pickup truck?" Dusty shook his head. "Even the worst hunter in the world wouldn't make that shot. It's not even hunting season."

Mule Head said sheepishly, "Well, you know how poachers are."

"Mule Head, think before you talk," huffed Chaw.

"Don't forget about someone from his past," said Jules. "Sean had quite a career in the Marines hunting down criminals in the Middle East."

"What do you know about that?" Dusty was skeptical.

Jules straightened and adjusted his head in an air of importance, "I know more than you think."

The other three groaned. "Typical bullshit," Chaw muttered.

Sean walked in about that time, and Mule Head lit up, "Speak of the devil."

As Sean headed toward the counter, Dusty yelled, "Hey, Sean. Come over and have some breakfast."

Sean saw the railroaders and knew they enjoyed gossiping. "No boys. I don't have time."

"Come over. We'll buy you some coffee." Pointing, Dusty added, "Mule Head, grab that chair for Sean."

He walked over. Anita came to pour him some coffee, and Dusty said, "Get Sean a cup to go when you get a chance, and put it on my check. He's in a hurry."

After Sean sat, Dusty asked, "Sean, what's this all about being shot at? It's all over the newspaper. What's the inside story?"

"You know, Dusty, it's an ongoing investigation. I can't talk about it right now."

"Who do you think it was?"

"Really, I can't talk about it now. It was a close call, but I've had closer."

"Well, Sean. There's a lot of talk going around. Everybody is wondering who would do such a thing," said Chaw aiming for the inside scoop.

"Well, a lot of it is wild speculation, but rest assured, we will get to the bottom of this."

Anita arrived with his to-go cup. Sean thanked Dusty for his coffee and bid everyone goodbye.

"Well, this must be serious stuff. Seems like it's really shook Sean up." Chaw said as he took a sip of coffee.

"Yeah, I guess getting shot at would do that," Mule Head replied.

Jules disagreed, "No, Mule Head. I could see it in his eyes. That young man is not shook up. He's just determined."

Syd stopped by Sean's office to tell him that she had learned something about Cooper's whereabouts on the morning someone attempted to shoot Sean. It turned out that, instead of being home in bed, Cooper was having breakfast at Frau's around 8:30.

"That's interesting. He told me and Alex he was sleeping. Was he with anyone?"

"No. According to the owner, he sat at the bar and ordered a breakfast and coffee. He wasn't there long. Just enough time to eat his food. The owner said Cooper wasn't talking much, which was unusual for him."

"Mmm. Let's take a ride and see what he has to say."

Cooper was changing the oil in his truck when Sean and Syd pulled up. He warily watched them walk toward him and waited for Sean to speak.

"Cooper, when I was up here last and asked you where you were on the morning someone shot at me, you said you were asleep. That's not true. Want to tell me where you were?"

Cooper's eyes widened as he seemed to think. "When was this?"

Sean gave him the date.

Cooper appeared blank, so Sean asked, "You remember having breakfast at Frau's?"

He shook his head. "Oh yeah. I remember now. I was out looking for a job."

"Early in the morning?"

"Yeah."

"Who were you interviewing with?"

Cooper's voice notched up, "Hell, no one. I was looking for a job. I was driving around to see if there were any postings up in any of the businesses. I didn't see any, so I came back here."

"Why didn't you tell me this the first time we talked?"

"Hell, I don't know. I guess I didn't think of it. Usually, I'm sleepin' then, but I woke up and couldn't git back to sleep, so I decided to drive around and see if anyone had anythin' posted in their windows or out front."

"What time did you leave here?"

"What's this shit about? I ain't goin' to say no more. I ain't done nothin' wrong." He turned back toward his truck.

As Sean and Syd headed back to the station, they discussed Cooper. Cooper was perplexing. On the one hand, he came across as a bumbling misfit, but on the other hand, he had embezzled from the Thompsons. Most would think that exhibited stupidity, but he had figured out a way to do it under the Thompsons' noses and had gotten away with it for a while. In Sean's mind, the verdict was still out on whether Cooper was shrewder than most people gave him credit.

It was a cold, cloudy November day. Suzy was sitting on the front porch of her deceased parents' house waiting for Morgan, who had gotten a key. The windows were boarded up, and the electricity had been disconnected. She had brought a couple of flashlights for them to search for property and bank records. She knew it would be cold in the house and had warned Morgan. She could probably light the coal furnace in the basement, but she didn't want to mess with it. Hopefully, this wouldn't take too long.

A truck pulled into the driveway, and she recognized it. Her heart nearly stopped. *Oh no! What is he doing here?* Surely Rose wouldn't have told him she was here. She quickly dialed Rose, but no one answered. *She must have taken Tootsie to the park. Oh, God. What am I going to do? He's seen me. I can't hide.*

Her grandpa made her uncomfortable—to the extent she feared him. Although her daddy never admitted it, she felt even he was intimated by Zeke.

As he limped toward the porch, he puffed, "Hey there, Suzy Girl. Didn't know whose car was on my property. What are you doin' here?"

"Hi, Grandpa. I'm surprised to see you, too. What made you decide to drive over?"

"Well, I'm glad you're here. Your daddy never gave me no key. Guess I should have told him to. I reckon you have a key."

He was now at the bottom of the steps. Her heart was racing. He stopped, catching his breath and looked around the front yard. "So, this is where it all happened, huh? Hadn't wanted to come here with the feds around." He looked up at Suzy. "You goin' to ask your grandpa in for a visit, Suzy Girl? Maybe, we can talk 'bout the property and all."

"Let's sit on the porch, Grandpa. The heat's not on. It's even colder inside than out here."

He nodded and hobbled up the steps. He slowly sat in the chair.

"I guess Rose gave you those papers?"

"Yeah."

"Suzy Girl, you and that baby's life is with us. We take care of our own. Your daddy and momma would want you to be with us."

"Grandpa, you will always be part of my family, just like you have been after we moved here. I've got a good job at the hospital. I like the people I work with. Besides that, I'm getting married. Pete's in the Army, but he is supporting me and Tootsie. As soon as his time is up, we're getting married."

"Well, I ain't met that boy. Your daddy didn't seem to want him 'round, but if that's who you want, you and he can live ov'r there with us. I already told you I'd buy you a trailer to live in."

Suzy watched Zeke pull out a pouch of tobacco and stuff a wad in his mouth. He continued, "I don't want you stayin' ov'r here after what happen'd to your daddy and momma and Aaron." Zeke's voice grew harsh. "Ain't right what happened to them. These people here let 'em be killed. That damn sheriff—from what I heard, he was friends with that commissioner. Hell, even one of his deputies killed my boys and grandson. That new sheriff ain't without blame either."

Just then, Morgan's car pulled in. Zeke jerked his attention to the car. "You expectin' someone?"

Suzy stood up and waved big to let Zeke think it was a friend. "Yes, that's my friend, Morgan. She and I were going to go through some things, like momma and dad's clothes. The church is having a clothing drive. There's no reason to hold onto those things."

Morgan slowly got out of her car and waved. Suzy yelled, "Hi, Morgan. My grandpa was over here and decided to stop by. I was just telling him that we were going to go through some things for the church drive."

"Oh, hi."

Zeke got up and said in a low voice, "You're not planning on takin' somethin' else, are you? Don't mind you helpin' the church, but I don't want nothin' else taken." It was obvious to him that they couldn't get much in their two cars. "Anybody else comin'?"

"No."

"Okay, you get you momma's clothes and Aaron's if you want, but don't touch Tony's things. You hear me?"

"Yeah."

"Don't come back up here again 'til the judge sorts this all out," he admonished.

He hobbled down the steps. He looked at Morgan but didn't otherwise acknowledge her.

Morgan waited beside her car until he had pulled out of the driveway and drove off. When she got up on the porch, she could tell Suzy was shaken. "Are you okay? You look pale. What happened?"

Suzy told her the story.

"He didn't threaten you, did he?"

"I don't think so. I don't know why he came here. Maybe he was planning to break in. He said he didn't have a key. Let's go in and get this done—the sooner the better. I don't want to be here if he comes back."

"Suzy, I'm going to ask Boone about this. I don't think it's a good idea for him to be here, but I don't know if we can stop it until the property ownership matter is solved."

This really frightened Suzy. "God, Morgan, I don't know what he might do if we take some legal action to keep him off the property."

"Oh, we won't do anything without your permission, but I want to make sure we know what the options are. One thing we could do is to put up 'No Trespass' signs. Even if your grandfather wasn't making a claim, you don't want people up here. There's always curiosity seekers. With the government having removed its signs, people might start coming here."

"I hadn't thought of that, Morgan. I don't want people up here."

"I'll talk to Boone. We'll get some signs put up. With the way the government boarded up the windows, I don't think anyone can get past them. Same with the lock on the door, but we'll have someone look at that too to make sure the house stays secure."

"Okay. Thanks, Morgan."

Once they were in the house, Suzy locked the door. They got to work going through papers and records.

A couple of days later, Suzy was late returning home because she was meeting with Morgan to discuss the case. Rose had Tootsie in her high chair feeding her dinner when she heard someone knocking on the front door. She peeked out the curtain and saw Zeke Pinkston. *What is he doing back here again?* She opened the door. "Zeke. I sure wasn't expectin' you."

"Well, you said that Suzy worked durin' the day. I need to talk to that girl. Rocky and I drove by Tony's place earlier, and it's locked down like it's guarding the Mint. She ain't got no business doin' that."

"The way I see it, Zeke, you don't have no right on that property, but I guess you need the court to tell you that."

"Tell her I'm here."

Rose didn't want to tell him that Suzy was meeting with her lawyer about the land dispute. Rose saw Rocky leaning on the truck looking at them. "Last time you were here, I told you to call first. Anyhow, she ain't here."

Zeke looked skeptical, "What'd you mean, she's not here? Where's she at? I know'd it's late enough for her to be here."

"What's all this interest that caused you to start comin' here, Zeke? Funny, it's just been since the Feds let go of that property. You ain't been here as far as I know'd since you picked up the bodies."

Zeke looked at Rose. "Suzy and that baby are my kin, Rose. They belong ov'r there with me. That's what Tony would have wanted. The sooner she understands that, the better."

"Seems to me the property is somethin' different than Suzy and the baby." Her eyes peered into his.

Tootsie squealed out. "You best get along, Zeke. She ain't here, and I've got to get back to the baby."

"You tell her I want to talk to her," he said as he turned to leave.

Zeke settled into the seat. "That old woman not let you see Suzy?" Rocky asked as he started the truck.

"Suzy wasn't there. She wouldn't say where she was."

"Huh. Probably out partying. Let's head to Knucklepin's. See what the locals have to say."

"Good idea, Son."

At Knucklepin's, Rocky and Zeke each ordered a beer and found a table. It was pretty busy for a Thursday night. Five men had claimed a nearby table and were talking about how they were looking forward to hunting season opening up at month's end. They were discussing where they had the best luck and one of them said, "I kinda like huntin' over in those woods in Mader Valley, but I don't know if I'm goin' to hunt there this year."

"Why's that?" his buddy asked.

"The old sheriff, Mike Adams, has been over there almost every day. I drive by there on my way to work, and his truck is parked along the road."

"How do you know that's him?"

"I seen him a couple of times up at his truck."

"Wonder what he's doin'?"

"Each day, his truck is parked a little further up the road. I don't know, but I think he might be doin' something along that old rail line."

"Wonder what that would be?" asked another man.

"I saw a camera around his neck and some kind of book in his hand one time. He must be takin' pictures, but I don't know. He's by himself."

Zeke and Rocky had been listening. Zeke interrupted, "That's crazy to be out there like that. Good way to get shot." He and Rocky laughed.

The men looked over at Zeke. One said, "Yep. Good thing it ain't huntin' season. Bet he won't be out there after it starts."

Chapter 12

Sean was getting ready to leave the station for the evening when his direct line rang. It was Geri. “Sean, have you talked to Mike today?”

“No. Why?”

“He’s not come home, and I’ve not heard from him. He usually finishes up around three o’clock. I called Frau’s and Knucklepin’s, but they haven’t seen him. I just got off the phone with C.P., and he hasn’t heard from him. He was going to drive out to where Mike was working and see if his truck is there.”

“I’ll head out there and check. Call me if you hear from him.” Sean grabbed his rain gear and high-powered search light just in case.

It was starting to get dark and a light rain was falling, but Sean recognized C.P. standing by his car, which was parked behind Mike’s truck. “Hey, Sean, I just arrived. I don’t see any sign of Mike. I’ve yelled, but nothing.”

“Do you have any idea what part of the track he was working?”

“Yes. When Geri called, I grabbed the schematic. Let’s get in the car so it won’t get wet, and I’ll show you.”

C.P. pointed to the map. "Each day, Mike covers a two-mile stretch of track. This is the area he was working today. From where his truck is parked, it looks like he walked straight down and then worked north for two miles. This is one of the farthest points from the road to the track. It's almost a quarter-of-a-mile."

"We need to search the woods. I'm going to call in the other deputies. We need search lights. I'm also going to call Harold Greene with the state police and ask him to bring in the search dogs. I've got a light. I'm going to walk back in there and head up the track. C.P., if you don't mind, stay here and when the deputies arrive, show them where to start searching."

"Sean, it's dark and rugged terrain. We're expecting heavy rain to set in. Maybe you should wait until others arrive so you're not in there alone."

"Mike may be hurt. I'm not leaving him. I'll be fine."

Sean didn't have a good feeling. Mike would know not to be caught out late in an area like this. Sean was concerned that he was injured and couldn't make it out. Even if he had his cell phone with him, there wasn't service in much of this area. Sean called Cheryl and explained the situation. He asked if she would go stay with Geri. He headed into the dark woods, hoping his buddy was okay.

After about an hour, Arlo caught up with Sean. He said that all the deputies, even those off duty, had joined in the search. The state patrol officers were also coming down the track from the opposite direction. The dogs should be arriving in about another hour.

They searched all night. Heavy rains prevented the search dogs from picking up a scent. Despite his attire, the dampness and chill pressed against Sean's body, but desperation soaked his soul. The sun finally was up enough that they no longer needed search lights, but the drizzle made everything a spectrum of gray. Harold caught up with Sean, "Sean, I've got more troopers who just arrived. They're in formation to comb the area. You've been here all night. Why don't you take a break? You need some food and something warm to drink. We'll find him if he's here."

"He's here, Harold. I'm not stopping until we find him."

"Okay, Sean. Now that it's light, maybe someone will see something."

About forty minutes later, Sean was surveying the ground as he followed the track when he glimpsed something lying off to the side, partially covered by soaked leaves. On closer inspection, he saw it was a pen. He moved closer to the slope's edge. His heart sank as he scampered and slid down the embankment, just avoiding a fall. "Oh, God, no! Please, God, no!" He dove down and tried to pull Mike's body toward him, but something had a tight grip. His lifeless body was soaked and covered in debris. Knowing his friend was no longer with him, Sean gently wiped the leaves and dirt from Mike's face as pain pelted his heart. He leaned into the body to embrace him and howled in anguish. After a time, he wiped away tears and fumbled for his two-way radio.

While they searched for Mike, Cheryl had stayed overnight with Geri. Sean left the scene and drove straight to Geri's. He was dirty, unshaven and his coat and hat drenched. His face was ashen with grief—his eyes and nose were red and his features tight. When Cheryl answered the door, Geri rushed through the door onto the porch. When she saw Sean, she clapped her hands to her mouth and a shriek escaped as she folded. Cheryl and Sean lunged to break her fall. They helped her to the sofa. Cheryl sat beside her—holding her tight—and Sean knelt in front of her. "Geri" was all he could whisper. Sean wasn't even sure if she knew he was there. She had her hands over her eyes, sobbing with abandon. Sean was fighting emotions threatening to overtake him.

After her sobs began to quiet, he choked back his emotions, his voice hoarse, "Geri, I'm sorry, but I need to ask you something."

She eventually calmed enough where she could look at him through red, swollen eyes. "Do you know of anyone who might have wanted to harm Mike?"

She looked startled, "You mean someone did something to Mike?"

Tears were streaming down her face. Sean didn't want to get into the details now if he could avoid it. "It may have been an accident, but we don't yet know."

She was sniffling, and Cheryl went to get her some tissues. “I don’t know of anyone. He was sheriff a long time, but he’s been retired for nearly two years. He never said anything to me. What happened, Sean? How did he die?”

Geri saw Sean’s pain, and oddly, she quieted—not wanting to inflict more torment on him.

“He was shot, Geri.”

She stoically absorbed that in silence. Cheryl had returned and sat beside Geri. Except for the rhythm of the cuckoo clock pendulum, the room was veiled in quietness—and stillness. For a brief moment, they were frozen in time unaware of anything but the grief that had engulfed them. Sean finally stood and looked into Cheryl’s face, which bore the torment of their dear friend’s sorrow and Sean’s bereavement. Tears streamed freely down her cheeks.

“I’ve got to go,” he mouthed.

She nodded and kept holding Geri who seemed unaware of either of them.

She mouthed, “I love you.”

He simply nodded and turned, thinking he couldn’t be there one more second. *I can’t think about things right now. I’ve got to get back to the scene. I’ve got to find his killer.*

After a while, Geri lay down on the sofa, and Cheryl took charge. She knew people would be arriving, and of course, their children would be coming in. She called Bri, who she knew would take care of food. She didn’t need to call Milton, because by now, he would be on the scene. Once

Geri was calm enough, she assisted her in calling their children—Matt who lived in Montana and Miranda in California. A couple of hours later, a steady stream of friends began arriving.

By the time Sean returned to the scene, the entire area had been cordoned off. Sean's deputies wanted to help, so Harold had them managing traffic and crowd control. At Harold's word, a mass of state police was ready to fan out looking for evidence. Harold walked up to Sean, "I called in the state's forensics and coroner. Ronnie and DD should be here anytime. Once Ronnie finishes her forensics work, we'll turn over every rock until we find all traces of evidence."

Sean nodded. He was fighting hard to hold it together. Mike and Sean had been best friends all the way up through high school. Their friendship was rekindled when Sean returned nearly two years ago. The shock of finding Mike had resurrected the crippling loss he experienced when his best friend in the Marines, Clint Neely, was killed in the explosion that nearly took his life.

Harold continued, "I don't know if you noticed, but the backpack he was wearing was snagged on a branch that was lodged between rocks on the creek's edge. It kept the body from being washed downstream. It would have been hard to locate, particularly if it was swept to the river."

Rage jolted Sean. "Keep me posted with every detail. I am going to find the SOB who did this." Sean turned and walked off.

Ronnie's team pulled in, followed shortly by DD, both having driven in from Columbus. No one said much as they went about their grim tasks.

Sean pulled together all his deputies. Even those who were off duty had joined the search, working all night and hanging around until now. "What do you want us to do, Sheriff?" Alex asked. "We all want to help.

Sean was exhausted. "Right now, I've turned the scene over to the state police. They have the manpower to do what needs to be done here. There is one person I want to talk to right away, and that's Cooper Townsend. Alex, you and Syd bring him to the station. I'm going home to change clothes, and then I'll be in to talk to him."

Kim's chest ached from sobbing. She fought to control her emotions as concerned citizens called in disbelief, seeking solace. Moisture clung to her eyelashes and tricked down her cheeks. When Kim saw Sean enter the station, his face grim and pale, her composure again faltered. Sean didn't feel in any shape to deal with someone else's grief, but he knew that Mike and Kim were close. Mike hired her shortly after becoming sheriff.

He hugged and tried to comfort her. "Oh, Sean, I can't believe this. He nearly died about two years ago and now this. I can't begin to imagine how Geri must be feeling. And Matt and Miranda. This is so terrible." Her tears dampened his chest as he held her heaving shoulders. Her sobs gradually began to wane and she looked up at him through tear-filled eyes. "He was your best friend. How are you doing?"

"I'm going to focus on finding who is responsible for this. I can't let my feelings intervene. I know this is hard on you. You worked with him for years. You were like his right hand around here."

She wiped her face with a tissue. "He and Geri and their kids were like family. He'd call every so often after he started recovering and ask how I was doing. He called a few weeks ago and was upbeat. He told me that he and Geri were not moving to Montana. He told me that he was going to be spending time in Mader Valley on a project on the old railroad there. We talked about that." She had calmed. She sniffed. "He seemed happy. I can't believe he is gone."

Sean thought she was going to start crying again. "Kim, why don't you go home? It will be hard, but we'll manage," he said with a caring smile.

She looked at him and pulled herself together. "I can't go home, Chief. I need to be here. It's my therapy."

He nodded, "Okay, but if you want to leave, do so."

Syd was standing outside the interrogation room with a grim face. "Chief, Alex's in there with him. He's like he always is, carping and cussing. Just wanted you to know."

"Thanks, Syd. You've been up all night, but I need for you to talk to all the people out where he lives and see if anyone saw him yesterday."

"Don't worry about me. I'll leave right now."

Sean opened the door. Something about his expression stopped Cooper's forthcoming rant. He looked warily as Sean sat down across from him. Alex was leaning against the wall behind where Sean sat.

"What's happened? Why'd your deputies bring me down here?"

"You don't know, Cooper?" Sean snapped.

"Know what?" Pointing toward Alex, "He didn't tell me jack shit. Just ordered me into the car."

Sean looked hard at Cooper. "Where were you yesterday? I want to know every detail about what you did."

Cooper was skittish. "I was home all day."

"Did anyone see you, Cooper?"

"Hell, how could they? I was home. My truck was out front all day. They may have seen it, but I was inside all day."

Cooper was growing more fidgety, sensing something bad had happened, "What's this all about?" he asked glancing between Sean and Alex.

"Mike Adams, the ex-sheriff, is dead."

"Huh? What happened?"

"I thought you might tell me." Sean's eyes bore granite as he leaned toward Cooper.

"Waaaittt a minute," Cooper screeched. "I don't know shit about this. Why did you bring me here?" Panic flaring in his eyes. "You've been trying to pin somethin' on me ev'r since I got back. You came by the other day tryin' to pin me with someone shootin' at you. I ain't done nothin'!" he yelled as he stood and banged his hands on the table.

"Sit down!" Sean roared as he came out of his seat. Alex straightened, thinking he might have to restrain Sean.

Cooper blanched and sat down. He buried his head in his hands rubbing his head.

"You saw Mike outside Frau's the other day and threatened him since he told you he couldn't help clear your record. Didn't you?" Sean demanded.

Cooper shot his head up and looked at Sean. "No more than I said to you!" he shrieked. "Yeah, I was mad, but I didn't kill him! You tried to pin me with killin' that lawyer too. Found out I didn't do that! Well, I ain't done this!" he yelled.

Alex stood by quietly, but tense. He had never seen Sean on edge like this. Sean glared at Cooper for a long time while Cooper fidgeted and couldn't keep his eyes set. "If you're lying to me, Cooper, we will find out. Alex, take him home."

Chapter 13

After Alex and Syd each returned to the station, Sean met with all the deputies. He was curt, his temper threatening to boil over. The deputies understood that Sean was grieving and overlooked his terse words. They worked on possible suspects and motives. Cooper was at the top of everyone's list. Sean added Kyle to the list, because he was bitter at Sean about being forced to resign. Thinking back about Kyle, Sean remembered he had also blamed Mike for being fired. He even said Mike should have taken care of Ben sooner, that it was his job to do so, not his.

Alex said, "Chief, it's coincidental that you were shot at and then Mike was, but thing is, we don't know for sure if it's the same shooter."

"We don't. We've also been assuming that it is someone who had a grudge against Mike or me, but we can't rule out that there is someone who is shooting at people in Mader Valley. Mike and I both had a routine there. Maybe someone considered us interlopers and didn't want us there. It could even be a serial shooter, and if that's the case, he could start shooting in other parts of the county. It's even possible that Mike's was an accidental shooting and mine wasn't. At this point, we've got to keep open all the possibilities."

Arlo mentioned that Zeke Pinkston and his son, Rocky, had been seen in the area a number of times. "I'll add them to the list," said Sean.

"Chief," asked Syd, "do you think the attempt on you *is* related to Mike's death?"

"Until we know more about the guns used, it's too early to say."

Mack spoke up, "The other day I heard Kim tell you about that complaint that came in from Mrs. Ritter about that weirdo that lives out that way. He's a big hunter. Maybe he was hunting and shot Mike."

Alex interrupted, "But it's not hunting season."

"No, but from what I've heard about him, he hunts even when it's not hunting season." Mack went on to explain, "He lives off the grid and hunts his food. As loony as he is, he might be someone who is shooting at people he thinks are intruders in the Valley."

"Add him to the list," said Sean. Sean thought that Mack had a good point, particularly about a possible hunting incident.

After they talked a while longer, Sean said, "We've got enough to get started. Everyone clear on their assignments?" The deputies nodded their heads. "Okay, I want to know the *minute* you have anything to report. *Anything!* This will be top priority unless I say otherwise. Be prepared to give a status update at our morning meetings."

Sean was not in the mood to hand out accolades, but after everyone left to pursue their assignments, he wearily reflected on the input received from his deputies. They had considered ideas about possible persons of interest and were dialed into the investigation. He realized he had been dogmatic and brusque, but nothing was going to stand in the way of finding who killed Mike.

Sean drove to John Pawley's place. The mastiff came charging from around the side of the house, growling and barking, and stood snarling at the police cruiser. Sean got out eyeing the dog. He was glad he couldn't get past the fence.

About that time, Pawley came walking around from the back of the house in his birthday suit. Sean didn't see how the toboggan and boots kept him warm. Certainly, the holster equipped with a gun wearing low on his sinewy body wouldn't provide warmth. "Hush, Baby." The dog came and stood by Pawley and immediately quieted. "This is the second time you've been up here, Sheriff. More company than I've had in years. I haven't seen that nosey biddy drive by lately. I would have hidden behind the bush if I heard her jalopy coming though."

Sean had noticed a deer hanging from a large hook on the side of the porch. Sean nodded, "Been hunting?"

"Yeah. Got to get ready for the winter."

"It's not hunting season, John."

"Hell, that's why I've been hunting now. Don't want to hunt with all those hunters out there. They might kill me."

A forty-year-old pickup truck sat up ahead of Sean's cruiser. It was hard to determine where the faded paint ended and the rust began. "You drive that truck much?"

Pawley turned his head to look toward the truck, "Not if I can help it. Hell, gas is expensive. I try to limit filling the tank to four times a year if I can."

"You get any news here?"

"No, and I don't want any."

"I take it then that you haven't heard of Mike Adams being shot near here?"

"The previous sheriff?"

"Yes."

"No, I haven't heard that. Did he survive?"

"No."

"Mmm. That's tough."

"Yeah. Could have been someone hunting and shot him. Any possibility you might know something about that, John?"

Pawley's eyes sharpened on Sean. "No. I know the difference between a man and an animal. I don't make those kinds of mistakes."

"Sometimes, from a distance, it can be hard to know."

"I repeat. I don't make those kinds of mistakes."

"Do you have an alibi for yesterday?"

"I was hunting."

"Do you hunt in Mader Valley?"

"Not for deer. I have my special spot north of here that I'd rather not reveal."

Despite his intensity in finding a killer, Sean found himself thinking there was something surreal about standing outside in the middle of November talking to a person of interest who donned only a toboggan, military boots and a firearm. Pawley didn't seem cold.

"Okay, John. I don't want you to get cold standing there. I'll leave you to whatever you're doing. By the way, how did you decide on 'Baby' for that dog's name?"

Baby let out a low growl.

"I liked it better than 'Pooh.'"

"Hey Sean, this is Harold. We may have a break."

"What's that?"

"One of my deputies found a casing up under a small rock overhang just below the place where we think the shooter was standing when he took those shots at you. He may have given up trying to find it thinking you might come after him. From its condition, it doesn't look like it's been there long. That's what leads me to think it was from the shooter. I'll get this casing to Ronnie and see what she can determine. It's from a 308 Winchester round, which is consistent with the type of hunting rifle we think could have been used."

"Any evidence on Mike's killing?"

"One more thing before I get to that. I talked to Zeke Pinkston about someone shooting at you. This was before Mike was killed. He wasn't cooperative other than to say he and his son were home when someone shot at you. I don't know if you've been there, but it looks like a compound. Anyway, by visiting him, he's on notice that he's on our radar." When Sean didn't respond, Harold continued.

"Ronnie and DD have Mike's murder on the top burner. They plan to call you soon."

"Keep me posted on any progress about Mike's case."

"Will do, Sean. Oh, there is one interesting thing. I had some of my troopers fan out on the other side of the creek to see if the shooter had been over there. One of them found a very old hunting knife just downstream. Someone must have lost it years ago. I don't know what you might want to do with it, but I'll drop it off by the station later."

"Okay. I'll be in touch."

Chapter 14

Sean arrived home late. Cheryl and Buddy rushed to welcome him, but he dismissively rubbed his hand across Buddy's head and barely returned Cheryl's embrace. He was tired and pale. "Honey, dinner's ready. Come in and sit down. I just made some coffee. Sean mumbled and followed her into the kitchen. Buddy kept rubbing against his leg, and when Sean sat, Buddy plopped his head on Sean's leg. Sean finally acknowledged Buddy and began rubbing his head as Buddy's tail wagged.

Sean's fatigue and weariness were all too obvious. Cheryl carried the conversation trying to distract him. She told him that Matt and Miranda were arriving tomorrow. Bri and Kim were ensuring there would be plenty to eat, and friends had stopped by throughout the day. Sean's interaction consisted of an occasional inane comment.

"If you're alright, I plan to stay overnight with Geri tonight."

"Of course I'm alright," he snapped. Cheryl blinked, and Buddy got up from the floor and moved to put his head on Sean's leg again. They finished their dinner in silence, and Sean told her he needed to get back to the station.

The next morning, Kim buzzed Sean and told him that a man wanted to talk to him but wouldn't give his name. "Put it through."

"Sheriff, it's Clay from Koot's. I liked Mike. I also know that someone took a shot at you. I don't talk about things that happen here, but there's something I thought you should know. Something I overheard."

"What's that?"

"Zeke Pinkston came in Koot's one afternoon. This was before someone took a shot at you. He talked about still having some business even though Ben and Jeff were dead. He's still carrying a grudge about his family being killed. He didn't mention you or Mike that day, but I heard from someone else that he was bitter against Mike because of his connection with the men that killed his family. He doesn't think Mike was blind to what was going on back then and blames him. People like Pinkston won't stop until they feel they have righted a wrong, even if it's a misplaced notion."

"Alright, Clay. Thanks for the heads-up. I'd appreciate if you hear anything else that you give me a call."

Over the lunch hour, Sean talked by conference call to Ronnie and DD. "Sean," said Ronnie, "unfortunately, the bullet fragments we retrieved from the tire and your truck's side door don't tell us much. Harold thinks the 308 Winchester casing he found came from the shooter. We can't know that for sure, but it seems plausible.

Harold's people are still searching for the bullet that flew past your head, but he feels it's a long shot to find it."

Sean wasn't interested in who shot at him unless the shooter was the same person who had killed Mike. As it happened, they were ready to switch to Mike's shooting.

DD spoke, "Here's the thing, Sean. The bullet that killed Mike is also a 308 Winchester round. This ammunition is widely used, so it could be a coincidence, but if we can find the bullet that missed you, we could determine if the bullets were fired from the same gun. Now, Harold and Ronnie both think the shooter was waiting at a straight-a-way, and as Mike walked around the bend in the track, he took the shot. Mike may never have seen him. This shot was less than a hundred yards, so not nearly the range involved in your shooting.

"The bullet entered the sternum area. The shot was enough to mortally wound him. Given the bleeding, he died soon after being shot. Not that it would have mattered given the severity of the wound and his isolation, but his phone would have been useless since there was no cell service where he was found. Because the bullet entered from the front, he fell backward, landing on his backpack, which was still on him when his body was found. We are running the bullet through the data base."

Sean remained silent, so Ronnie spoke, "We think the shooter dragged his body to the embankment's edge and pulled it down to the creek. We don't know if more than one person was involved, but one person could have done this if he had the strength. We believe he expected the creek to wash the body in its current toward the river that flows south of Bekbourg, which would have happened, especially with the hard rains overnight, but the backpack's strap was hung on a large branch that was lodged under the water's edge. We suspect the shooter was in a hurry and left once he had the body in the edge of the water. Had the victim's body washed away from the shoreline, it could have taken days to find it."

When Sean didn't comment, DD and Ronnie glanced at each other. They couldn't see Sean, but they assumed he was listening. DD continued, "Given the contents in his stomach and the condition of the body, we think the time of death was in the early afternoon. He had eaten a lunch."

Ronnie asked, "Sean, do you have any questions?"

"No. I appreciate you putting a rush on this."

"I have a couple of other things I want to review, and then I'll contact you about returning his body," DD said. "We also want to say that we're sorry. We know that you and Mike had known each other a long time and were close."

"Thanks."

Sean was sitting at his desk when he hung up the phone. The photo sitting on the credenza caught his eye. He inherited it from Mike when he moved into the office. It was a photograph taken by the *Bekbourg Tribune* of them standing shoulder-to-shoulder in their football uniforms before the state championship game their senior year. Both looked determined to bring home to Schriever High the winning trophy, and the team did. Now, Mike was gone. Sean put his head between his hands and took a deep breath. He was glad that Cheryl had stayed over at Geri's last night. He knew he was terrible company. He was struggling to handle the grief, and his single focus was to find Mike's killer. It was difficult to deal with any distractions. He saw the hurt in Cheryl's eyes last night when he lashed out when she asked if he was okay. The deputies were giving wide berth, but he wouldn't rest until he found Mike's killer.

The nightmare that so frequently haunted him after Clint's death had replayed itself, forcing him awake in a scream with his body soaked in perspiration. Despite the passage of time, its vividness and gore had not diminished. Buddy had jumped up on the bed, routing his nose under Sean's hands trying to get petted—his way of showing support. *Oh, God. I hope those aren't returning.* They always left him drained. Kim had commented on his limp today, thinking he had injured himself searching for Mike. The shrapnel wounds were still painful, but they were particularly stark after a nightmare.

Chapter 15

Alex knew Sean was burning candles at both ends. He was at the precinct when deputies arrived for their morning shifts and there when they got off duty. He was tired, but no one around the precinct dared suggest that he get some rest. Another matter weighing on Sean's mind was the safety of his deputies. He had been shot at, and Mike—the former sheriff—was dead. He didn't know if the entire department was a target, but more than once he had cautioned all of them to be on alert and take precautions. Cheryl and Kye were probably vexed by his persistent reminders to be diligent, but they had the good grace to never show it.

As Alex and Sean drove to Zeke Pinkston's, Sean was in no mood for small talk. He was only interested in hearing about the deputies' progress in the investigation. The deputies were investigating the activities of Zeke and his son in Bekbourg. They were talking to neighbors who might know the whereabouts of Cooper when Mike was shot. They were canvassing gun stores in the region about guns sold there, and they were patrolling Mader Valley regularly, but so far nothing looked suspicious.

They were also talking to people close to Mike who might know something. The *Tribune* and local TV station were asking anyone with any information to contact the sheriff's office.

"Alex, everyone needs to double down on their efforts. Reiterate to the others if they learn of anything that might be a lead, I want to know immediately."

"Will do."

The gravel driveway would be easy to miss because of the overgrowth along the road, except for the battered mailboxes on wood posts leaning to varying degrees. A rusted gate hung on its hinges blocking the drive—except it wasn't secured. Alex got out and swung open the gate, allowing the cruiser to pass. Sean and Alex drove up an incline that had woods on one side and a field on the other where a couple of horses and some cattle grazed. They pulled into an opening. Straight ahead was a white clap-board house with peeling, smudged paint. Off to one side were three mobile homes with older model vehicles sitting around, a couple of which were on blocks and ready for the junk yard. Smoke circled above from the wood burning stoves that had been retrofitted into the shanty additions to the mobile homes and from the house's chimney. Firewood was stacked under a large covered shelter.

A vicious welcoming committee of Dobermans rushed the cruiser as Sean and Alex pulled up in front of Zeke's house. Sean and Alex waited, but Zeke didn't appear to call off the dogs. "Alex, get the spray canisters." Just as Sean and Alex were readying to open the doors, Zeke walked out and yelled a command. "Keep the canisters ready, Alex, in case those dogs charge."

The dogs retreated and perched near the porch. Because of an occasional low growl and the dogs' trained attention, Alex warily eyed the dogs. One of them looked like one that Alex had seen at Tony Pinkston's place the morning he was found dead. He wondered if Zeke had claimed the two dogs. Sean noticed a couple of window curtains pulled back on the mobile homes by curiosity-seekers.

"This is a surprise, Sheriff."

"Is it?" Sean replied when they got to the base of the steps.

Zeke leaned his head slightly, "That's not very friendly. I already told that state trooper that my boy and me were here when someone shot at you."

Zeke, where were you day before yesterday?"

Zeke squinted. "Don't see that's none of your business. I think you all better turn 'round and leave."

"Have you been in Mader Valley anytime within the last month?"

Feigning boredom, Zeke looked off in a distance. "Might have."

"I was told that you and another man were driving on Mader Road the other day. Mind telling me why you were driving up that way? It's a pretty isolated place. Not many houses. Not much traffic."

"Zeke smirked. "Bekbourg got surveillance on all its roads now?"

"What were you doing there?"

Zeke spat a tobacco wad. "I don't see how that's any of your damn business, but I don't see no harm in tellin' you. My ancestors used to own a farm in that area. I wanted to see what that property looks like now."

"You just suddenly got an interest in that property?" When Zeke didn't respond, Sean continued, "You have probably heard that Mike Adams was shot and killed."

"Yeah, I heard that. Sounds like someone don't like the job the sheriffs are doin' there in Bekbourg."

"Before he was killed, Mike told me that he saw you at Frau's and you were threatening him."

"I made it clear that I wasn't happy with him. He didn't protect my family. It was one of his deputies that killed them."

"You unhappy enough to kill him?"

He took his time spitting another tobacco wad. "He damn sure let 'em die under his watch, but as far as I know'd, he didn't order it."

"I understand that you have a son, Rocky. Where was he two days ago?"

"I don't think I like your question."

"I don't give a damn what you like. We're investigating the death of a former sheriff. Answer the question."

Zeke squinted, "Next time you decide you want to drive over here and insult me, you call our sheriff first. I'm goin' to call Elmer and tell him that the Bekbourg sheriff's department is harassing one of his residents."

"You do that, Zeke, but I'll tell him what I'm telling you. I'm not going to stop until I find who killed Mike, and I don't give a damn which county they live in."

Sean was determined to learn as much as he could as quickly as possible and that meant personally interviewing everyone under suspicion. Despite it being late afternoon, on their return from Tapsaw County, he and Alex drove to where Kyle lived. A single-wide trailer had a wood lean-to built on the front end on one side of the mobile home. His home was surrounded by woods and isolated from neighbors. "Mind if we come in, Kyle? We've got some questions."

Kyle stepped back, and they followed him inside. There were a few cardboard boxes sitting around. He cleared off a kitchen chair and moved it into the small living room where two upholstered chairs sat with a small table between them. A television sat on a plain wood cabinet in the corner.

"You moving, Kyle?"

"Thought I might. Thought I might find a deputy job in one of the counties nearby."

"Someone shot Mike in Mader Valley two days ago. Before that, someone took some shots at me. You happen to know anything about any of this, Kyle?"

He shook his head, "Nope, Sean. I don't know nothin' 'bout either of those."

"You didn't know they happened?"

"Well, I heard 'bout that with you. I heard at Knucklepin's, but I ain't been nowhere in a couple of days, so I ain't heard 'bout Mike. Is he okay?"

"No, he's dead."

Kyle looked surprise. "No, I didn't know that." He was chewing on his cuticle.

"You have any guns, Kyle?"

"Yeah, I've got a hunting rifle, but I don't hunt no more. It belonged to Dad. I also have a hand gun."

"You know of anyone who would want me or Mike dead?"

"No, I don't know of no one."

"You been to Mader Valley recently?"

"No."

"You don't harbor any hard feelings toward me about leaving the department?"

Kyle glanced at Alex, who didn't react. "No. I'm looking for another job."

"I'd like to see your guns."

Kyle looked at Sean and Alex and for the first time since Sean had known him, he pushed back, "I don't think so."

"Why's that?"

"Just 'cause, Sean."

"What kind of rifle do you have?"

Kyle's head shook. "Ain't goin' to say no more."

Sean stood, and Alex followed suit. "If you decide to move, you let me know where you'll be."

"I'll do that, Sean."

"If you think of anything that might be helpful, we need to know."

Sean was suspicious about Zeke's claim that his family once owned property in Mader Valley, so he asked the county property department to research it.

When Kathy Isaac from the property department called, she confirmed that a Magnus Pinkston had once owned thirty acres along Mader Valley Road. He sold it in 1911 to Stefan Frank, who was a large property owner in that area.

Sean's suspicions were not dampened. *Even though it turned out to be true that Zeke's family once owned property in Mader Valley, his claim that he was cruising the area to look at ancestral property seems awfully convenient.*

Chapter 16

Cheryl ran by the *Tribune* to catch up on things. When she entered the front door, she could see right away that their receptionist was frazzled.

"Hi, Cheryl." Patti Richards greeted Cheryl but didn't wait for a reply. "The phone's been ringing off the hook. Milton told me to talk to you." The jean-wearing, middle-aged receptionist was great at multitasking. Her short, bleached blond hair sprang around her round face. She wheeled her chair around the mini corridor behind her desk as though she and the chair were one. Her only wardrobe statement, her eyeglass chain, danced along the sides of her face from her brown-rimmed glasses planted on top of her head. Her desk was piled with clutter including used tea bags in plastic wrap. *Thank goodness*, Cheryl thought, *she doesn't expect me and the rest of the staff to reuse coffee grounds the way she reuses tea bags*.

Pointing to pink note slips pierced on an erect spike, Patti remarked, "People around here are going nuts about the Mader Valley ghost. You wouldn't believe how many people have called to see what we know about the legend. I know we've written some articles over the past, especially around Halloween, but they are wondering what really happened to Mader."

"What do you mean?"

"Well, they know that a man named Mader died there. That's why it's called 'Mader Valley,' but there are all sorts of rumors about his death. They all want to know the details. This business about Mike being killed and the sheriff being shot at there has stirred the hornet's nest. Some of the callers are starting to call it the 'Valley of Murder.'"

"Mmm." Cheryl sat in front of Patti's desk. "I remember hearing about the ghost legend when I was young, but I never knew the story behind the legend. You know, with this much interest, this might be one of those historic stories that I've been talking about running in the paper."

Gathering the pink slips, Patti handed them to Cheryl, "There's definitely an interest. I've already been telling people we were looking into it. I'll tell them to watch for the story."

Despite her weariness, Cheryl grinned and stood. "I'll get started right now." She empathized with Milton who said he felt like saluting around Patti.

The phone rang, diverting Patti's attention. Cheryl heard as she walked through the door, "*Bekbourg Tribune*. What can I do for you?"

It had been a long day, but on his way home, Sean stopped by to check on Geri. For her sake, he was glad to see her house buzzing with people. A team of women was working in the kitchen. Danny

Chambers, who had played football with Sean and Mike, his son Drew and Matt were sitting on the porch despite the cool evening. Geri and Becky Werner, Geri's best friend from high school and owner of the large dealership in Bekbourg, were in the living room. Sean talked a few minutes with Danny, Drew and Matt and then walked into the living room. He spoke to Becky and then sat down on the sofa next to Geri. "Hi, Geri. It looks like you've got a lot of people taking care of things around here." Becky excused herself and went into the kitchen.

Geri's lips attempted a smile. "I'm blessed to have such dear friends. I insisted that Cheryl go home and get some rest. She was up all night with me night before last, and I know she didn't get much sleep last night either."

"She was glad to help, Geri. Everyone wants to help."

"Everyone has been so generous and caring, Sean. Bri brought over the biggest bunch of pastries and dishes that she and Max prepared. Mary has been by twice and brought dishes. Kim is organizing with the church for us to have food for several more days. I'm glad for all the support. It helps."

"Well, if there is anything we can do, let us know," he said as he stood.

"I will, Sean, but you look awful. I'm worried about you. How are you doing?"

"We'll get through this, Geri. I'm trying to find who did this. That is my way of dealing with things."

Geri got up and gave him a weak smile and walked into his arms—tears glistening in her eyes. "Let me walk you to the door."

Just before he was to step out on the porch, she took his hand. "Sean, Mike loved you like a brother. He always said you were his best friend. He told me that again the other day after he got back from you and him having lunch at Frau's."

"Thank you for telling me, Geri. One thing that is the absolute truth is that you were the love of his life, and he knew every day that he was a very lucky man."

He kissed her on the cheek and squeezed her hand. When he got to his car, he fought the spill of tears.

When he arrived home, Cheryl and Buddy greeted Sean when he walked through the door. He hugged Cheryl tight as Buddy ran circles around them with his thick tail swatting their legs. Once Cheryl stepped back, Sean gave Buddy a hug and patted his head. They all walked into the kitchen where Cheryl already had dinner ready. Trying to make amends for the way he had barked at her the night before, he asked, "How did you have time to fix all this? I just left Geri's, and she said you had only recently left." He noticed she had dark circles under her eyes.

"We owe this delicious pot roast to Bri and Max. They are keeping us and Geri's family fed."

"I'm glad they're helping. Geri told me that you hadn't slept in two nights."

"Well, I'm sure the same is true for you. I noticed you limping and rubbing your thigh. Did you have one of those dreams last night?"

"Yes, but I don't really want to talk about it."

They talked for a few minutes about the people that Sean had seen at Geri's and what was happening. She told him that C.P. had been there for a couple of hours earlier in the day. "He insisted on paying for all the funeral expenses. Geri balked, but in the end, C.P. convinced her it was because Mike was working on a project for him."

Sean told her it had been a long two days. He told her about driving to Tapsaw County to talk to Zeke Pinkston.

"You think he had something to do with it—off the record, of course?" She tried to keep things light.

He managed a grin, "Off the record—I don't know, but I thought I should pay him a visit."

"Well, he has been over here some recently."

Sean remembered seeing him with Rose the other day. "I'm glad you raised that just now. I'm going to talk to Rose and see what she can tell me about Zeke being here."

"One other thing. The newspaper has been flooded with calls with people asking about the ghost of Mader Valley. With Mike being killed there, it's engendered interest."

"Mmm. I don't want people to exploit Mike's death with some ghost legend. I sure as hell don't want people to start talking about Mike's ghost."

Cheryl was quiet while she took a couple of bites. "You know, Sean, you raise a good point. None of us want that. Through the years, people have talked about the ghost of Mader Valley. The legend has grown. It's almost like a cult. People go to Mader Valley sometimes for seances. Teenagers go there especially around Halloween. Sightings of Mader's ghost have been reported over the years."

"That's my point."

"Maybe, I should research the legend. See what's in the old files at the newspaper. If I can find some information, I could run some articles about what happened to Mader."

Sean didn't want to think any more about a ghost legend. He noticed a book lying on the counter. "Is that the book that Milton and everyone were talking about the other day?"

"Yes, I found a copy at the library and was a third of the way through it when that happened to Mike. When Bri and Max stopped by, I told them about it. They are going to read it. It's really good. Sally heard us talking about it, and she found a copy in the bookstore."

Sean smiled a little. "Sounds like the start of a book club."

"It could be. Everyone is so busy right now, but they are into the book. I ought to consider a 'Book of the Month' column."

"I thought you were going to start a column on bridge?"

Cheryl's smile did not conceal her weariness, "I am. Kye's weekly bridge games gave me the inspiration to add a syndicated bridge column in the *Tribune*. There are quite a few people around here who play bridge."

Sean stood and pulled Cheryl up into his arms. He needed to feel the comfort she brought, but he also just wanted to hold her. "You are always thinking. You've got terrific ideas for the *Tribune*. I appreciate you being there for Geri and the kids. Thank you."

They kissed and kept each other in their arms as cleaning the kitchen became a forgotten chore.

Chapter 17

Cheryl and Milton were in the conference room at the *Tribune* drinking coffee. "I'm going to delve into our archives, Milton, and see what I can find about the origins of the Mader ghost legend. Sean mentioned something last night about not wanting people to equate Mike with Mader."

"How's he doing?"

Cheryl paused. "He won't admit it, but it's been hard. He's haunted by it. They were best friends throughout their youths. The bond was made more special by their football. They spent *hours* running passing formations. Sean once told me that it was like magic how in sync his throws and Mike's catches were. Sean knew where Mike would be on the field. All he had to do was throw in Mike's direction, and Mike was there to catch it. Their lives were knitted together. Even Mike's death won't break the strings that bound him and Sean."

Cheryl drank some coffee before she continued. "Added to that is the pressure Sean is putting on himself to find the killer."

"Plus, someone tried to kill him."

"Yes, but he's carrying other worries, Milton. He's concerned that the shooter might try something close to home, and Kye and I could be in danger. He's even wondering if his deputies could be targets—if it's some deranged person who is anti-law enforcement. He told me it could even be a serial shooter around Bekbourg. He's got to be careful. We know he's a target. If he's distracted, he could . . . . God, I don't even want to think about it."

"I know telling you not to worry would be wasting my breath, but remember, Sean's a professional. He saw a lot during those years he was investigating crimes for the Marines. He knows not to let down his guard. I know that the victim being Mike complicates it, but he'll work through things. It may take some time. It's probably a good thing that he has something like catching the killer to focus on."

"I guess you're right. It bothers me to see how obsessed he is."

"You both have a lot on you. You have been a huge support to Geri."

"You've made that possible, Milton. The paper is running like a well-oiled machine. Patti told me that we are printing extra copies with the stories you've written on Mike's death and the investigation. I am so grateful you are here."

A grin hinted on Milton's lips, "I'm having fun. I haven't been here long, but Bekbourg feels like home."

Cheryl teased, "Maybe Martha has something to do with that?"

Cheryl laughed as a blush rose on his cheeks. "Yeah, maybe." Milton put a stick of gum in his mouth. Since suffering a heart attack a few years ago, chewing gum had replaced cigarettes.

"Not to change the subject, but people are curious about the rumored renovation of the old Schumacher Cigar Box factory. We wrote a short story about the building being bought and the Fischner Construction Company filing a permit application to refurbish it, and people started calling wanting to know about its history and what was going on. I've asked Lilly to review our old files and see what she could find out about its history. When it was constructed, it was the crown jewel of Bekbourg.

"Konrad Schumacher brought in an architect from Boston to design the cigar box factory in the Richardsonian Romanesque style. Many public buildings constructed in the later part of the 1800's adopted this style, such as courthouses, churches, and train stations. A beautiful example is the Trinity Church in Boston. As you know from the cigar box factory, stone exteriors along with gabled roofs and towers are incorporated into the design. I really like the large round stained-glass window that centers the central tower in the front of the Schumacher factory. Schumacher's mansion also reflects this style. Two beautiful structures that Bekbourg can be proud of."

"The factory was boarded up when I was growing up. I always thought it was a shame that such a dominating presence stood empty. What's the word on the buyer and the plans?" Cheryl asked.

Milton shrugged, "Haven't been able to find out. The purchaser is Livingstone Trust. It's a private trust, so we don't know much about it. Cole Fischner is tight-lipped about the owner and the renovation plans. Anyway, we are going to run some stories about its history, including copies of photos of the workers inside making the cigar boxes and pictures of the boxes themselves. We have old photos of Konrad and interviews from the old papers."

Chapter 18

Kye Davis played bridge each week with three other retired school teachers—Milly Couture, Ann Parr and Lucia Delgado. After a six-hand round, they switched partners and started a new score. After three rounds, the winner was determined by whoever had the highest individual score. Ann and Lucia had just finished a round with a 700 point rubber and a partial game. Ann served more coffee as they shifted seats where Kye would be paired with Lucia.

"Okay, Dear," Kye said to Lucia, "It's now our turn. I haven't had a good hand all day."

Ann who was the dealer said, "Sorry, but I plan to deal a good hand to me and Milly."

Milly watched the cards being dealt, "I'm ready, Ann. Deal me a two no-trump opening hand. I won't be greedy."

They all smiled.

They knew that Kye rented one side of the duplex to Sean and Cheryl. "Kye, do you know if Sean is close to finding out who killed Mike?" asked Lucia.

"No, Dear. I haven't seen them long enough to talk to them. Sean is late coming home and early leaving. Cheryl has been spending a lot of time at Geri's as well as at the paper."

"I wonder if Mike's shooting is related to Sean's shooting?" asked Ann.

"That's a good question. We sure can't have Sean injured," Lucia said as she frowned at her cards.

Milly was drinking her coffee and had not yet looked at her cards. "What do any of you know about who bought the old cigar box factory?"

"Or what their plans are?" asked Ann. "Kye, has Cheryl said anything? The paper ran the story about it but just mentioned a trust company as the buyer."

"No, I've not had time to talk to her, but I did hear something interesting."

"Oh, what's that?" inquired Ann, who was sorting her cards.

"Well, you know that Fischner Construction is going to do the renovations. Karl's health is not good, so Cole has taken over running the company. Noel came into the property division in the county office the other day trying to find out who the owner was. He was pretty short with Kathy from what I heard."

"Why on earth would he be upset with Kathy?" asked Lucia.

"Why was Kathy upset?" asked Milly who was hard of hearing.

"Milly, Ann is ready to bid."

"Oh, let me see if Ann dealt me a good hand." She put down her cup and picked up her cards.

"Noel Fischner was upset that someone had bought the old cigar box. He wasn't upset at Kathy."

"Who was upset at Noel?" asked Milly as she sorted her cards.

"No one, Dear. Noel was upset at Kathy."

"Oh. That's too bad. He shouldn't act that way toward Kathy," said Milly, as she too was scowling at her cards.

"Well, isn't that kind of like Noel to be like that?" asked Lucia.

Ann said, "He's always been temperamental, but I wonder if it has something to do with his brother doing the work on the building? Even when those boys were in school, I thought Noel was jealous of Cole."

"That may be right," Milly said as she bid a "pass."

"Well, at least I can open," said Kye. "One heart."

Chapter 19

Sean went to see Rose. "Come in, Sheriff. I was just getting ready to give Tootsie a snack." Tootsie was holding on to Rose's dress hiding behind her legs and peeking out at Sean. He smiled at her, and she ducked further behind Rose but continued to look up at him with her big eyes. "Let's go to the kitchen. I'll get her settled, and we'll get caught up."

After Rose got Tootsie settled in her high chair with her snack, they sat and drank coffee talking for a few minutes before Sean asked, "Rose, Cheryl told me that Zeke has been by here to see you and Suzy. Does he come by often?"

She explained how his visits started once the federal government decided it didn't want the property. "He has been here several times. You saw him here that one day. He was by himself then, but usually that younger boy of his is driving. I especially remember the last time they were here. The visit was bad enough that day, but then I heard the late news on TV about Mike Adams missing."

This caught Sean's attention. "About what time of the day was he here?"

"It was later in the afternoon. I'd say about four o'clock or thereabouts. He was wanting to see

Suzy, but she wasn't here. He didn't ask to see Tootsie that day. I guess he knew I wouldn't let him."

"Was his son with him then?"

"Yeah. I always look to see. He must do the drivin' when it's them two."

"How did Zeke seem? Was there anything unusual? Anything about his clothes or about his son that you noticed?"

"No, it was 'bout as always."

Mack's wife was in a particularly foul mood, and the peanut butter sandwich for dinner he figured was proof. "I hope you're happy that I'm not going on the trip with my bridge club. I made up an excuse that my sister is ill and I may have to go to Athens to stay with her for a few days. I just don't believe that the money could have dried up like it did? Are you in trouble, Mack? What's goin' on?"

"Nothing's going on, Loretta. Your spending finally caught up with us. All this fancy stuff around here. That yearly trip you go on. The well finally ran dry. It's not me doing anything with the money. I don't hardly spend a dime."

"I can't believe that he demoted you. You've been there longer than anyone. You should have been the sheriff, not him."

"Let's not go back over that, Loretta. He's the sheriff."

"Well, Mike wouldn't have ever demoted you. He counted on you. You were the assistant sheriff, for goodness sake. Seems Sean managed to push Mike and you both aside."

He finished his sandwich and started to go watch TV. "Let it go, Loretta."

After he left the room, Loretta fumed. It was only a matter of time, if they didn't already know it, that people would learn Mack had been demoted. She hated to be humiliated like this. Well, she would think of ways to undermine that pompous over-the-hill football star. People will see what a mistake it was to elect him sheriff and maybe Mack could run for sheriff next time.

Chapter 20

Suzy and Morgan had finished discussing the case when Morgan said, "Suzy, I would like to take you to dinner. You're my client. What do you say?"

"I'd really like that a lot. Let me call Ma Maw and make sure she is okay with it."

Rose was thrilled that Suzy was doing something for a change other than work and her home life. Morgan and Suzy walked to Max's bistro. Even though they were in a professional relationship, they had begun to develop a friendship. During dinner, Suzy told her about Pete and their plans. She learned that Morgan worked for a firm in Columbus her first two years out of law school.

"Timing is everything," Morgan laughed and explained that Boone was looking for a young attorney, and she sent a copy of her resume. She told Suzy that she had a boyfriend during law school but he took a job in D.C., and the long-distance thing just didn't work out. She was so busy at the law firm she didn't have time to make friends, much less date. There wasn't anyone special in her life.

After they ordered dessert, Morgan asked, "If you could do anything you wanted, what would you want to do, besides marry Pete?" They laughed.

"I don't really think about things like that, Morgan. I'm trying to keep my head above water with my job and then taking care of Tootsie. I'm looking forward to marrying Pete when he finishes his first enlistment."

"I realize all that, but you must think about what interests you."

"Well, I like working at the hospital. I'm part of the cleaning crew, but I watch the nurses—how they care for people. They work hard and are really dedicated to their patients. I guess if I could be anything I wanted, I'd be a nurse."

Morgan's smile was radiant, "Great! Then let's figure out how you can do that."

Suzy laughed out loud. "What? Are you crazy? I can't do that."

"Sure you can. I bet Hillsrock Community College has a program. It may even be part-time, so if you want, you can still work at the hospital."

Optimism momentarily jolted her but then her buoyancy was dashed. "There is no way I can afford to go to school."

"There are ways, Suzy. There are grants and scholarships. If you want to be a nurse, it can happen."

She had never allowed herself to dream about the future beyond Pete and Tootsie. "Oh, my gosh. Do you really think so?"

"I sure do." Morgan and Suzy talked about the possibility of her becoming a nurse.

Chapter 21

"Sean, I'm very sorry about Mike. I know that you and he go way back."

"Thanks, C.P. and thanks for coming by." They sat in Sean's office.

"What can I do for you?" C.P. asked.

"Mike told me some about what he was doing for you, but I'd like to hear it from you."

"Sure. I'd appreciate if you kept this to yourself. I'm planning to make an announcement soon about some of my plans, but the part that Mike was working on is down the road, if it ever happens.

"Back in the 1840's the City of Bekbourg built the West Virginia Bekbourg & Cincinnati Railroad Company, the WVB&C, from Cincinnati to Wheeling, West Virginia, to move coal, lumber, and other goods. It was a way for the local businesses to get their goods to markets and a way to get supplies delivered. The line was also used for passenger trains. After building the railroad through the center of town, the city also built a switching yard, freight house and passenger depot. All are still here today.

"Then, in 1905, owners of the Maryland Virginia & Ohio Railroad Company, the MV&O, which served regions in Ohio and Appalachia, decided they wanted to expand rail service, and the WVB&C offered a strategic fit. The city was unwilling to sell their railroad, so the MV&O offered to lease the system under a long-term arrangement. From the city's perspective, MV&O's lease proposal relieved it from operating a railroad while continuing a revenue stream. Over time, the institutional memory that Bekbourg owned the rail line faded, and people, including the employees, identified the rail system as being part of the MV&O.

"A merger between the MV&O and a larger company in the 1990's formed the Ohio Maryland Virginia Consolidated Railroad Corporation, the OMVX. Because of the size of the two railroad companies, there were some parallel rail lines and redundant train yards. The new company's vision was to streamline operations and capitalize on efficiencies. This meant closing less profitable lines and consolidating facilities. Where there was overlap in employees and facilities, decisions had to be made about cutting workforces and closing depots and yards. The WVB&C was one of those lines that didn't fit into OMVX's long-term plan. Over time, service was curtailed.

"When I worked on the OMVX, I came across this information about the lease. That is the reason I returned to Bekbourg, Sean. I want to buy that line., There have been a lot of moving parts in trying to put the deal together, not the least of which is getting the financing arranged." C.P. breathed a sigh of relief. "Things are looking up. I finally got word last week that the financing is coming through."

"That would be welcome news around Bekbourg, C.P. The railroad workers have been concerned about what was going to happen to them. My dad works for the milk plant, and he's been concerned about the economic impact to the plant if they lose the rail transportation."

"Well, you know how these things are. It's not done until it's done. There are still some things that have to be worked out and approvals obtained under the Railway Labor Act and with the Federal Railroad and Surface Commission. That's why I don't want this to get out just yet. A critical part before I can move forward is that I need to get the city to agree for me to buy the line."

"How does the spur line that Mike was working on fit into this?"

"It's a separate matter. The city doesn't own it. The spur line was built in the 1880's by a lumber and mining conglomerate that had an operation north of here. They built the spur line to bring their lumber and iron ore down to the WVB&C here in town to be transported. Over time, the lumber portion of the business ended because the trees were lumbered out. Later, the mining operations ceased, and the spur line wasn't needed. It's laid dormant all these years.

"It looks like the state is moving forward with building the lodge and cabins and conference center at Peatmont State Park. Years ago, the state had plans to do that, but when the economy hit a downward cycle, those plans were put on hold.

Bekbourg has reinvented itself as a tourist destination. My goal is to turn that spur line into a scenic railroad between here and the state park. However, this is on down the road, Sean. My first priority is to buy the WVB&C. Another thing, I don't even know if it is feasible to do what I want to do with the spur line. That's what Mike was doing. He was doing an initial evaluation of the condition of the line. If the integrity of the line is good, I plan to bring in an engineering firm to do a complete feasibility study to see what work and financing is necessary."

"Do you have any reason to think someone is opposed to what you are planning to do with the spur line?"

C.P. raised an eyebrow, "I hadn't considered that, but no, I don't think so. I contacted the heirs of the lumber and mining company, because that is who owns the spur line. We entered into a letter agreement where, if I decide after conducting the evaluation and feasibility studies, that I want to make an offer, we will attempt to negotiate a sale. I think they are hoping I decide to buy it because they don't have any use for the line. It's just sitting there."

"So you don't know of anyone who would be opposed to what Mike was doing for you?"

"No, not at all."

All the deputies were present for their morning meeting. "Our investigation is going nowhere." Sean looked around to make sure he had their undivided attention. “We need to shake things up. Let’s review what we know.”

Mack spoke, “That man who lives near Irma Ritter in Mader Valley—he’s obsessed with guns. I bet he’s got a gun that shoots a 308 Winchester bullet.”

Alex spoke up, “How would we find out? From what I know about him, he’s a recluse. I’d be surprised if he told us if he has one.”

“Sheriff, I’ve talked to people all around where Cooper lives and places he might go, like Knucklepin’s and some other bars. I haven’t found an alibi. I can’t find any information that he owns a rifle. The only gun he ever mentioned was a 9 mm, which he said disappeared when Ben Clark arrested him. That gun never showed up.” Syd reminded everyone.

“We searched his place when Owen Donaldson was killed and didn’t find any firearms,” Alex responded.

“Maybe he keeps them somewhere else.” Syd commented.

“Chief, did Forensics have any thoughts on whether Mike’s shooting could have been a hunting accident?” Arlo asked.

“There are lots of people around here that have hunting rifles,” said Darrell.

“The shooter pulled the body to the creek’s edge. They think he was hoping the creek would wash it downstream. The 308 Winchester bullet is used by a lot of people,” Sean reminded them.

"But if it was accidental, why would the shooter have dragged Mike's body to the creek?" added Darrell.

"If it was an accidental shooting, the shooter may have panicked and wanted to try and hide the body," offered Syd.

"Yeah, and if it was intentional, he wanted the body to disappear—at least for a while," said Alex.

"Whoever shot at me was experienced. We need to check the area shooting ranges and see if we can learn anything there." Sean looked around the room.

"I'll do that, but if someone owns a lot of property, they could practice there." Darrell said.

The continued discussion was a rehash. Sean was frustrated. "We need to broaden the scope of our investigation. We need a break. Talk to people you have already interviewed. Press them on their memories. Find other people who might know something. Darrell, revisit the gun stores again and see if you can find dealers around here that sell in flea markets and talk to gun dealers in Tapsaw County. If something doesn't break soon, I'm turning the whole damn investigation over to the state police. They have the resources and personnel to turn over every stone."

Mike's memorial was well attended. A community of love and support surrounded Geri and her children. Held the day before Thanksgiving, the burial was limited to a small gathering of family and close friends. Sean and Danny were among the pallbearers. Miranda had made arrangements for her final exams so she was able to stay with Geri until after the holidays. Mary told Geri not to think about coming back to work at the foundation until she was ready and not before the first of the year.

On Thanksgiving Day, Sean's parents hosted dinner for Geri and her children along with Sean and Cheryl, Sean's sister and her family and Kye.

Syd and Arlo ran into each other at Frau's, each getting a cup of coffee. They sat down at a table. "Any luck finding out about Cooper?" asked Arlo.

"No, I've talked to all the neighbors in the area, and they didn't know anything, but I've got some other ideas. During the investigation this past summer into Owen Donaldson's death, I talked to some people who he hung out with years ago. I'm going to circle back and see if I can find out something useful. It might be a long shot, because after Cooper was released from prison, he doesn't appear to have renewed old acquaintances. What about you?"

"I've been running down any information I can find about any firearms Zeke or his son, Rocky, own and about Rocky. He's a lot younger than his brothers, Tony and Ray. It's not surprising they don't have any firearms registered, and none of the gun stores around here and surrounding counties have any reports of guns purchased by them. Given his decrepit condition, I don't think Zeke could have climbed up to the perch where the shooter aimed at the sheriff or walked down to where Mike was killed, but Rocky could have. I've talked to some guys Rocky hung out with during high school. That's like pulling teeth. They wouldn't say much. He dropped out his junior year. When they were boys, they shot at cans on fence rails and other targets and hunted. So Rocky's been shooting firearms from an early age. He doesn't appear to have any close friends now."

"What did they say about his accuracy?"

"They said he was a 'damn good shot' both with hunting rifles and hand guns. They didn't remember the type of ammunition he used or the guns he had."

"Well, if it was intentional, whoever shot Mike was a good aim. It was a fatal shot. Of course, some hunting rifles have scopes."

"That's a good point. We don't know if the shooter used a scope. But my guess is that whoever was shooting at the sheriff used a scope. The bullets just missed him, and those were about three-hundred-yard shots. He was lucky."

"Thing is, we don't know if we're dealing with one shooter or two," Syd said.

"I know. It's odd though that it was both the past and present sheriffs. That makes me think it's the same person."

"Yeah, but even if it is, we don't know why. Did the shooter have something specific against both of them, or was it something like the sheriff said, they were both hanging out in Mader Valley?

The sheriff hasn't ruled out that it could be someone who has it in for law enforcement."

Arlo drained his cup. "I know one thing. We need to get a break soon. The chief jumped down all our throats at the morning meeting. He wants the killer found."

"Yep, he sure does. He said he's going to turn over the entire investigation to the state police." Syd drank the rest of her coffee and got up to leave, too. "We better get back at it."

Chapter 22

Cheryl pulled the inventory file and started identifying boxes. Her research into the Mader Valley ghost folklore took her back to some of the earliest *Tribune* files and notes. She researched the courthouse records and reviewed the library documents. She also sought Kye's insight into who might know something through family memoirs.

"Well, Dear, I ought to know more about the legend than I do. You know it happened in the valley where the old railroad spur line ran. Maybe a good starting point is one of the older railroad workers. If Cecil was still alive, he would probably know more. There is someone who comes to mind. Martin Jackups. He's from a long line of railroad workers."

"Oh, I know Mr. Jackups. That's Annalee Carter's grandfather."

"That's right."

Martin Jackups had been a friend of Cheryl's grandfather, and she had seen him when she first returned to Bekbourg. Cheryl knocked on his door. "Come on in and have a seat, Cheryl.

Annalee told me that you needed my help on a story you're writing."

"Hi, Mr. Jackups. How are you doing?"

"As spry as a fox in a hen house," his eyes twinkled. "Annalee keeps me up on you. I'm glad you stayed in Bekbourg and even happier that you bought the *Tribune*. Mattie and Seth did a fine job, but you're breathing new life into it."

Cheryl laughed. "Thank you. I'm happy to be back."

"Good. I bet part of that reason is our new sheriff." He grinned and winked. Cheryl laughed out loud. "Now, tell me how I can help you."

Cheryl was still chuckling. "What did you do for the railroad?"

"Well, I worked for the railroad for nearly fifty years. I worked along the track when I was a section hand. The railroad nickname for that worker is a 'Gandy Dancer.' I was responsible for a two-mile section of the rail. I would walk it every day, tightening bolts and making sure everything was in order to keep the trains running. When there was a big repair job, all the section hands would work together to get it fixed. I was a section foreman when I finally retired. There were twenty section hands reporting to me. I'm a fourth-generation railroad worker. I don't know if you know this, but I knew Sean's grandpa. He was a conductor."

"Oh. I didn't realize that."

"Yep. We were there at the same time. Well, enough about the good old days. How can I help you?"

Cheryl told him about the Mader Valley story she was working on. “The old spur line runs through Mader Valley. I thought you might have heard stories passed down about what happened since Mader was found there.”

“I never worked on the spur line. It was a privately-owned line for a mining and lumber company. But, I heard a few things.” Martin told her what he knew. “There’s someone else you might want to talk to. He’s an engineer. Getting close to retirement age. His name is Jules Leroux. He also is a fourth-generation railroader. He loves old railroad history. He might know more than I know.”

Cheryl contacted Dusty Shaw and got Jules’ information. When Jules heard what Cheryl wanted to talk about, he was eager to assist. They met at Frau’s. When he saw Cheryl enter, he walked up to her, “Ms. Seton. It is my pleasure to meet you. I am Jules Leroux at your service. The fair Anita has given us the perfect table where we can discuss your research into the Mader Valley Ghost.”

Cheryl smiled to herself. Dusty told her that Jules would be glad to help, but “be prepared. He thinks he’s a Frenchman.”

“It is very nice to meet you, Mr. Leroux. Thank you for giving me your time.”

When they reached their table, he seated Cheryl and sat down, promptly putting the paper napkin on his lap. “I understand from our mutual friend, Dusty, that you are Sean’s intended. He is a lucky and fine man. I am glad that he is okay.”

“Thank you.”

Anita came and took their order.

"Now, please tell me how I can help with your story."

As it turned out, Jules knew a great deal about the history of the railroad operations at the time that Jarvis Mader died. He also had heard talk from his father and grandfather about what his great grandfather told them about Jarvis Mader. With his flair for the dramatic Jules helped fill in many of the gaps for her research.

Chapter 23

On election night, the sweep by the Reform Party candidates brought excitement and optimism as a new era began for the city, which had been under the thumb of the county for so long. That euphoria, however, took backstage on the first day of December, as the pall of Mike's death loomed large over the swearing-in ceremony. No one stayed around to celebrate or extend their congratulations. Briefly after Bri was sworn in, the out-going mayor ushered her around City Hall, introducing her to the staff and discussing the mayor's responsibilities. They entered the mayor's office, and he suggested, "You sit behind the desk."

She smiled but moved to the small round table. "Let's sit at the conference table."

He picked up a file and handed it to her. The filed contained reports and memos to assist with the transition. They discussed the pressing items. He then handed her a file with a large red "URGENT" printed on it. "Bri, we received these two letters last week. I gave Tessa copies; she can give you more details. For the past few years, the OMVX Railroad Corporation and the city have been in talks about what was going to happen with the two-hundred mile rail line that runs through Bekbourg." He explained the railroad's history. "Many people are concerned that we were going to lose rail service altogether. Under the lease, we get paid an annual guaranteed amount, which increased each year based on an escalation clause, plus a percentage of revenues for transit over the WVB&C tracks. Thank goodness for that minimum guaranteed payment, because our revenues would be negligible given the decline in the number of rail cars running on the line.

"The lease is due to expire in a year. We kept hoping they would extend the lease, and we thought they might. When the discussions first started, the OMVX was telling us that they would remove any improvements they had made over the years, mostly the track and signals, but that is worth millions of dollars. At the time, our city attorney was having health problems and was retiring, but when Tessa came in as city attorney, she reviewed the lease and all the files. By the way, she's our resident expert on this. Anyway, she said that the lease states that any improvements belonged to the city, so the OMVX backed off that claim.

"They were never clear on what they wanted. After we told them the assets were ours, they started talking about some rail service continuing past the lease terms, but we couldn't nail down anything specific. Well, last week, we received this notice from the OMVX Railroad to terminate the lease. Under the terms of the lease, they were obligated to give us a one-year advance notice if they were going to terminate. Not that I believe it is feasible, but we have one year to figure out how to run a railroad if we don't want service to stop. In this other letter, the OMVX offered to enter into another arrangement, but hell, I don't know why we'd sign up for that. It reduces the annual payment to the city by half, and then, they aren't committing to run the train beyond another year. The only benefit I see is that they are agreeing to bear the costs of shutting down the railroad, which could be a lot, since they would maintain all the road crossings even though the train isn't running and some other things. Removing all the fixtures would be costly. However, Tessa believes it is a one-sided proposal, because even though they would carry the costs of closing down the operations, they get the assets, which means they would retain the salvage value of all the rails and related assets. We would keep ownership of all buildings and the land. They are giving us until the end of the year to accept their proposal.

"Anyway, this is something that needs immediate attention. The City Council will need to make some decisions on this."

Bri glanced at the letter thinking, *from the frying pan into the fire.* "Okay, I'll talk with Tessa."

"Well, like I told you the first day we met after the election, I'm here to help. Let me know if you have any questions. I enjoyed my eight years, but it's time to pass the baton."

Because of Mike's death, Bri and Max opted not to have a celebratory dinner. Since C.P. was the only guest currently staying at the B&B, they asked him to join them. Max prepared a crown roast with all the trimmings and served an expensive bottle of wine that Dillie had sent from her vineyard. Bananas Foster topped off the special dinner.

C.P. helped them clean up the dishes, and they moved to the cozy parlor where the fireplace warmed the room. Max served cognac. C.P. said, "Max, a five-star restaurant has nothing on the fine feast we had tonight. I appreciate you and Bri asking me to join you. Being your guest at the B&B has many fringe benefits."

They chuckled. "We were glad you could join us," Max said.

"Yes, we are glad you could be here," agreed Bri.

"Bri, I hesitate to bring up a business matter this evening, but it's rather pressing. If you prefer not to talk business tonight, I could come by your office tomorrow if your schedule permits."

"Now is a good time. What's this about?"

"Should I leave?" asked Max.

"Not at all, Max. I'm sorry to be raising it this evening after such a fine meal and pleasant company. I put off raising it until now for a couple of reasons. One, of course, was that I didn't feel right raising it with Mike's passing. Also, with the imminent change of power in the mayor's office and at the City Council, I thought it best to deal with those who were going to be in charge for the long-term."

"Of course."

"Did you know that the City of Bekbourg owns a railroad?"

Bri arched her brows, "It is funny that you would ask me that."

"Oh?"

"Just today, the mayor showed me a letter where the OMVX Railroad served notice on the city to not renew its one-hundred-year lease. Contemporaneous with that termination notice, they also made an offer to enter into a new agreement, but from what I understand, it doesn't sound like a very good offer. I need to talk to some people and get more information."

"So, they have sent that notice?" C.P. was relieved that the termination notice had been submitted. He didn't know the terms of OMVX's proposed new arrangement, but he hoped the city would prefer his offer.

"Yes. It came as a surprise to me that we owned a railroad, but you seem to know all about it."

"Yes. Outside of the city officials, I don't think many people realized it. The lease is a revenue source to the city, but it's never been talked about around the railroad. I didn't know about it until I started to merge the MV&O with the other larger railroad in the 90's that created the OMVX system. We had to evaluate all of our rail holdings between the two systems and decide which ones were most strategic to the combined system. At the time, the OMVX determined that, long-term, its rail system in northern Kentucky offered the greatest strategic fit and started diverting more rail service there. It didn't make economic sense to run parallel lines, and the decision was made to slowly phase out the

Bekbourg railroad. During the evaluation process, I came across the lease document, so I knew that it was coming up for expiration. By the OMVX providing the termination notice, the lease will end in a year."

"That's my understanding. I don't want to see the railroad shut down, but we are going to have to figure out how to keep in running."

Max asked, "How will you do that? Can the city run a railroad?"

"Well, it did in the 1800's until the lease started. I can't even begin to think what might be involved."

"That's what I wanted to discuss with you," said C.P.

It was Bri's turn to say, "Oh?"

C.P. smiled. "The good news is that the OMVX has opted to not renew the lease. That allows me to put in motion my plans, if the city approves, to buy the railroad."

"What? You want to buy the WVB&C?"

"I want to keep it running and have ideas for expanding service around here and negotiating interconnection agreements with other rail lines to increase the freight hauled over this line. I have financing lined up that will keep people employed around here. Of course, there are regulatory approvals that I need to obtain. To make this work and keep operations running when the lease expires, I need to move ahead with filings and contracts. The reason I am raising this with you is that I plan to meet individually with the city council members and tell them what I'm telling you. Hopefully, everyone will see this as a good thing for Bekbourg. Then, I'll bring my proposal to purchase the line before the full council. Once I have the council's approval, I can take it, along with my proposal, to the agency in D.C. to seek its approval. I have a packet upstairs in my room that outlines everything along with background materials. When we're finished here, I'll get it for you. I ask you to keep it to yourself right now until I can meet with all the council members. We will go public when I present it to the full council."

"I will talk to the city attorney and see what is involved. This is a big development for the future of Bekbourg."

After Bri talked to the city attorney, Tessa Compton, and after C.P. talked to each council member, the city issued a press release to the *Tribune* with a meeting agenda. The *Tribune* followed up with the story:

Plan to Keep Local
Railroad Open

Bekbourg City Council is currently in negotiations with Chester Paul Traylor, former Executive Vice President of the OMVX Railroad Corporation, to sell to him the WVB&C Railroad

Company. This comes on the heels of the OMVX notifying the city that it was not renewing their long-standing lease and of its plans to close down local operations.

Mr. Traylor, a native and local resident, intends to take over operations of the WVB&C, which had been under a one-hundred-year lease to the MV&O Railroad Company. It had been acquired in the 1990's by the OMVX Railroad Corporation. At the time of that merger, there were rumors that the division running through Bekbourg was at risk of shutting down because it paralleled another railroad to the south and traffic could be diverted to that line.

Since the merger, traffic has dwindled and this line was used mostly for local freight. Mr. Traylor plans to breathe new life into the railroad by expanding rail service in the region to local businesses—as well as increasing through-service with connecting lines.

According to Mr. Traylor, there are many details to be worked out and regulatory approvals are needed, but his plan is to keep the railroad operational.

According to the city spokesperson, when the OMVX notified the city of its intent to terminate the lease, it also tendered a proposal for a new arrangement. The council will also discuss that proposal at the same meeting. The OMVX offer does not guarantee rail service beyond a year.

In exchange for assuming all costs for shutting down the railroad, it proposes that the ownership for all rail assets, with the exceptions of land and buildings, be transferred from the city to the OMVX. The city spokesperson declined to provide an estimated salvage value for the railroad assets other than they were of significant value—well into the tens of millions of dollars.

Anita, a waitress at Frau's, could tell that something was going on. The railroad gang was in an unusually boisterous and animated mood. She walked over to take their orders and heard one say, "Can you believe this? It doesn't look like the old railroad is going to close after all."

She asked, "What's going on this morning?"

"Haven't you heard?" rejoiced Dusty. "Looks like the railroad is going to stay in business. C.P. Traylor is going to buy it and keep it open."

Anita smiled, "That sounds like good news. Now, what are you having for breakfast?"

After they gave their orders, Mule Head said, "How come they are going to let him buy this railroad? Wouldn't it just be in competition with the OMVX. If they are going to shut it down, won't C.P. buying it take business from them?"

Dusty said, "Don't you know they don't really own it? The city owns this section of the railroad, and the OMVX only leased it."

Mule Head said, "Never heard that before."

"I didn't know it either until I read it in the newspaper," Dusty gulped his coffee.

Chaw asked, "Jules, did you know anything about the lease?"

"Well, of course I did. I knew the city owned the railroad from Cincinnati to Wheeling. In 1840's, the city wanted to be part of the railroads that were moving west. Bekbourg didn't want to be left out, so they decided to build their own railroad. By the time they finished, it stretched from Wheeling, West Virginia, to Cincinnati, Ohio. Its name is in recognition of West Virginia, Bekbourg and Cincinnati.

"Back near the turn of the century when the MV&O was consolidating their routes, they were tired of paying the high cost of using the WVB&C and decided to try and buy it. The city didn't want to sell it but didn't want to continue running a railroad, so in 1905, they ended up leasing it to the MV&O for a hundred years. Most people eventually forgot that Bekbourg owned the rail line, and for all intents and purposes, it became part of MV&O, which was later merged into the OMVX. It obviously doesn't fit into their current plans, and I don't know if they are happy with it remaining open, but the city can do with it whatever they want. I'm just amazed that C.P. is planning to buy it. It's not the most profitable railroad around. We'll just have to see."

Their jubilance started to wane. Dusty said, "I guess that means that business won't be as usual and that I would have to resign my seniority to work for C.P."

Jules agreed, "Yes, as would I, but nothing has come out about how this would affect the crews who operate this railroad."

Dusty's decision was made. "If I can get a job on this, I'm going to take it without hesitation."

"I'm just a few years from retirement," said Jules, "so I'm not sure what I'll do. I'll have to look at the terms of any labor agreement."

Chaw took a sip of coffee, "Well, I'm sure glad I don't have to worry about it. I have my payoff coming. I'm goin' to retire as soon as all that comes through."

Mule Head said, "Yeah, I don't think it will affect my disability, but it will be a whole new railroad."

"It will sure beat driving to Cincinnati or Wheeling every time I have to go to work," said Dusty.

Anita brought over four plates of steaming eggs, bacon, and hash browns and set them down. Jules said, "I don't know how you do it, my fair Anita. Superb as always."

Chapter 24

Arlo knocked on Sean's door, "Got a minute?"

"Sure, Arlo. Have a seat. What's going on?"

"You asked me to find out where Zeke was on the day Mike was shot. Well, he and his son were at Knucklepin's on the evening Mike was shot."

"They must have gone there after leaving Rose's house."

"Must have. The bartender said that Zeke and Rocky sat at a table near a group of men. Percy, the bartender, gave me one of the men's names. I finally got to talk to him today. He went out of town the next day. He remembers people drifting in that night and bits and pieces being mentioned about Mike missing and the police looking for him. But, before anyone knew that Mike was missing, the men at his table were talking about Mike being seen in Mader Valley. One man had seen him, and they were wondering what he was doing there. They were joking that he probably wouldn't be doing that once hunting season started. Well, Zeke was listening, because he broke into the conversation and said something like it was crazy that Mike was there, since that was a 'good way to get shot.'"

Sean arched his brow.

Arlo continued. "Percy also said that Zeke and his son stayed fairly late that night. With people drifting in and talking about Mike missing, Zeke was interested in what people had to say about the search for Mike. He thought it a little odd since they are from Tapsaw."

Sean wanted more information about the Pinkstons. Zeke and his son were in town the day Mike was shot and happened to stay late listening for updates about Mike's search. However, no one knew where they were when Mike was killed.

A hardware store with a lawn and garden department had posted a sign for seasonal help. As he was driving by, Cooper saw the sign and stopped in and asked to apply. The clerk gave him an application and told him that if he could complete it, the manager might be able to talk to him while he was there. Before starting with Koot's, Cooper worked cutting grass for a small lawn care business. His hope was that if he could get hired for this seasonal work, they might keep him on when planting season started.

The manager stopped reading the application when he came to the part about Cooper's conviction. He looked up at Cooper, and Cooper had a sinking feeling that he was getting ready to be rejected yet again.

"Mr. Townsend, I'm sorry, but we are looking for someone with a different type of experience. I need someone who has familiarity with tools and household projects. Your experience doesn't work."

Cooper was frustrated with all the rejections. He knew that the real reason he was being told "no" again was because of his criminal record. "That ain't the real reason you don't want me. It's 'cause of me bein' in prison. That's it every time I talk to someone 'bout a job. But I wasn't guilty. That's what people need to understand. I was framed. Those damn sheriffs know'd it. The one that was killed, he wouldn't help me clear my record and the new one won't either." Cooper slapped his hat on his leg as his voice grew louder. "They just as well be dead. They don't help no one anyhow."

The manager was concerned that Cooper was getting out-of-control and wanted to diffuse the situation. "I'm sorry, Mr. Cooper. I need someone who can help with the seasonal sales we have going on—things they need for decorating their homes and special gifts. I see that you have experience with yard work. I'll keep your application, and when planting season and yard season arrives, if a space is available, I'll keep you in mind."

This was the most positive news Cooper had heard during all his interviews. He looked at the manager, "Okay, well, I'd like that. I always liked that kind of work. If I don't have nothin' by then, I'd be interested."

After Cooper left, the manager called Sean. He explained about Cooper stopping by and the interview. "Sheriff, I know you are trying to find who killed Mike and shot at you. He was steamed when I told him that I couldn't hire him. I don't know if this means anything, but it appears to me that Mr. Townsend blames you and Mike for not helping him with clearing his record. When I told him that I couldn't hire him, he said that you and Mike 'just as well be dead,' that neither one of you helped anyone."

Sean thanked the manager for calling. Maybe it was time to question Cooper again. He had a motive. He blamed them for not clearing his record, but a stronger motive against Mike. Mike was the sheriff when he was arrested, and Ben worked for Mike. Cooper blamed Mike for Ben arresting him and to Cooper's mind, framing him. He felt that Mike didn't work hard enough to prove he was framed. Cooper wouldn't face the fact that he himself was to blame. First, he was skimming off the Thompsons at Koot's from the deliveries, and second, when he was arrested, he never told who or why he was being framed. It was virtually impossible for Mike to investigate his claim.

Cheryl and Milton attended the city council meeting. Bri had allotted extra discussion time for C.P.'s proposal to buy the WVB&C from the city. C.P. explained his plan to work with local businesses to increase rail services as well as possibly building new spur lines to offer new service for commodities and supplies and increasing access to markets. C.P. had spoken with Becky Werner about constructing a short spur line to deliver vehicles directly to the dealership. He had met with the local concrete manufacturer about new rail options.

Because the railroad had provided a major transportation means since the opening of their factories a century ago, the milk and paper companies were heartened by a new owner who would infuse new investments and add services. The local railroad employees were cautiously optimistic, but they wanted to know more about the employee terms, although having the railroad continue to run through Bekbourg was better than the line shutting down. Some local representatives appeared at the council meeting in support, while others submitted letters favoring the sale to C.P. No one appearing at the meeting was in opposition.

The city council members agreed that C.P.'s proposal was more beneficial to the city than the OMVX offer. C.P.'s proposal gave them a way to cash in their railroad asset while also helping the local economy and businesses. The city didn't have the expertise or infrastructure to operate a railroad. The council unanimously approved moving forward with the sale of the WVB&C to C.P.—subject to satisfactory regulatory approvals.

Chapter 25

Cheryl and Milton were sitting in the *Tribune's* small conference room. Between them, they had almost drunk a pot of coffee. "Cheryl, between the murder investigation and the railroad saga, our circulation is well above our projections."

Cheryl smiled, "I know. That's one of the reasons I'm trying to add things while people are reading that will keep them buying the paper even after these stories start to wane."

"That's a good strategy. The 'Bridge' and 'Book of the Month' columns are good ideas. I also think the plan to start a series on the history of the railroad will be popular. Speaking of which, how's the Mader Valley ghost project going?"

Cheryl grinned and opened a file and handed him some papers. "Here it is. Let's run it in four parts. I think you are going to like this. It took a while to piece it all together, but I think people will find the story interesting."

Milton skimmed the pages while Cheryl drank her coffee. His eyes were bright when he laid down the file. "This is good work. Let's run Part One in tomorrow's edition."

Valley of Murder

The Legend of Mader Valley:
Fact and Fiction – Part 1
by Cheryl Seton

So powerful is the folklore of the demise of Jarvis Mader that the valley bears his legacy, Mader Valley. His violent death and the unsolved crime have captivated residents of Bekbourg County for over a hundred years. Many teenagers and adults have braved the darkness of the night, hoping to witness his ethereal presence.

Rumors and superstitions have been attributed to Mader's ghost haunting the valley and roaming the railroad track.

A story in the Bekbourg Tribune, November 12, 1942, reported that a "Hobo was found dead along the Mader Valley railroad track. The sheriff was so unnerved by the eeriness of the dead man that he brought the doctor to the scene. The dead man's eyes were wide open, as if he had seen a ghost. The doctor could find no evidence of foul play."

In 1955, a tragedy befell a family when, unbeknownst to each other, two brothers were hunting in Mader Valley. One swore to the sheriff that he saw "a white figure floating behind the tree line above the creek." So startled by the ghostly figure, he panicked and shot, killing his older brother.

The ghost of Mader was reported to have swooped in front of a pickup truck filled with teenagers one night in the fall of 1964. The teen driver swerved and ran off the road. Two died at the scene. One was crippled for life. The other five recovered from their injuries. The driver lived with the horror of seeing the ghostly appearances in his dreams until he could no longer bear the torment and took his own life.

In 1977, the remains of a man were found off the creek's edge in Mader Valley by a man running his hunting dogs. The medical examiner determined that he had been frozen in the snowdrift that covered the ground for much of the winter. While the sheriff suspected a woman and her boyfriend for the death of this man—her husband—they vehemently denied culpability and blamed his demise on the Mader ghost. No charges were ever filed.

Since the recent death of Mike Adams and the attempt on Sheriff Sean Neumann's life, both occurring in Mader Valley, the Bekbourg Tribune has been inundated with calls about the legend. In order to discern facts from fiction, I have researched archived files from the Tribune, the sheriff's department, and the Bekbourg County Library. I want to extend my sincere appreciation to Jules Leroux and Martin Jackups for their contributions to filling in many of the gaps as I have attempted to piece together the basis for the legend. Given that Jarvis Mader's death occurred in 1895, I could not locate all of the information to provide a completely factual account, in which case, I filled in with what I think were the most probable facts. Part 2 will appear in an upcoming publication.

Chapter 26

The following day, Noel stopped by Bri's office. "Hi, Noel, or should I say, Commissioner Fischner?" she asked smiling.

"Hi, Bri. Mayor," he grinned. "I like your office. Are you settled in?"

She laughed. "I'm learning a lot. I've got a tremendous amount to learn, but everyone is very helpful. How about you?"

"Yeah, there's a lot to learn. Say, there are a couple of business matters I wanted to talk to you about."

"Oh, alright. What do you have?"

"Well, the first thing is that before the changing of the guard, the city council approved a construction permit to make changes to the old Schumacher factory. There's a new owner. I'd like for you to take another look at that. I'm not sure the permit conforms to code."

Bri was confused. "Who is the new owner?"

"Livingstone Trust. I don't know more than that. It's a private trust."

"Who is the contractor?"

"My father's firm."

"I don't understand, Noel. What doesn't conform to the code?"

"I'm looking at whether the county has some jurisdiction over the factory, but I don't want the city to get the wool pulled over its eyes."

"Why would the county have any involvement in this? The factory is located in the downtown area. That's easily within the city limits."

"There may be other things to consider."

This is strange. The contractor is his family's business. He doesn't have a specific code violation reference, and the building is entirely within the city limits.

"What is the other thing?" Bri asked.

"It's the proposal by C.P. to buy the railroad. He got the city council approval, but he didn't bring it to the county. I don't see how the city could have approved it without the county looking at it."

"The city owns the railroad, Noel. The county isn't involved."

"Well, I'm going to look into this too. Before the city acts on things, we should be coordinating to make sure there aren't county issues. I think you should give me a courtesy heads-up. I don't think the commission should be surprised by things like this. Even if something is exclusively within the city's jurisdiction, I think we should work together to make sure actions are in our mutual interests."

"What are the other two commissioners saying about this?"

Noel dodged her question, “It’s pretty clear that the city has an obligation to keep the county apprised of things.”

To spare spurious debate, Bri refrained from asking if he thought it was a reciprocal obligation for the county to run its business by the city. The city and county had different governing responsibilities, and while she supported the two governmental entities coordinating where citizens across both would be impacted, she had no intention of allowing city affairs to be subordinated or dominated as they had been in the past. She wasn’t happy with his attitude, but she wanted to make sure she was on solid legal footing before responding to him. She was going to talk to the city attorney. “I’ll look into these matters, Noel. I’m still learning, so I can’t give you an answer until I look into it further.”

“Okay. We ran on the same Party ticket. I think the city needs to work closely with the county commission. We don’t want to run into gridlock problems.”

“I’m running late for a meeting, Noel. We’ll talk later.”

“Oh, okay. I better run too. I’ve got some things to do, too. See you later.”

Bri was waiting when Cheryl walked into Max’s bistro. “Max, it’s starting to look like the holidays around here.”

Max laughed. “Stop by the B&B on your way out if you want to see spectacular decorations. Bri out-did herself this year.”

After having worked in Cincinnati for many years, Max and Bri had moved to Bekbourg over ten years ago to pursue their dreams. They purchased the boarded-up former boarding house in downtown and restored it into a stunning Bed and Breakfast. They also bought the building next door, and Max turned it into a chic lunch and dinner bistro that offered exotic coffees that drew people throughout the day.

Bri smiled, "Well, I have Max to thank. We spent an entire day decorating trees and hanging garland and wreaths."

"The lights along Main Street are really pretty." Cheryl appreciated the city's efforts to bring the holiday spirit to the downtown.

"They are," agreed Bri. "The city works department always does a good job."

After their food was served, Cheryl told Bri that the *Tribune* was planning to run a series of articles about the community's support for C.P. buying the railroad. "We've interviewed businesses that are evaluating upsides in their business plans. We're also reviewing the *Tribune* archives to run stories about the history of the railroad and how its history is woven into the fabric of the city."

"I'm glad, Cheryl. I had no idea the city even owned the railroad. Thank goodness C.P. was here with a plan. It would have been detrimental for the railroad to shut down, but I don't know how we could have possibly found a way to keep it running, especially with just a year to figure it out. I've already decided that one of my first priorities is to get a handle on all the budget items so we can be more proactive and not have something like this pop up and bite us."

Cheryl grinned. "You sound like me talking about getting a handle on the *Tribune*, although the Trotters left things in pretty good shape with their file inventory. The employees are top-notch. Of course, having Milton has made all the difference in the world."

"There are good people that work for the city. I didn't mean to imply otherwise. It's just that I need to get a handle on things. In the past, the city kowtowed to the county's edicts on most things."

"That is true. The Thompsons didn't want an independent city council—they wanted it under the county's thumb."

"That's right," said Bri. "That's one of the reasons the Reform Party was formed—so the city council makes decisions that are in the city's best interest. That doesn't mean we don't cooperate with the county, but it needs to be mutual. That's why I'm surprised at Noel."

"What do you mean?"

"Well, Noel came to see me right before I was to meet you. It was odd, Cheryl." She told her about Noel. "He wants me to tell him about city business ahead of acting on the items at our weekly meetings."

"Huh? The *Tribune* posts the agenda items ahead of each meeting. He can see the topics there."

"He wants more. I think he wants to oversee the city's business, which amounts to usurping our decision making. He also is asserting that the county may have jurisdiction on things that are clearly within the city's purview."

"Like what?"

"The construction permit for the Schumacher renovation, for one, and C.P.'s proposal to purchase the WVB&C."

"How can the Schumacher renovation be a county matter?"

"Exactly. I don't see how the railroad sale can be either. The current lease is between the city and the OMVX Railroad Corporation. The city owns the railroad. Although the rail line also runs through the county, I don't see how that makes it a county matter."

"What are you going to do?"

"I'm going to talk to City Attorney, Tessa Compton, and see what she has to say."

"What do you think is going on with Noel?"

"I don't know, but he was elected commissioner, not king."

They both laughed.

That afternoon, Bri stopped by Tessa's office. "Tessa, there's something that I wanted to ask you. Is now a good time?"

"Of course. Please have a seat."

Files were stacked on her desk, on a book shelf and even along one wall. Colored sticky notes were hanging off the phone and along the edge of her desk. She was tall and slender—a striking woman with dark, shiny hair that feathered along her caramel face. Her multicolored blouse was set off by the black jacket with gold buttons. Bri felt shabby next to Tessa and made a mental note that perhaps her earth-mother wardrobe wasn't sophisticated enough for her new position.

"Thanks, Tessa. I have a question about the overlap between the city and county. The new commissioner, Noel Fischner, came by earlier today and thought I should have run by him this matter about the railroad since the tracks run in the county. He also thought the county might have some jurisdiction over the old cigar box factory—which the city recently issued a permit for the renovations. Is any of this true?"

"Of course not. First, I've been reviewing all the files pertaining to the railroad. The city built the railroad and owns it one-hundred percent. There were no investors. The county doesn't have a scintilla of jurisdiction over the railroad. Same thing applies to the Schumacher factory. It is located entirely within the city limits."

Tessa was self-assured. Bri couldn't help notice the beautiful stone ring on her ring finger. As she spoke, her long fingers professionally manicured with red nail polish moved like a mesmerizing dance in rhythm with the musical clinking of her gold bangles.

"Mayor, when I first took this job, I couldn't believe how the county commissioners ran rough-shod over the city. At first, I'd go to the mayor and tell him that the county didn't have legal authority over a city matter, and he'd just blow it off and say that he didn't want to create waves. It was like a breath of fresh air when the Reform Party emerged and promised that the city would operate independently of the county but work for the mutual benefit of the citizens. That's the way it should be. Did Commissioner Fischner indicate if the other two county commissioners are aligned with his position on these two matters?"

"I asked him that, but he was noncommittal."

"Sounds like he hasn't talked to them about it. I wouldn't have been surprised if it had been one of them, but I *am* surprised that Commissioner Fischner is the one raising this, because he was instrumental in starting the Reform Party movement. My advice is, now that some of that old guard at the commission is gone and new players, such as yourself, are in place in city leadership, I'd not let that camel get its nose back under the tent."

Bri laughed. "I'll take that advice. What do you think about C.P. Traylor buying the railroad?"

"We need the railroad here. I have observed the decline in rail service just in the three years I've been here. I've reviewed the OMVX proposal, which doesn't commit to continuing to operate the line. Frankly, I think the reason they even made the proposal is the value they see in the rails and related equipment. Under their proposal, they agree to bear the costs of shutting down the railroad in exchange for the salvage rights for the rails and related assets. Those include the copper wiring, rails, ties and all other hardware, which is a valuable asset to the city.

"If we don't have a way to keep the railroad running, we could hire a company to remove and sell the assets on our terms and timetable and give them a percentage as a fee. We would still come out ahead. Despite what the OMVX would try to convince us, we have leverage in our negotiations with them. But, the best news about all this is that we have another offer. I would turn my efforts to Mr. Traylor's proposal. His is a bona fide offer to take ownership of the railroad and make a go of it. We don't have a railroad department." They both laughed. "My feeling is that his offer is reasonable. I don't see a reason to entertain the OMVX proposal."

"What about them saying that if we don't accept the proposal by the end of the year, they are withdrawing the offer?"

"Poppycock. They want the assets. Before I started here, they were trying to bluff their way by claiming they owned the improvements they had made during the lease. Fortunately, that was not what the lease said. Time is on our side. Even if the deal falls through with Mr. Traylor down the road, we can work something out with the OMVX if it's in our best interest to do so."

"Okay, I feel a lot less panicked than I did when I first heard about this railroad situation." Glancing toward a diploma on a wall, "I see you graduated from a prestigious law school. Are you from Bekbourg?"

"Not even Ohio. I grew up back east and attended college and law school there. During law school, I met Derrick. After he graduated, Boone Carter recruited him to join his law firm. He was the only black attorney in Bekbourg until I moved here. We maintained a long-distance relationship while I worked. When I visited him, I really liked it here. One of us had to compromise if we were going to get married and be together. I guess Boone must have put in a good word, because when the city attorney retired, I was offered the job out of the blue. I thought, 'it's now or never,' so I said 'yes.' I've been the city attorney now for about three years."

"I know this is a personal question, but do you like it here?"

"I do. It's a slower pace than I was used to and, frankly, it was frustrating at times dealing with the situation that existed before this election. But, I can see that you and the new council members are planning change, and I always like change."

They both laughed. "I have a feeling you and I are going to be working together on a lot of things."

Tessa smiled. "I look forward to it."

Chapter 27

Kim was talking with Arlo when Harold Greene entered the precinct. She stopped in mid-sentence to address him, "Hi, Officer Greene. Sheriff Neumann is expecting you. I'll tell him you're here."

She buzzed Sean and spoke into the phone. "Sir, he'll be right out. Would you like some of our famous police-house coffee?" she grinned.

Arlo had spoken to Harold while she was on the phone with Sean. He said, "Kim makes a mean pot of coffee, Chief."

"I can't pass that up."

Kim smiled. "Good. How do you take it?"

"Black."

Arlo excused himself, and Kim poured Harold's coffee. Sean came and greeted Harold, "Thanks for coming by. Let's go back to my office."

Sean closed the door. "Have a seat. How are things going?"

"Fine. How is your investigation going?"

"I can't see we're making much progress. I've been re-reviewing the progress reports from my deputies, but there's not much to grasp onto. I've asked them to circle back on their interviews to see if anybody remembers something else on the second go-around. Darrell's checking out gun ranges and gun stores, but without a gun, there's not much to go on. Arlo is chasing down information on the Pinkstons. Same with Syd on Cooper, and Alex is looking into Kyle."

"What about old cases that Mike handled? Any old grudges from those?"

"I've asked around, but other than Cooper, no one knows of anything. I even called the deputies who used to work here, and they didn't know of anything. Maybe it's someone who relied on Pinkston's drugs, such as a dealer, who suffered losses when Pinkston's drug business was shut down. Someone like that might carry a grudge."

Harold thought about that. "I guess that's a possibility. You have any leads on that?"

"No. Since nothing is shaking loose with our preliminary list of suspects, I've started thinking about other possibilities."

"Is that something you would like for me to check into?"

"It's probably a wild notion, but why don't you see if any names pop up."

"I'll get started on that right away. I'll call Lucky and see if he's got any thoughts or possible leads in that direction."

Harold un-wrapped a brown paper package. "This is what I wanted to drop off. It's that hunting knife we found when we were looking for evidence in Mike's death." He held it up for Sean to see.

"That thing must have been there a long time. Any idea how old it is?"

Harold smiled. “I don’t have any idea. I didn’t have any forensics run on it because I could tell by looking at it that it wasn’t related to Mike’s case. Just a guess, the knife could be a hundred years old.”

Harold wrapped it back in the paper. Sean said. “Thanks for bringing it by.”

Sean, Cheryl and Buddy were walking along Main Street admiring the holiday lights hoisted on the light poles and affixed to awnings and door frames. The cold and misty air gave truth to the approaching seasonal celebrations, although Sean didn’t want to fall under the spell. He was alert to pedestrians and passing cars wondering if he and Cheryl were targets. Heck, if it was a serial shooter, anyone could be a target, but he was beginning to think that was the least likely of all the possibilities. There had been no shootings since Mike’s death.

Cheryl suggested the stroll because she thought they both needed to take a break from the weight of everything. “Here, hold Buddy’s leash. I’m going to run into Max’s and get us each a cup of hot chocolate with lots of marshmallows AND whipped cream.”

He grinned at her exuberance. She returned with two large cups of steaming aroma. He couldn’t help but enjoy the moment. “Are you sure there is hot chocolate below this mound of white stuff?”

She giggled. “I even asked Max to add peppermint schnapps.”

“Oh, well, that makes it complete.”

Cheryl giggled again. Cheryl took a slurp and had a whipped cream mustache. Sean grinned and did the same. Cheryl laughed so hard Sean thought she might spill her delicacy. He couldn't help but chuckle. She looked like a teenager with her faux fur rimmed knitted hat and her jacket and scarf with jeans and laced-up snow boots. The tension knitted throughout his body began to loosen, if only for this brief magical time. His gloved hand took hold of hers, and they strolled toward the end of the street where the church's large Christmas tree was being admired by others. Several of the shop owners where standing on the sidewalk, handing out candies and treats.

They came to an older couple dressed in Mr. and Mrs. Santa outfits standing in front of an antique store. Sean and Cheryl stopped to talk with them for a couple of minutes and then ventured on. Sean said, "When I joined the Marines, that building was in disrepair. All the windows were boarded up. That couple retired and moved here a couple of years after Bri and Max did. They restored that building and opened the antique business. Mom and Dad told me that they are doing well. They are active in their church and donate to the fundraising gala each year."

"Maybe I should interview them for the paper. Maybe I should think about doing spotlight articles for the local businesses."

Sean turned to her and smiled. "Always thinking."

Happiness radiated from her. This stunning woman had enthralled him since he had first observed her at a murder investigation news briefing.

Sean said, “I may need to talk to them on official business soon.”

This surprised Cheryl. “Why’s that?”

“When the state police were looking for evidence in Mike’s shooting, one of the troopers found an old hunting knife. Harold brought it by the station. It’s probably a hundred years old. It’s amazing that it was in as good of shape as it was having been in the elements all these years. Even a red ring around the handle is still recognizable.” He smiled, “I may even run a ‘lost and found’ notice in your newspaper. If I can’t find the family it belongs to, I could take it to that antique store and donate the proceeds to Mary’s foundation.”

They had come to the large Christmas tree. Cheryl had grown silent. At first he thought she was simply admiring the tree, but when he looked closer, he saw that she was deep in thought, oblivious to the surroundings.

The deputies were assembled for the morning meeting. Sean wasn’t yet there, so Arlo was telling them about Harold coming by to see Sean.

Syd asked, “Do you think he was here because the sheriff is getting ready to turn the investigation over to the state police?”

“I don’t know, but the sheriff was expecting him.”

“How do you know that?” asked Darrell.

"I heard Kim say that the sheriff was expecting him."

Mack asked Alex if he knew anything about it. Alex told them that he didn't. He wasn't even aware that Harold had come in.

Sean walked in, and the deputies got quiet. During the meeting, they discussed their efforts, but it was clear to everyone that they weren't making much progress. Sean's impatience was on display. No one had the courage to ask him about Harold's visit and whether he was pulling the investigation away from the department.

Chapter 28

Several people around town were bridge players. Kye played bridge weekly with Milly, Lucia and Ann, but she was happy to fill in at another bridge game if a substitute was needed. Because of her love of the game, she accepted an invitation to play at Loretta Harris's house, but this wasn't her favorite group. It took much longer to play three rounds because they liked to talk about trips they were either planning to take or had taken. Another dynamic at play was an underlying competition between June and Loretta—made evident by an occasional catty remark. However, the main reason she didn't enjoy the group was because of the gossip. If it was run-of-the-mill gossip, she didn't mind that. In fact, she liked being in the know, but some of their gossip was mean-spirited and some seemed spun from whole cloth.

Kye commented, "Loretta, I like the pattern on the cups and saucers. I've never seen this before. Is this a new pattern?"

"Why, yes. I was recently in Columbus and saw those and just had to have them. I've got some sugar cubes if you would like some in your coffee.

June started serving tea, and I thought sugar cubes were so 'English like,'" she cackled.

"No, Dear. Just some cream will be fine."

The bidding ended with Loretta winning the bid with a four spade. Kye played an ace of diamond, because she had the king. After she took those two tricks, she led with the suit in her partner's bid, and suddenly, they had three tricks and only needed one more to set Loretta. This flustered Loretta. "June, we may not make this. You shouldn't have bid at the three level. I thought you had more points."

"Well, I assumed you had thirteen points, Loretta."

Loretta went down one trick. Kye knew she was annoyed. "Let's take a break. I made a crumb cake," exhaled Loretta.

The women were delighted because Loretta was a good pastry cook. After they were settled, Kye listened to June, "Loretta, this crumb cake is delicious. We are going to miss you on our trip. It's too bad about your sister. How's she doing?"

"As well as can be expected. I hated that I couldn't go this year, but family comes first. If they need me, I want to be there."

Kye said, "I'm sorry, Loretta. I didn't know about your sister. We will add her name to the prayer circle."

"Thank you, Kye. I say a special prayer for her every night."

June asked, "Kye, do you know if the sheriff has any suspects in Mike Adam's death?"

"No, I don't know anything more than I read. I certainly hope they solve the case soon."

Loretta smirked, "Well, he might not be looking too hard if what I heard has any truth to it."

"What on earth does that mean?" Kye's eyes widened.

"Well, it is awfully suspicious. Mike was the sheriff all those years. People liked him. Then Sean returns and ends up being sheriff. Mike and Geri decided not to move to Montana. Maybe he was some competition to Sean. Maybe he was planning to run against Sean next time around."

Kye's stern teacher's expression surfaced, "Surely you're not suggesting that Sean was somehow responsible for Mike getting shot?"

June jumped in, "Loretta. I agree with Kye. That's ridiculous. Someone also tried to kill Sean. Sean couldn't have shot at himself from up on the hill."

Throwing her head back, Loretta smugly retorted, "How do you know he didn't take those shots and then act like he was a victim?"

Kye felt her blood pressure rising, "Loretta. These are vicious rumors. I can't believe anyone would start such a thing. Certainly, no one should be repeating them."

Rolling her eyes, she feigned disinterest. "Well, I'm just repeating what I heard. Let me clear away these dishes, and we'll play the next round. Hopefully, my next partner will do a better job of bidding."

Chapter 29

"Okay, Morgan. Walk me through all the evidence you have," Boone said as he walked in and sat down at the table.

Morgan was ready for their meeting. She was prepared to show him the documents and records that Zeke had produced in response to her document requests and discuss with Boone the questions she planned to ask Zeke during his upcoming deposition. She explained the property was in the names of both Tony and Ruby Pinkston. They had made two payments, the first half on the day of closing, and the remaining fifty percent a year later. "Zeke has his hand written note that says he loaned Tony the money. It doesn't have a date when it was written, and it makes no reference to whether he loaned the money in one lump sum or in two payments."

"So, is there any indication that Zeke knew there were two payments made?" asked Boone.

"No. And if he loaned them the money in one lump sum, why did they not just pay for it all at the time of closing?"

"That's a good question, Morgan. What do the bank records show?"

"Well, that's another interesting point. Tony and Ruby's bank records don't shed any light on this. As the closing date approached, Ruby deposited enough money for the first payment in their checking account. They didn't have a savings account, and there are no records about other bank accounts anywhere. The checking account seemed to just be used for household purchases. All of their vehicles were older models, and when they bought them, they were used. I didn't see anywhere in the bank statements that they wrote checks for those. It appears they mostly paid cash for things."

"I guess I'm not too surprised about that," Boone said. "What about Zeke's bank account? Did you find any evidence of him withdrawing money that would indicate he loaned Tony and Ruby the money?"

"No. He doesn't have a bank account."

"Where did the money come from then if he loaned it?"

"I don't know, but that is one of the questions I plan to ask."

"Right. Does he work? How would he get the money to loan it? What did he say in response to the written interrogatories you asked him?"

"He said he got it from farming."

"Okay, Morgan, make sure during the deposition you ask him where he keeps his money that he gets from farming. Ask what crops he grows and how he sells them. Don't push on this, just ask, because we know that he was a major marijuana grower at the time Tony and Ruby were murdered. I never heard if he stopped since the DEA was all over the cartel's operations here, and of course, he is not going to admit to growing marijuana if he's still doing that. Ask if there is any other source of income. He'll probably deny it, but let's ask. Find out how he pays for his farming supplies and where he buys his supplies. I don't think they will tell you how he pays for them, but let's see what we can find out. We need to see if there is any evidence that he had enough money to loan Tony and Ruby."

"Will do."

"Another thing. Ask questions about his handwritten note included in his pleading that he claims is proof that he loaned them the money. When did he write it? Why did he write it? What was his understanding of how Tony and Ruby planned to pay for the property? Probe about any conversations he had with them about their buying the property. The heart of his claim is that he loaned them the money. We need to discredit his allegation."

Morgan drove to Hiram's office in Tapsaw County to depose Zeke. When she arrived, Zeke and Hiram were in a small conference room with the court reporter. She introduced herself.

Zeke looked hard at her. "You're the girl that was with Suzy at my boy's house that day."

She turned to Hiram, "If the recorder is ready, I'm ready to start the deposition."

Neither Zeke nor Hiram were friendly to her, but she wasn't there to socialize. She was prepared for the deposition. She had thoroughly analyzed the documents and records, and she had prepared her list of topics that she intended to cover. She had outlined the questions she planned to ask Zeke and had the documents she planned to show him in the order of her questions. She was perspiring even though the small conference room was cool. Morgan didn't want them to sense her trepidation. This was the first deposition she had ever conducted by herself, and she had only sat in on a couple. This would be her only chance to depose him, and she needed to make the most of the situation.

After the preliminary questions, Morgan asked, "Mr. Pinkston, here is a copy of the handwritten note attached to your pleading in this case that says that you loaned Tony the money to buy the property. Did you write this?"

"Who else would have?"

"Yes or no, Mr. Pinkston. Did you write this note?"

"Yep."

"Why did you write it?"

"Well ain't it obvious?"

"Please tell me why you wrote it."

"To show I loaned Tony the money to buy the property, which he never paid me back, so that makes the property mine."

"Did you ever show Tony the note?"

"No. There wasn't no reason to. He and I had an understanding."

"When did you write the note?"

"Ah hell, I don't know. What's that got to do with anythin'?"

"Was it around the time your attorney here filed the pleading claiming you loaned the money?"

Zeke's shrewd eyes looked at her. "No, it was back when I loaned Tony the money."

"Did you loan him the full amount?"

"Yeah. How else could he have afforded the place?"

"Did you give him the full amount in one payment?"

Hiram leaned over and whispered something.

Morgan said, "Counsel, I'm asking him. You are interfering with my questions."

Zeke said, "He paid it off in two payments. That's what his bank records show, and that's what my brother Earl told me."

Morgan made a note to ask Earl, because he didn't mention talking to Zeke about this.

"But did you loan him the full amount or break it into two separate loans?"

"I loaned it in two separate amounts."

"Why then did you have just one hand written note?"

Zeke looked hard before replying, "I didn't see no need to write two notes sayin' I had loaned the money to Tony just 'cause I loaned him the full amount in two different payments. The one note I wrote covered it. It said I loaned him the money to buy the property."

"Did you write the note when you loaned the money for the first payment or at the time of the second loan payment?"

"Hell, I don't know."

"You don't know?"

"I guess it was before the first payment."

"You guess?"

"Okay, damnit. Before the first payment."

Morgan made a note to follow this up at the hearing because his testimony was weak on this point. If he wrote the note before the first payment, how could he be so sure Tony would need additional funds? Why not write two notes? Zeke's note never mentioned that there would be two loans. Zeke eyed her with suspicion as she wrote her notes.

"Why did Tony not pay it off in the first payment?"

"How the hell should I know?"

"He didn't tell you?"

"No, that was his business."

"Was it because you couldn't loan him the full amount?"

"Hell no."

"So you could have loaned him the full amount?"

Zeke sensed a trap, but had already gone down that road. If Zeke had the ability to loan the entire amount and had loaned him the full amount, why would Tony need to break the payments into two?

"It's none of your business 'bout my finances, Girl."

"You can call me Ms. Ramirez, Mr. Pinkston. Please answer the question."

"What question?"

"Could you have loaned him the full amount?"

"I ain't goin' to discuss my private affairs."

Morgan made a note. She was entitled to this information, but she already had the answer.

She looked at Hiram, "He is obligated to respond, Hiram. This is clearly within the scope of this case, but I'll move on for now.

"Did Tony or Ruby ask you to loan them the money?"

Zeke thought for a minute. "He didn't come out in so many words, but I knew he wanted the property, and so I told him I'd loan him the money."

"Did you have any reason to think they wouldn't repay you?"

"No, but that's why I wrote the note in case they didn't pay me back. I would have the land."

"How long did they have to repay you?"

Zeke paused. "We didn't decide that."

Morgan was trying to get information. Details like there not being a time limitation to repay the loan were pertinent, but they were better being brought up during the hearing.

"Was the loan to Tony and Ruby?"

Zeke didn't like these questions. He was realizing that she was smart and trying to trap him. "That don't matter. I gave Tony the money to buy the property."

"You said you wrote the note when Tony bought the property, is that correct?"

"We're not goin' over that again, are we?"

"Mr. Pinkston, please answer the question. Is it correct that you wrote the note when Tony and Ruby bought the property?"

"Yep."

"You gave Tony the money. Is that what you said?"

"Ah, hell. Yes. How many times do I got to repeat it?"

"And Tony deposited it in the bank. Is that correct?"

"Huh?" Zeke looked questioningly at Hiram, who was doodling on a pad.

"If you gave it to Tony, wouldn't you assume he took it straight to the bank and deposited it?"

Zeke stared into Morgan's eyes. He detected a trick question.

"Let's back up. Did you give him cash?"

"Yep."

"Both times?"

"Yep."

"Mr. Pinkston. It was a lot of cash. He wouldn't just leave it sitting around, right? You told me you gave the cash to him. I'm asking you if you know if he took it straight to the bank and deposited it."

Zeke wouldn't answer.

"Let the record reflect that Mr. Pinkston is not answering the question." Morgan knew that Tony didn't deposit the money. It was Ruby.

"Hiram, this is bullshit."

"Let's move on, Counsel. This is getting tiresome." Morgan had made her point and moved to the next line of questioning.

"How much did he and Ruby repay you?"

"Not any."

"Over a four-year period, they didn't repay any of the amount?"

"No."

"That didn't worry you?"

"Well, he told me he would, and his word was good enough."

"But there isn't any record of him saying that anywhere?"

"I got my note. That's proof."

"Your handwritten note?"

"Yeah."

"You say the deposits into the bank soon before each payment shows that the money came from you."

"That's what I said."

"But, you can't prove that, can you Mr. Pinkston?"

"My word is proof. Besides, Tony didn't have the money to pay for it. He lived up there with me. I paid for everything."

"Tony didn't have any money except what you gave him?"

"That's right 'cept for what he made in farming, and that wasn't much."

"Well, for the second payment, he had been living on the property in Bekbourg for a year. We know that his business was selling marijuana and meth. The federal authorities said his drug business could supply this entire region. He didn't just build that big a business after he moved to Bekbourg. The marijuana business was already going on. You weren't involved in his marijuana business before he moved here, were you, Mr. Pinkston?"

Zeke knew this was a set up. "No. I don't sell drugs." Morgan knew that wasn't the truth, but he wasn't going to admit that.

"Well, where would your money have come from? You don't even have a bank account."

Zeke stared at her.

Morgan pointed to a response to an interrogatory question, "In this response, you say that you don't have a bank that you use. Where do you keep your money?"

"That's none of your damn business."

"Mr. Pinkston. You had to have gotten the money from somewhere when you loaned it to Tony. You said you don't have a bank, and there are no banking records that show you withdrawing the money or giving it to Tony and Ruby. The money came from somewhere. I'm asking where it came from."

"And I said that's none of your business."

Morgan knew that during the hearing if this came up, the judge would require Zeke to answer, because it was on-point with the case.

"What is your source of income?"

"Farming."

"What crops do you grow?"

"Different things."

"Like what?"

Zeke was growing impatient with the detailed questions. "Surely you know what grows on farms."

"I'm asking you what you grow, Mr. Pinkston."

"Corn."

"Is that all?"

Hiram interrupted, "This is irrelevant. He told you he farmed. That's all you need to know."

"He claims he loaned a large amount of money for Tony and Ruby to buy the property. I have a right to inquire about the source of his income to know how he had the funds to make that loan."

"You best move on. He told you he farmed and grew corn."

"Mr. Pinkston. The income tax returns produced during discovery show that you don't earn enough money to have that kind of cash just laying around."

Hiram interrupted. "He is not required to answer that."

"So you're objecting to him answering?"

"Yes."

"I don't agree. I'm making a note, and this is something we may take up with the judge in a motion to compel. You are not cooperating in answering relevant questions."

Hiram shrugged, "That's up to you."

"Mr. Pinkston, did you charge Tony interest?"

"Hell no. It's family."

"Do you have any credit cards?"

"No."

"Have you ever had any?"

"No."

It was a long, grueling day. Zeke and Hiram raised obstacles at every turn. Zeke dragged his feet on responding, and the deposition lasted almost double the time that it should have. When he did answer—usually after Hiram raised a pointless objection—Zeke answered in the shortest phrases he could. Many times, she felt it was like dropping bread crumbs for a duck to follow. She had to ask the next question to get the next word or phrase to finally complete the line of questioning and move to the next topic. At other times, his answers were vague or obtuse or intended to sidetrack her in another direction. He was condescending to her.

She never displayed the uneasiness she felt over it being her first deposition. She never showed her dismay with the games Hiram and Zeke played or Zeke's insulting remarks. At times, she had to remind Hiram that his client was required to answer the questions. Spewing a list of boiler-plate reasons, Hiram would argue with her that Zeke didn't need to answer, but she was dogged in her persistence. During a couple of testy exchanges with Hiram over Zeke's refusal to respond, she threatened to call the judge right then and there and get his ruling. In the end, Hiram knew that her questions were legitimate for depositions and that the judge would instruct Zeke to answer.

On her return to Bekbourg, she felt drained but also took pride in having conducted her first deposition. More importantly, she had answers to the questions she needed for the hearing. She was grateful to Boone for showing confidence in her. She didn't want to let him or Suzy down. Soon, she would have to defend Suzy and Rose in Hiram's depositions. She had learned today that Zeke planned to be present. She wasn't worried about how they would do in the depositions. All they had to do was tell the truth, which they would do. Zeke's purpose in attending was to intimidate. Morgan also suspected that Hiram would be obnoxious in his questioning. If he was a jerk, she had to prepare them to remain focused and calm.

Morgan and Boone discussed whether they should object to producing Rose for questioning, but they felt the judge would likely rule that she could be deposed as she was Ruby's mother and might know something. Judge Bergmann didn't have patience for discovery disputes, and they didn't want to risk prejudicing their case before it got to the hearing. Where Suzy was anxious about appearing for a deposition, Rose wasn't. She told Morgan that she didn't know anything about the property or how Ruby and Tony had paid for it— "They can ask me anything they want."

When Tony and Ruby Pinkston were killed, they had a checking account, but it had never carried a balance over a thousand dollars. Although neither Tony nor Ruby had a job, random cash deposits into that checking account supplied funds used for living expenses, such as paying utility bills, groceries, car insurance and property taxes. Ruby and Tony must have paid cash for gas, because there was no record of them having a credit card.

Zeke didn't admit to giving them money except for the payments needed for purchasing the property.

The weakness in Suzy's case was the source of the money that simply materialized to be deposited in the bank each time the two payments were due. There were no records to show where the money came from, and Zeke was claiming he gave Tony the money. By the same token, it was a weakness in Zeke's case, because he could not prove he had that much money. Nothing was conclusive on this point. One big difference in the two sides was that Zeke was alive to make the claim, and both Tony and Ruby were deceased, so there was no one who could refute Zeke's position with first-hand knowledge.

Suzy and Rose had just finished cleaning up after dinner when they heard someone rapping on the door. Suzy opened the door to find Zeke standing there. Even though it was cold, Suzy didn't want to invite him in. She grabbed a coat off the coat tree and opened the storm door and walked out on the porch. "Hi, Grandpa. This is a surprise."

"Girl, that girl that I saw that day at your daddy's house is an attorney." He could have chewed nails with his anger.

Suzy blinked at his hostility, "Yes, that's right."

His tone threatening, "I don't like liars. Don't ever lie to me again. Family don't lie to each other."

Suzy didn't retreat and remained poised even though she was trembling. As she spoke, she hoped her voice wasn't quaking. "I didn't lie to you, Grandpa. Yes, she's a lawyer—a good one. But she and I are friends. I want to become a nurse, and she is helping me know what steps I need to take. She's my friend."

Zeke's penetrating leer sought to unlock the statement's credibility. Although she maintained eye contact, it was disconcerting to gaze into his glower. "A nurse? What put that idea in your head? Hell, you don't need to be no nurse."

Suzy did not lift her eyes from his.

Rose opened the door and saw Zeke. "What are you doin' here?"

"I'm talkin' to my granddaughter. We have some business."

"It's okay, Ma Maw. We're just talkin'."

Rose scrutinized them both and nodded but left the front door open so she could peek through the storm door.

"She was damn nosey, Suzy. This is causing a rift in my mind, and I don't like that. This has gone far enough. If you know what's good for you, you'll drop this nonsense and move over with me where you belong."

Suzy asked, "Why are you tryin' to get the property, Grandpa? What do you have against me havin' it? Pete and I have talked about farming it when he gets out of the Army. I know you'd like for us to move over with you, but this is my home now. I'm goin' to enroll in the local college and work on becoming a nurse."

"I don't want no hard feelin's with you, Girl. You is all that's left of Tony's family, well, you and that baby, but I don't like your attitude 'bout this. I've been thinkin'. We don't know how that judge will rule. Maybe we can have it where we jointly own it."

Suzy didn't want any part of that. She knew he would control everything. Joint ownership would be tantamount to forfeiting her rights to the property, but she wanted to finesse her response to avoid setting him off. When she was expecting Tootsie, her daddy had threatened to kill Pete if he didn't stay away from her. Tony had always been deferential to Zeke. She had Tootsie and Rose to consider. "Let me think about it, Grandpa. It's not something I can decide right now."

He started to get up. "Don't wait too long to let me know. I hope you'll see that's a good solution. I'm gonna end up with that property one way or another."

The next day while they were sitting on the porch, Rocky asked his dad, "How'd things go with Suzy? You think she'll be willin' to share the land?"

"She wouldn't commit. That girl can be stubborn like Tony was."

"Bet she's not as tough though. She'll break. Ain't no way she won't back down once you threaten to take Tootsie."

Zeke thought for a minute. "I don't know 'bout that, Son. She's got more backbone than I would've thought. I'm not sure she scares easy, and she's show'd she's feisty hirin' that lawyer and all."

"Guess that shows she's got Pinkston blood."

Zeke continued to chew his tobacco. "I guess it does. Say, did you hear anything last night at Knucklepin's 'bout any of those shootings in Bekbourg?"

Rocky lit a cigarette. "Not much. I overheard a couple of men talkin' about the old sheriff's shootin', but I didn't hear talk about any suspects or about the cops' investigation."

"Well, give it a few more days and make another trip and see what people are sayin'."

"Sure."

Chapter 30

Sean was working late, so Cheryl invited Kye to join her for dinner. They were discussing the book by G. Keb, which they both had enjoyed reading. Cheryl said, "Bri just finished it, and she really liked it. Max is going to read it next."

"One of the things that's interesting to an old English teacher like me is the writing style. Some of it reminds me of something I've read before. I wonder if the author has written books under a different pen name. I'd like to know, because I'd like to read some of his or her other books. Interestingly, I don't even know if the author is a man or woman. Maybe everyone should get together and discuss it once we've all read it."

"That would be fun," agreed Cheryl. "Maybe that can be the first book in my 'Book of the Month' column."

"Dear, I'd be glad to be one of your reviewers."

"Oh, that would be great, Kye. I'm also working on a syndicated bridge column. You play bridge, and it seems like a lot of people around here play."

Kye frowned.

"You don't think that's a good idea?" Cheryl asked.

"I think it's a very good idea, Dear. I'm sorry, but when you mentioned bridge, it brought a sour taste to my mouth. Something happened today, and I've been debating whether to tell you, but I think I should."

"What happened?"

"Like you said, there are several bridge players around town. I play with three retired school teachers each week, and there are several groups like ours who play. When someone can't play, it is easy enough to find a replacement. Well, June asked me to fill in for one of the women in her group, and I did. I kind of wish I hadn't. Do you know Loretta Harris?"

"No."

"She is the wife of one of the deputies, Mack Harris. I shouldn't be unkind, but she is not one of my favorite people. She is showy and a gossip. Anyway, during the game today, she suggested that Sean might have been behind Mike's death."

"Whhhaatt?" Cheryl was incredulous.

"I know, Dear. That was my reaction. I'm not part of that group, so I probably shouldn't have said anything, but I couldn't help it. I told her that was the most ridiculous thing I had ever heard and asked her who told her such a thing. The other women were looking at her, too. I guess she felt she had stepped in something, so she tried to back pedal by saying that there was some talk going around that Mike might have been planning to run against

Sean in the next sheriff's election when he was fully recovered and that Sean might not have liked that. She added that it was odd that Sean so quickly took over Mike's job."

Cheryl was exasperated. "Did she say where she heard it?"

"She didn't say, but I told her that it was a terrible thing to repeat. The other two women said they had not heard it. I told her that I didn't think something so mean-spirited should be repeated. The other women agreed. I could tell she was in a snit, but I couldn't let that pass."

"Thank you, Kye, for trying to squash that malicious rumor." They went on discussing other matters, but after Kye went home, Cheryl stewed. She decided to visit Loretta Harris and see if she could learn more about the rumor's source.

The next day, she called Loretta. "Mrs. Harris, this is Cheryl Seton, the new owner of the *Bekbourg Tribune*. I understand that you are a member of a bridge club. I am thinking about starting a syndicated bridge column in the paper and would like to meet with you and get your ideas."

Loretta was flattered that Cheryl would call her, and it also gave her a chance to show off her house. She invited Cheryl to her home the following day.

Loretta thought that if she impressed Cheryl, she might include her in newspaper features. She made her special lemon squares and used the new cups and saucers to serve coffee.

"Please have a seat, Cheryl, and make yourself comfortable. I am so glad to finally meet you. My husband works with Sean, but I'm sure you know that. It's high time we met."

"I'm happy to meet you, and thank you for inviting me over. I understand you are knowledgeable about bridge, and I wanted your thoughts about a column I am planning for the *Tribune.*"

As Loretta served the coffee and lemon squares, Cheryl surveyed the living room. "You have a beautiful home."

"Why, thank you. There's only so much I can do on a deputy's pay, but I make do. Before you leave, I'll show you around."

"I'd love to see it. How long has your husband worked for the sheriff's department?"

"Oh, he's been there longer than anyone. Over thirty years. Mike was the sheriff, and with him being a big football hero, people here would always support him, so Mack never ran against him. Mack's very experienced. I always thought we should move to the big city. I think he would have been elected chief with all his experience. But, we decided to raise our two children here and ended up staying here. Mack knows practically everyone in the county, and that's very important to being good in that kind of job. The new sheriff," Loretta seemed to catch herself, "but you know this. He's been away for, what is it, twenty years?"

"Yes, but during that time, he was in a special criminal investigative unit and investigated crimes in many parts of the world."

"Yes, I suppose that can be helpful in a small town like Bekbourg."

Loretta's comment provided Cheryl an opening. "I agree. I certainly think his training will help in finding who killed Mike." Cheryl watched Loretta. "With your husband being in the department, people must ask you about things the department is investigating."

"Well, of course. They are always asking my opinion on things."

"Have you heard anything about who they think may have killed Mike?" Cheryl asked as she nibbled a lemon square morsel and murmured, "Mmmm. So delicious."

Loretta smiled and considered her answer as she took a bite of lemon square and sipped her coffee. "Oh, I have my opinions like everybody, but I'm careful what I say. I think it's best if we just see if they arrest someone. Well, enough about that. What can I tell you about bridge?"

They talked about bridge, with Loretta explaining how the ladies enjoyed their weekly games and how much she enjoyed hosting them.

"I noticed the pictures on the table there. Is that your bridge group?"

"Oh, yes, it is. Let me show you."

They walked over to the round display table. "Every year, we go someplace for a 'girls' long weekend,'" she said, putting her fingers in quote marks. "Nothing too fancy, just a place to have fun and maybe play a little bridge. We've been doing it for years." Cheryl noticed that all of the locations were in gambling venues.

"Since we're up, let me show you the rest of the house."

"Oh, I would love to see it."

The house was one-story and despite the spacious rooms, Cheryl could not help musing that it was like maneuvering through an overly-stocked novelty shop. Loretta guided Cheryl through the kitchen, den and down a long hall—which led to four bedrooms. When she opened one of the bedroom doors, she chuckled, "This is Mack's man-cave. He won't let me touch it other than to vacuum and dust. I guess most men like *one* room where they can have their things." Cheryl noticed some law-enforcement things, like hats, wind breakers and other uniform-related things. There was also a fully stocked gun cabinet. A worn recliner faced a small television sitting in the corner.

When they returned to the living room, Cheryl thanked her for her time and the delicious refreshments. "I am glad I talked with you. I've learned a lot about bridge."

"You are welcome. Keep me in mind if you ever want to do home or cooking features. I am glad to contribute where I can."

"I will do that. Thank you again."

Cheryl found it interesting that Loretta didn't repeat the ludicrous rumor about Sean, but she probably thought better of it since it was common knowledge around town they were engaged. Unfortunately, she still didn't know the rumor's source. It was so outlandish as to defy any sense of credibility, so why start it? Cheryl wondered if Loretta herself had started the rumor, but why would she? Loretta struck her as someone who was an attention hound. It could be as simple as she liked to gossip to give the appearance of being in-the-know, but why stoop to such a rancorous tale?

That evening, Cheryl told Sean about her visit with Loretta. "It's a nice home, but for my taste, it was claustrophobic with all the furnishings and accessories. She told me that she had raised their two children and never worked outside the home. She goes on annual trips with her bridge friends to different casinos. I didn't know deputies made that kind of money."

Sean was preoccupied. His interest rose some when Cheryl told him about the rumor that Loretta was spreading. "She wouldn't repeat it to me, Sean. Kye came on strong with her, so she may have decided not to repeat it again. Anyway, I couldn't learn the source."

"Who knows? I wouldn't put any emphasis on it. Anyone who knows the history between me and Mike would know it has no basis in fact or reality."

Chapter 31

"Hey, Sean. It's Lucky." Sean smiled. One of these days he was going to ask him how he got that nickname.

"Hi, Lucky. How are you?"

"Doing good. I've got some information for you." Lucky was with the FBI out of their Columbus office. He and Sean had worked together on cases when Sean was in the Marines.

"Great. Shoot."

"First, I talked to Boze. We've both looked into the Miguel Esteban organization. He's still operating, and his nephew, Dante Esteban—alias Dante Gomez—is in Colombia. None of the U.S. intelligence or law enforcement agencies has any word that the Esteban cartel has a hit out on you, at least not currently."

"Okay. I guess that's one box we can check."

"Yeah. I also did some digging on John Pawley. He grew up in Bekbourg. You probably knew that. After he graduated high school, he attended a small state school in Ohio and then dropped out and joined the Marines and served in Vietnam. He was awarded two Purple Hearts. He was a sharp shooter, and Sean, his reputation was that he never missed. He's an expert in handling a sniper's rifle."

"Mmm. He likes his guns. Mike told me that he probably had an arsenal. Have you been able to find out anything about Zeke Pinkston's son, Rocky Pinkston?"

"Yeah. Just getting to that. He's twenty-four-years old. Lives up there around Zeke. He never completed high school. Rocky's had some odd jobs but nothing sustainable. I suspect he works for Zeke. Neither he nor Zeke have any firearms registered, but they are probably well stocked. I'm going to keep digging on him, but one thing of interest is that he hangs around with a militia group. It's on our radar."

"No doubt then about his familiarity with firearms."

"No doubt," Lucky agreed. "Say, Harold called me and told me about your theory one of the shooters might be someone who was put out of business when Tony Pinkston's drug operation was destroyed. He and I have both been looking into that, but so far, nothing is coming up. We'll keep looking, but I wanted you to know. Have you found anything interesting?"

"Haven't even made it to first base, Lucky. We know the bullet found in Mike was a 308 Winchester round. Beyond that, we don't have a weapon, no real lead on a suspect, and don't know if it is the same shooter. Harold believes it's the same shooter. He keeps reminding me to be on alert, because he thinks I'm still a target. His theory is that the shooter tried for me and missed, so he made sure he got closer to Mike when he shot him. He thinks the shooter is biding his time."

"If Harold's theory is right, do you know why he'd be after both you and Mike?"

"Cooper is the only one who expressed the same motive against both of us. Pinkston, in his way of thinking, has reasons against both of us. His grievance against Mike is that his family was killed while Mike was sheriff and because he believes that Mike and Jeff were close. Of course, Ben worked for Mike, so that may be another strike against Mike in Zeke's mind. With me, it would likely be because of a run-in we had. Kyle has a motive against me for forcing his resignation and a grievance against Mike because he didn't fire Ben—who Kyle patrolled with. Kyle is shifting blame for his failure to report Ben to Mike."

"Well, speaking of Kyle, I did some research. I didn't find a lot. He was married for a couple of years several years ago, but they got divorced and she left town. No kids. From everything I could find he seems to live a quiet life. He has no service with the military."

"I don't know much more about him," said Sean. "He hangs out some at Knucklepin's. Even the other deputies don't seem to know much about him, but of course, except for Darrell, they haven't been here very long."

"You'll crack this, Sean. Something will give. I'll help any way I can. Just call."

Kim buzzed Sean. "Hey, Boss. While you were on the phone, a woman called. She only wanted to talk to you."

Sean got the phone number and returned the call. She asked Sean if they could meet somewhere where they wouldn't be seen. She didn't want anyone to know she was talking to him. She told him that she might have some information about the shootings. Sean suggested that they meet at a drive-through on the east side of town. He was waiting at a picnic table on the edge of the parking lot. She saw him and walked over. "If this is okay, we can sit here, but if it's too cool, both tables are open inside."

"This is fine, Sheriff Neumann. Like I said on the phone, my name is Brooke Ratcliff, and I work at the Pavilion. I'm sorry to drag you out here, but, you see, I was seeing Kyle for a while, and I didn't want to take a chance that word might get back to him that I talked to you. I don't know if any of the deputies knew we were seeing each other."

"You make it sound like it's in the past."

"It is. I broke it off after what happened. He was so drunk I don't think he remembers much about that night. It was soon after that when I stopped seeing him. I moved back to Bekbourg not too long ago to help take care of my mother. We had only seen each other a few times."

"Okay. What is it you wanted to tell me?"

"I met him after work at Knucklepin's to get something to eat. He was angry. Kyle had just quit his job that day. I didn't understand what had happened, so it was kind of hard to follow him. He felt it was the old sheriff's fault that a deputy named Ben got fired. He felt the old sheriff let you push him around and call the shots. The part that has been bothering me is that Kyle said it was too bad that Ben didn't finish the job against the old sheriff or you. I was curious so I finally went to the library and read about those events. I don't want to cause any problems where there aren't any, but I decided it was best to tell you and let you decide."

"Can you remember anything else?"

"No. He called me a few days later to see about getting together. I told him that my mom needed me, and that I couldn't see him again."

"How did he react?"

"He didn't really say anything. Something like 'okay.' Didn't seem to care. I haven't talked to him since."

"I appreciate you telling me. Was he ever violent around you and threatening in any way to you or anyone?"

"No. Never. I would have broken off before that night if he had been."

Suzy was walking to her car after getting off from work when Rocky walked up. "Hey, Suzy."

Suzy jumped. "Oh my God! I didn't see you. What are you doing here, Rocky? You scared the shit out of me."

"Sorry 'bout that, Suzy. I didn't mean to do that. I wanted to talk to you."

"Okay, let's get in my car. It's cold standing out here."

"Okay."

After they were sitting in the car, Suzy opened the conversation. "This is a surprise, Rocky. What's it about?"

"Suzy, I don't have to tell you that Pap is hell-bent on getting that property."

Suzy sighed. "Oh, I know. Why is he wanting it? What is going on?"

"I can't get into that, Suzy, but you know how he can be. This can't be easy on you. I've always thought of you as a little sister, but I can't take sides against him."

"Does he know you're talking to me about this?"

"No. I know he offered that you and he share it. That seems reasonable to me. You interested in that?"

"No way. You know I wouldn't have any rights if we did that. Rocky, that property belonged to Daddy and Momma. It rightfully belongs to me. Pete and I are going to get married when he finishes his first term. We have talked about farming that property. It gives us something to start with. It may be all we ever have except what we earn."

Rocky looked out the window into the darkness. "I take it you're not going to back off?"

"No, I'm not."

"Well, just be prepared, Suzy. He won't stop until he gets what he wants."

They talked for a few minutes about other things before he got out of her car.

Chapter 32

Percy, the bartender at Knucklepin's, knew his customers, and after serving two beers to Cooper, he slowed service, and after four beers, Cooper was done for the night. That was the way it usually worked, but Percy had already decided that he was cutting Cooper off after three tonight.

Cooper liked sitting toward the middle of the bar where it was easy to flag down Percy for a refill. Cooper had been grousing about a variety of things since he sat down, and after two beers, he was on a roll. It was a fairly slow night for people seated at the bar, with only two other patrons sitting at the far end. The bowling leagues played tonight, and Knucklepin's was a favorite stop.

Mack Harris walked up to the bar to order the beers for his bowling buddies as Cooper was railing that, "That damn sheriff is harassing the hell out of me." Percy handed the beers to Mack with a half-ear to Cooper. "Damnit, he's trying to frame me just like that dead sheriff did. I lost six years of my life in that hellhole 'cause he didn't do his damn job. Hell, he was in cahoots with them rotten Thompsons." Cooper took a long, noisy gulp from his third beer. "Well, he got what was comin' to him, and this new sheriff's damn lucky he's not six feet under. Assholes like that can't run forever."

After Mack walked back to the table with the beers, Percy headed to Cooper. He had heard enough to know that Cooper was on the verge of getting out of hand. "Cooper, your tab just closed. You need to pay up and get on home."

Cooper glanced sharply at him. "It's too early for you to be kickin' me out."

Percy shook his head. "Come on, Coop."

"Ah hell," he grunted as he pulled a couple of singles from his shirt pocket and slapped them on the bar. He slid off the bar stool and announced, "I'm goin' to take a leak," as he ambled down the hall.

Sitting at the other end of the bar were Rocky and Kyle. Rocky eyed Cooper as he passed by, "You know anything about that?"

Kyle sipped his boilermaker. "He's been singing that song ever since he got back."

Rocky downed the rest of his whiskey and laid money on the bar. About that time, Cooper headed out the door. "Time to shove off," Rocky muttered as he got up to follow Cooper out the door.

Mack came into Sean's office after his day off, "Sheriff, you got a minute?"

"Yeah, Mack. Have a seat. What's up?"

"I dropped by Knucklepin's after our bowling game the other night, and Cooper was there. I went to the bar to order beer for the men. He was spouting off his mouth like he usually does, but he said some pretty rough things about you and Mike. He was blaming Mike for spending six years in prison and you for harassing him. Even said Mike was in cahoots with the Thompsons. He's saying you're trying to frame him like Mike did. He said Mike got what was coming to him and that you couldn't get away with it either. He was angry, Sheriff."

Sean asked, "Can we collaborate this with anyone else who was there that night?"

"Oh, yeah. Percy heard it. Hell, he was loud enough that everyone up near the bar heard him for sure. I don't know if my bowling buddies heard it back at our table. They didn't say anything about it if they did. I'll tell you who was sitting at the bar and must have heard it and that was Kyle and Rocky Pinkston."

Sean's attention peaked, "Kyle and Rocky? Were they sitting together?"

"Yeah. I didn't go over and say anything to them, because I was in a hurry, but yeah, they were sitting beside each other."

After he left, Sean leaned back in his chair. Sean didn't know what to make of the fact that Kyle and Rocky seemed to know each other and how this fit into the investigation. Well, he was tired of sitting on his ass. Cooper had made threats before the shootings and was still making incriminating statements. A couple of days ago, Syd had learned from talking to an old buddy of Cooper's that, during high school, they used to target practice at the quarry and that Cooper was a good shot with his friend's rifle. Cooper didn't own a rifle back then, and his friend's rifle, which he still had, didn't match the murder weapon. Maybe Cooper didn't think they would search his place since they had done so during the summer. They had enough to get a warrant. He'd start there and see if anything turned up.

Sean obtained a search warrant, and he along with Alex, Syd and Mack went to Cooper's. Sean banged twice on the door before Cooper answered. He looked at Sean and then spied the three deputies behind him. Sean said, "Cooper, we have a search warrant to search your place." Even though Cooper was well acquainted with them, Sean identified the three deputies.

"What the hell?"

"Why don't you and I have a seat here?"

"Ain't no way I'm staying in here while these yahoos ransack the place." He grabbed a coat, and Sean followed him outside to make sure he didn't take off. There were a couple of old lawn chairs where they sat during the search. Cooper was cussing and fuming. "This is damn harassment. I don't have a damn gun. You ought to know that. You tore up the place once before."

"Cooper, we didn't tear up your mother's place. You've been sounding off around town about blaming Mike and me for not helping clear your record. You were even heard blaming Mike for going to prison, saying he was in cahoots with Ben and the Thompsons. You say things like that, Cooper, we have to investigate."

Cooper screwed up his face, ready to let go again, when all three exited the trailer. "Nothing in there, Chief," said Alex.

Cooper whooped, "Hell no, there ain't nothing in there. I told you so."

Alex ignored Cooper, "Syd's going to search the truck, and Mack and I are going to search the shed out back."

As they walked away, Cooper glared, "This is plain bullshit. I got rights. I ain't goin' to put up with this shit. Every time somethin' happens, you assholes try to blame me."

Cooper kept fuming while Sean ignored him. Syd came walking over, "Sheriff, I've searched all through the truck, including underneath and in the wheel wells. I didn't find anything there."

"Shit," murmured Cooper.

"Okay, Syd." She stood off to the side.

After a few minutes, Sean saw Alex and Mack walking from around the mobile home, Alex carrying a rifle out in front of him. "Sheriff, we found this up in the rafters in the shed out back."

Cooper looked up and saw Alex carrying the rifle and jumped up and bolted down the yard. Sean jumped up to give chase, but, despite Cooper's gangly sprint, his gamey leg prevented him from gaining on the fleeing Cooper. Out of the corner of his eye, he saw Syd whiz by and throw herself on Cooper's back, causing him to tumble forward. She had Cooper restrained by the time Sean got to them. She finished putting the handcuffs on Cooper as he struggled and shrieked, "It's a frame! You're framing me!"

She and Sean yanked Cooper to his feet and manhandled him to the cruiser, all the while he was wildly screaming that he was being framed. Once they got him in the back and closed the door, they leaned against the cruiser catching their breaths. They could still hear Cooper bellowing.

Mack and Alex walked up, Alex still holding the gun.

"It's a Remington 742. That's one of the guns listed by Forensics that could have been used against Mike," said Alex.

Mack added, "Sheriff, it looks like we got him."

Sean's heavy breathing had almost returned to normal. He pushed himself off the cruiser and said, "Give me the rifle, Alex. I'm going to run it up to Columbus for Ronnie to do a ballistics check. Take Cooper to the station and put him in a cell."

As keyed up as he was over Mike's death, he didn't want to do anything he would regret. The drive to Columbus gave him time to decompress and think through things.

When Sean arrived back at the station, Alex told him that Cooper was locked in a cell and was demanding to talk to an attorney. "Another thing, he's threatening to sue the department."

"Let him try," Sean barked as he walked to his office.

Next morning, the *Tribune's* headlines that a suspect was in custody on suspicion in Mike's death rippled through the town. Anita served many tables at Frau's where it was the topic of conversation. Percy heard a variety of opinions. Knowing that Cooper had served time and had been bad-mouthing Mike, some people believed they had the right man. Others "could have sworn" that the Pinkstons were responsible. Still others thought his murder was the drug cartel's handiwork. Emerging, however, from the widespread opinions was a consensus that Mike's killer was behind bars, and many thought he too was responsible for shooting at Sean.

Two days later, Ronnie Vin called Sean. "It's a match, Sean. The bullet we found in Mike came from the Remington you brought in. It's an older model—fourteen years old. What about a scope?"

"A scope?"

"Did you find a scope?"

"No, why?"

"There are recent markings of a scope mount on the gun.

"Mmm. That's odd." Sean wondered why it wasn't still attached to the rifle.

"Do you know how accurate a shooter he is?"

"Not really. We have a witness who said he was a good shot with a rifle in high school. The only gun I've ever known him to own was a 9 mm hand gun, and if you believe him, it was stolen from him when he was arrested several years ago on a drug possession charge."

"Well, even experienced marksmen use scopes, but if he wasn't very experienced, that would explain why he had a scope, but the question is: why wasn't it with the gun?"

"That's a very good question."

"There were no fingerprints on the rifle."

Sean thought that was interesting. *If Cooper had the gun hidden, why wipe it down?*

"There's one other thing. The casing that Harold found lodged under a rock near where he believes the shooter stood taking shots at you—it's from a 308 Winchester round. That's the same bullet type that killed Mike. We don't have an intact bullet that was shot at you, so we can't be sure this is the gun used against you. It's an awfully big coincidence that the casing also came from a 308 Winchester round."

The headline in the morning's edition of the *Tribune* was:

Suspect Charged in Murder
of
Former Bekbourg County
Sheriff, Mike Adams

Bekbourg didn't currently have a public defender, so Derrick Compton, an attorney in Boone's law firm, was appointed to represent Cooper. He pled not guilty at the hearing and was returned to jail to await trial.

The deputies were relieved that Mike's killer was behind bars. Although there wasn't any other evidence in Sean's case, there was a general feeling, at least among the deputies, that Cooper was responsible for both crimes. Since the casing found near where they believed the shooter stood in Sean's shooting was the same as the bullet found in Mike—both a 308 Winchester round—there was a strong similarity between both shootings. Besides that, Cooper had made incriminating statements about both Mike and Sean. The state police was still looking for the bullet that missed Sean's head, but the deputies didn't have any other leads to pursue.

In the morning meeting following Cooper being charged, Sean told Syd that she should continue to see what she could find out about Cooper's movements and see if there was anyone who knew how or when he got the rifle or knew anything about a scope. "Selling the scope could have been a quick way to raise some money, so see if you can find out anything about him selling it." He also told the deputies that there was a strong presumption that Cooper was the one who had shot at him, but there was no proof and that they should continue to look for leads. Sean wasn't optimistic about finding any evidence, but he didn't want to stop looking.

After that morning, the topic of the shooter tapered off in the morning meetings, because Mike's killer was in custody, and no evidence had surfaced in Sean's shooting.

Chapter 33

The Legend of Mader Valley:
Fact and Fiction – Part 2
By Cheryl Seton

The time period was 1895. The nation was enduring another economic crisis, the Panic of 1893, which lasted to 1897, caused in great measure by the return of the monetary policy to the Gold Standard.

Jarvis Mader lived in Kinniconick Hollow—near Garrison, Kentucky, with his young wife, Elsa, and their four young children. He was employed by the Kinniconick Railroad to cut trees and make railroad ties. Economic times were hard. Some of the railroads didn't survive, and the Kinniconick Railroad was one of them. Jarvis Mader lost his job and had no land to grow things and no other source of income. The closure of the railroad was a devastating blow to the area. There were no jobs, and men from the area had to look elsewhere for employment.

Jarvis had gotten wind that the lumber and mining company in Bekbourg County was looking for men to cut lumber for railroad ties and mine iron ore up in the hills. Because he had experience cutting wood for ties, he thought it worthwhile to travel to Bekbourg. He was reasonably optimistic that he could get hired. He sold his gun and left the money with his wife to support the family while he was gone. He told his wife that he would be back by Christmas and would send money as he got paid.

He set out walking on what he figured was a ten-day trip. He took the ferry across the Ohio River and headed north, mostly sleeping outside unless someone was generous enough to allow him to bed down in their barn. The big problem was he had no money. He had left everything back with his wife. All he had with him were a couple of changes of clothes, some food, and a hunting knife that his parents gave him when he and Elsa married—one that had a red ring around the edge of the knife's guard.

Jarvis didn't return home to Elsa and their children by Christmas.

Chapter 34

The court reporter sat at the far end of the small rectangular conference room ready for the deposition to start. Zeke and Hiram sat on one side of the table, a yellow legal pad with notes lay in front of Hiram. When Morgan and Suzy entered, neither man stood. Suzy looked at Zeke, "Hi, Grandpa."

"Suzy."

Morgan laid her file on the table. "We're ready."

Morgan had counseled Suzy to try and ignore Zeke during the questioning and warned her that both men might try to intimidate her. Hiram launched in with a clipped, demanding tone. He asked what Suzy might know about her parents' finances and about how they paid for the property. She reminded him that she was just fourteen years old when her parents bought the property. She didn't know anything. She had never heard them discuss how they planned to pay for the property. Occasionally, her mother would mention needing more money put in the bank, but there were never any arguments between her parents about money.

"Well, if you don't know anything about this, how can you say your grandpa didn't loan the money to your daddy and momma to buy the property?"

"For the same reason I don't know that he did."

"What have you taken out of the house?"

"Well, after Momma and Daddy and Aaron were killed, the police, after a while, let me go in and get my things and Tootsie's things. They watched what I got."

"You didn't take anything that belonged to your momma or daddy?"

"No. The police wouldn't let me take anything other than what I took."

"That's not all you took, is it?"

"What do you mean?"

"Your grandpa here said that he caught you up at the house, joined there by your attorney."

"Well, that was after the police said I could go back into the house."

"Had you been there before your grandpa caught you with her up there?"

"No. I was just there that one time."

"You knew that your grandfather claimed he owned the place. I don't see you had any right to be there. What did you and your attorney steal from the place?"

"Wait a minute," interrupted Morgan. "Suzy didn't steal anything. Nor did I, for that matter. She had every right to be there. By law, it belongs to her."

"I'm asking what she stole."

"And I'm not going to let her answer as long as you phrase your questions that way."

Zeke piped up. "Well, might as well call it what it was—stealing from her own grandpa. That's against the law to steal. The sheriff here might have somethin' to say 'bout that. Hiram just wants to know what was stolen so I can file a report with the sheriff."

Suzy had paled. Her hand trembled as she tried to drink some water.

"Hiram, another outburst by your client, and I will halt this deposition. He is out of order."

"Now wait just a damn minute," Zeke sat forward. Suzy leaned back in the chair, but Morgan moved forward. "I have every damn right to hear what this lyin', thievin' granddaughter of mine has to say."

"We're going to take a break," Morgan rose and said as she gathered her file. "Come on, Suzy." She turned to look at Hiram, "Anything else like this happens after we resume, I am going to withhold Suzy from any further questioning." She then told the court reporter she could take a fifteen minute break.

Once they got back to Morgan's office, Suzy collapsed into a chair bending forward with her arms crossed holding her stomach. "Do you think they can have me arrested for going into my parent's house? Oh, God. I don't know about all of this."

"Look, Suzy. You are doing fine. Sheriff Neumann isn't going to arrest you for going into that house. Your grandfather and his attorney are trying to bully you into giving up. I know this isn't pleasant."

Suzy interrupted. "This is torture, Morgan. I hate it."

"I know it isn't easy, but Suzy, don't give up. You owe it to yourself, Tootsie and Pete. Just hang in there and remember. They are trying to frighten you and bully you. Just keep telling yourself that and answer the questions, but try not to show you're scared. You have been doing a great job. Let's go back in there and show them what you got."

Suzy looked at Morgan for a minute. She sat up and pushed her hair away from her face. "How much longer is this going to last?"

"I think they are about through. He's asked all the questions about what you knew about the source of the money used by your parents to buy the property. You ready to finish this?"

Suzy nodded.

When they got back in the room, Hiram and Zeke were returning from the outside where Hiram had smoked a cigarette.

Looking at Morgan, Hiram said, "You're unduly interfering with this deposition. I ain't having this again. I'll call the judge if I have to."

Morgan squared her shoulders, "It's your client that is interfering, and if he says another word to my client during her deposition, I will end this. Also, Hiram, I will not allow you to continue to badger her or allow her to answer a question where you accuse her of a crime."

They stared at each other, and Morgan said, "I suggest that we get started so we can finish. Mrs. Waters will be here at two o'clock. You wanted to get this done in one day, and we accommodated that request."

"Okay, Ms. Pinkston. At the insistence of your attorney, I'll change the way I ask the question, but that's not to say I don't stand by what I said earlier. What did you take from the house that day that Mr. Pinkston here caught you and your attorney at the house?"

Suzy looked at Morgan to make sure that she didn't have an objection. When Morgan continued to write something on her pad, Suzy responded, "The only reason we were there that day was because my grandpa filed this case and claimed he owned the property. Like I told you before, I had never heard Momma and Daddy talk about that. If there was anything that might speak to it, my attorney and I thought it might be in the house—in their papers. We looked through where Momma kept all her files. She's the one who did all that sort of thing. Daddy never dealt with paperwork. We took all those papers."

"What else?"

"Momma also had a picture of her holding Tootsie on her nightstand, and I took that—even though the glass was cracked. I also took a picture of Momma and Daddy on their wedding day. That's all I took."

He sat back in his chair, "You mean to tell me that you hadn't been in the house since the police first let you in, and that's all you took?"

"Yeah."

He raised his eyebrows. Suzy looked at him but didn't back down. "What happened to the papers?"

"Morgan has them."

Hiram looked at Morgan. "I want to see everything that was in those papers."

"I produced to you everything that was responsive to your data requests, which included everything that pertains to this lawsuit. Everything else is irrelevant. We have no obligation to show you any of the rest."

"Well, when we win, everything that was in the house is Mr. Pinkston's. Those papers will belong to him as will those two pictures your client stole."

"We'll cross that bridge if and when that point comes."

"Ms. Pinkston. Have you been back to the house since that time you were there with your attorney?"

"No."

"Well, how come all those 'No Trespass' signs are everywhere and the doors are locked like prison doors?"

Morgan spoke up, "Precautions were taken to prevent trespassers from coming onto the property and breaking into the house. With the federal government removing theirs, it was necessary."

"Once the judge rules in our favor my client will expect the key to those locks to be immediately turned over to him. Counsel, I will also demand an accounting of everything that has been removed from the property by your client." Hiram turned back to Suzy. "You know, don't you, that your grandmother's deposition is scheduled right after this?"

"Yes."

"Who are you throwing Tootsie off on since your grandmother can't watch her?"

Morgan objected, "That has nothing to do with the property. Suzy is not going to answer that."

Zeke had obviously put Hiram up to asking the question, because he snarled, "Well, she better have better answers than that when I file to take custody of that baby. She's always leaving her. Rose is an old woman. She ain't fit to care for her. I ain't goin' to stand by and see my great grandchild neglected by an unfit mother." His dark eyes bore into Suzy's.

Before Suzy could respond, Morgan spoke, "Counsel, I take it you don't have any additional questions on the property?"

"Oh, I got lots more questions, but I'm saving those for the hearing."

"Okay, then. Mrs. Waters and I will be back at two o'clock."

Suzy and Morgan went to her office. Suzy's eyes were wide. "Oh, my God. He's going to try to get Tootsie."

"Look, Suzy. This is all a game they are playing. Don't buckle under this pressure. It will be okay."

Suzy sat up straight, and for the first time since Morgan had met her, Suzy's lips formed a determined line and her eyes narrowed, "There is no way in hell, Morgan, that I will ever let him get Tootsie. I'll leave here. If I can't be where Pete is, I'll find some place, but he's not getting Tootsie."

"Suzy, don't let him get to you. He's trying to pull your chain. He doesn't have a leg to stand on in getting Tootsie. You and Pete are her parents, and you are taking excellent care of her. You're both working hard. Let's stay focused on this property matter."

"Is there any chance Grandpa can bribe the judge?"

Morgan arched her brows, "I've never heard any rumor like that about Judge Bergmann. If that was a possibility, Boone would know, and I've never heard him say anything like that."

"Well, I overheard Daddy talking to Ray and Victor about paying a deputy for help with things, so he probably learned that from Grandpa."

"What type of things?"

"I never heard that."

"I'll talk to Boone just to make sure. What deputy?"

"Ben somebody. He's dead. He was one of the killers that night."

"Now, Mrs. Waters, you said that you were close to your daughter. That she called you every night after she cleaned up the kitchen. You mean to tell me that she never talked to you about her and her husband's finances?"

Rose sat straight at the table with her arms resting on the table and her hands clasped. "Don't go puttin' words in my mouth. I said that her callin' me every night happened after they moved over here. While they were livin' in Tapsaw, she usually just called every Sunday evening."

"Okay, but even before they moved to Bekbourg, she called you every week. A daughter tells her mother everything. She didn't tell you that Tony needed money from Mr. Pinkston to help buy the property?"

"Never heard that one."

"She never told you that they ran short of money?"

"Nary once. Ruby never talked about money things."

"Well, surely, once they moved over here, she did. You talked to her *every* night. The second payment was coming up. That was a lot of money. You're telling me that she never mentioned where the money was coming from?"

"Nope, sure didn't."

"She never mentioned that her husband needed money from his father to make a payment?"

"Nope."

"You're telling me that you didn't know that Mr. Pinkston loaned them the money to buy the property?"

"Not only did I not know that, but I ain't got no reason to even think that he did. As far as I know, Tony and Ruby never borrowed any money. I never heard her mention a loan or makin' payments."

"They ever ask you for money?"

"Nope, never did. As far as I know, Ruby and the kids never wanted for a thang."

"Is Suzy working this afternoon?"

"Hiram, I'm not going to let you get started into that line of questioning," interrupted Morgan. "That has nothing to do with the property."

Zeke spoke up, "Well, it does have to do with the care of my great granddaughter."

"Who is being well taken care of," Rose spat before Morgan could object.

"So, you're saying she ain't with Suzy?"

Rose wasn't going to let Morgan stop her. "I ain't saying nothin' except she is, like always, being taking good care of."

"Rose, I know'd that granddaughter of mine is out catting around. She wasn't there those two evenin's I stopped by. She ain't fit. That little girl belongs over with her family who'll see that she's taken care of."

"Zeke, that dog won't hunt. Suzy is the best momma around. She got that from her momma. She takes exceptional care of Tootsie. She is responsible."

Morgan wrestled control of the conversation. "Hiram, we're not going to discuss things that are not relevant to the land. Now, do you have any more questions about the property?"

"No."

"Okay, then we're done."

After Rose and Morgan returned to her office, Rose said, "I know you probably didn't want me to say anything about little Tootsie, but I can't sit by and let them say things 'bout Suzy that aren't true. That girl loves that baby. She is so good to her. She is working hard to give Tootsie a good life."

"I know. I've seen her with Tootsie. Just so that I know for the record, who is keeping her? I assume Suzy went back to work after her deposition this morning."

"She did. It's Ruth Pinkston that is keepin' her. That is Earl's wife who sold the property to Suzy's parents. Earl is sick, and I sometimes take Tootsie over there on our walks and spend some time with them. They never had no children, and they love it when I bring Tootsie over. I don't want Zeke to know that, 'cause he might start stopping by there, and they don't need him doin' that."

"Do you know what he was talking about when he said Suzy was out two evenings when he stopped by?"

"I sure do. I wouldn't give him the satisfaction of letting him know where she was, 'cause it's none of his business, and I know he's just tryin' to harass her. Both evenin's she was meetin' you. One of those times, you both went to dinner."

Later that afternoon, Boone stopped by Morgan's office. "How did the depositions go today?"

They went fine, I think. Two things that stood out, though, are that Zeke is accusing us of breaking into the house when we went there to find the financial records and stealing them." Boone arched a brow. "He also seems to be planning to accuse Suzy of neglect and fighting her for custody of Tootsie."

Boone sat in a chair. "I'm all ears."

Morgan described the depositions, and they discussed the case. As they were winding down, Morgan said, "Suzy is concerned that Zeke might bribe Judge Bergmann. I told her that I didn't think the judge was like that, but that I would ask you."

"That's the way I would have responded too, Morgan. I've never had reason to suspect him of doing something like that. Now, I don't always agree with his rulings. He has his biases. Behind his back people refer to him as the 'hanging judge' because he throws the book at people found guilty of serious crimes, and even petty crimes. Owen Donaldson always thought he had a hill to climb when he brought a case against the county or when he was representing a plaintiff against a company on some environmental issues."

"Do you think he'll have any bias in our case?"

"No. But, he respects attorneys who are prepared in court. That doesn't mean he will rule in their favor, but he shows impatience with sloppy lawyering."

When she told him about Ben working for Tony Pinkston, Boone made a note to tell Sean.

Chapter 35

Noel Fischner sent a letter to the city council stating that he was opposed to the city's approval of a construction permit for Fischner Construction's renovations of the Schumacher factory. He requested to be heard at the council meeting. Since Cole was the general contractor listed on the permit application for the project, he was notified and given an opportunity to speak. The *Tribune* reporter tasked with covering city hall saw the agenda item:

> *Commissioner Noel Fischner requested to be heard on building permit approved for Fischner Construction for Schumacher Cigar Box factory renovations.*

Around town, people took notice when a county commissioner contested a permit already granted to his brother, who happened to be the president of a notable family-owned construction firm. In turn, this raised the profile of the Schumacher project. People speculated who was behind the Livingstone Trust and what business was going into the old factory. Intrigue and suspense circulated around town.

A week later, the *Tribune* saw a spike in circulation as people purchased newspapers to read about the city council's ruling.

City Council addresses
Commissioner's
Protest of Permit Approved
For Family-owned Company

One of the agenda items on this week's city council meeting concerned a permit previously approved by the city council for Fischner Construction to renovate the Schumacher Cigar Box Company factory previously owned by the local order of nuns. The sale took place approximately two months ago, and the purchaser is listed as Livingstone Trust.

Fischner Construction is listed as the general contractor with major renovations planned within the structure. Cole Fischner, President, said that only cosmetic repairs were planned to the building's exterior.

While Commissioner Noel Fischner, brother to Cole, requested that the council reconsider the permit approved by the previous council, he is not protesting a construction permit approved for the Schumacher mansion.

The objections raised by Commissioner Fischner concern the noise levels resulting from the construction, the congestion from construction worker vehicles around the factory during the work, and the ability to adhere to code requirements given the age of the factory. He additionally requested that the owner be required to disclose the intended purpose of the business to ensure it meets ordinance requirements.

At one point during the hearing, he suggested that the county commission might have jurisdiction, at least joint-jurisdiction, over the permitting process. Tessa Compton, City Attorney, rejected any notion that the county had jurisdiction over the matter.

Cole Fischner addressed each issued raised by his brother. He said that, except for the exterior repair work, for which there would not be substantial noise levels, the work would be confined to the interior of the structure, so noise levels around that part of town would not be a problem. As far as the workers' vehicles, they would be parking in the oversized lot near the factory, so residents and visitors would not be inconvenienced. He submitted a detailed list of the work along with how each project would comply with codes. One of the council members questioned him about the intended purpose of the business. He satisfied the council that it would not be used in any way that conflicted with any ordinances, but that if that question arose at some future date, it could be addressed then. But, he reaffirmed that nothing would be contrary to the city ordinances. He assured that the renovated factory would again be a source of pride for the downtown.

The city council unanimously reaffirmed the permit as originally approved. Construction is expected to begin within two weeks.

Chapter 36

During the 1990's when C.P. discovered that the City of Bekbourg owned a two-hundred mile stretch of railroad that had been leased to MV&O and was coming upon the one-hundred year primary expiration date of January 1, 2005, it planted an idea that maybe, one day, he could buy that line and own his own rail system. A year ago, he retained a long-time friend, Grayson Macafee, who assembled a team of advisors, including investment bankers and financial institution representatives. C.P.'s plan was to be ready to step in if the OMVX terminated the lease. It was important to keep the railroad running and not let it lapse into a dormant period where schedules, business alignments and relationships were interrupted.

Grayson Macafee, a transactional attorney in Washington, D.C. who specialized in railroad mergers and acquisitions, headed up the team charged with identifying and addressing all the legal and regulatory approvals and contracts as well as coordinating with the investment banker for financing and investor matters.

C.P. needed approval from the Federal Railroad and Surface Commission to purchase the railroad. However, prior to filing the application with the commission, he and his team wanted to meet with the advisory board's arm of the commission in a pre-filing meeting to explain C.P.'s plans. This would give them the opportunity to walk the advisory board through the major facets, such as the financing arrangements, the interconnection routes, and the competitive benefits to customers and consumers. A major issue would be the railroad union matters, but since the employees would be governed under the national agreement, he hoped that would not be a sticking point. He and Grayson discussed the fact that the OMVX had tendered an offer to the city, but they thought the city's approval of C.P.'s offer should effectively neutralize OMVX's argument that its proposal should be considered in the alternative.

After this pre-filing meeting, the next step was to file the comprehensive application with the Federal Railroad and Surface Commission. Knowing protests would be filed, he and his team had worked hard over the past year to anticipate those issues and nail down the details. C.P.'s goal was that within a year, he would get final approval to move forward with owning the railroad.

C.P. had been in back-to-back meetings with the local businesses and noticed that Grayson had tried to call him three times. He knew something was up. Grayson's assistant put C.P.'s call right through.

"Hi, C.P. How are things in Bekbourg?"

"Moving right along. I've had productive meetings with the local businesses. Most are willing to file in support. What's new at your end?"

"I'll give you the good news first. I've got the pre-filing meeting set up next week. I can always push the meeting back if we have to, but you wanted to move full steam ahead since there are several moving parts and time is of the essence."

"Good. If all goes well, we can file before the Christmas holidays."

"Right. That leads me to the second thing, which may not be such good news. Do you know Lester Sims?"

"Yes. Why?"

"He is a department head on the commission's advisory board and pretty influential. He pulled a few strings and is going to be at the meeting and will be involved in the process."

C.P. let out a groan, "Ah shit."

Grayson chuckled, "Sounds like you and he have mutual feelings for one another. When one of my attorneys called to set up the meeting, he said that when Lester found out you were involved, the conversation went downhill."

"I bet. There's no way to avoid dealing with him?"

"No. Like I said, he is one of the department heads."

"He is going to be a pain in the ass."

"Well, we knew that this wasn't going to be a bed of roses. The OMVX is going to put up a fight. They aren't going to want the competition from you."

"That's all true, but Sims. I can't believe it. I didn't know he was there."

"Yeah. He took the position about a year ago. Anything else we need to discuss?" Grayson asked.

"No. I appreciate you getting the meeting set up quickly."

Chapter 37

The Legend of Mader Valley:
Fact and Fiction – Part 3
By Cheryl Seton

Jarvis didn't return home to his family by Christmas. Elsa was worried about him and concerned with the responsibility of four young children. Herman Mader, Jarvis's older brother, along with other family members, supported Elsa and her four children, but Herman knew he owed it to his brother's wife to learn of Jarvis's fate. Herman was slightly better off economically than Jarvis, so as soon as the weather warmed up in the spring of 1896, he traveled by horse to Bekbourg in search of Jarvis. Although Bekbourg had felt the economic pinch from the Panic of 1893, its economy had fared better, and the lumber and mining company was still operating.

When Herman arrived in Bekbourg, he visited the sheriff's office, but no one there knew anything about Jarvis. Jarvis was a giant of a man who always wore an unusual wide-brimmed hat. Herman described Jarvis's appearance to everyone he talked with, hoping to jog someone's memory. He asked around town to see if anyone remembered seeing Jarvis—but to no avail. He finally checked at the railroad depot and talked with the freight agent who collected money for freight and passenger service.

His spirits lifted when the freight agent vaguely remembered a fellow fitting Jarvis's description being upset because he didn't have a nickel to ride the train to the lumber and mining company on the upper end of the old spur line. The agent told Jarvis he would have to walk but warned him to stay off the railroad right-of-way. The railroad detectives would run him off, and if they caught him, they would beat the hell out of him. The railroad didn't want hobos on their property.

Herman thought that the railroad detectives might know something about Jarvis, so he asked the agent where he might speak with them. The freight agent pointed to a small office across the street but told him that they were not usually in the office. Their work required that they travel on the trains, and he would have to wait until they returned to town to talk with them.

Since Herman didn't have anything better to do, he waited for two days outside the door for their return. On the second day, he noticed two large burly men getting off the train that was returning on the old spur line from the lumber and mining operation. He approached them and told the two men that he was looking for his brother. They weren't friendly, but he persisted in explaining when his brother had arrived in Bekbourg and that he planned to seek employment with the lumber and mining company at the end of the old spur line. To play on any sympathy they might have, Herman told them that Jarvis's wife and four young children were waiting for his return. One of them finally decided to cooperate and said, "Yeah, I vaguely remember seeing someone that matches that description up the line. We yelled at him and ran after him, but he ran off. It was getting late, so we let him go. He was an idiot to be out there that late. That's our job to keep trespassers off the right-of-way. That was the last we saw of him."

Herman didn't feel the railroad detectives were very forthcoming, but at least he got a sliver of information.

He asked them, "If I pay the fare, would you show me about where you saw him?"

"Sure, but we're not going back up that way for two days. If you're here then, you can ride up. But we can't be exactly sure where it was that we saw him since it was getting dark that evening."

Two days later, Herman got on the train and rode up to the area where the railroad detectives thought they had last seen Jarvis. They told him he could walk back to town along the track, that they wouldn't do anything to him.

He walked along the creek bed, but the water level was high so he couldn't cross it, but he didn't think his brother would have crossed over to the other side. Herman spent the day searching the area, but never found any trace of Jarvis. He walked back to town.

The following day, he caught the train heading to the camp where the workers for the lumber and mining company stayed to see if Jarvis had ever made it there. He talked to different people, but no one remembered seeing Jarvis.

Herman knew that his brother would never abandon his family. It appeared that he never made it to the camp. If he had gone on to another city to find work, he believed that Jarvis would have found a way to contact Elsa. He stopped back by the sheriff's office and told him that he had no luck in finding his brother and gave him contact information in case something turned up. With a heavy heart, Herman had to return to Kinniconick and tell the family the bad news.

Chapter 38

County Prosecutor, Tyler Forquet, called and asked Sean to stop by his office.

"Sean, Derrick called me. You know that Cooper said that he didn't have an alibi."

"Yes."

"Well, that may not be true. His mother has been in Chillicothe tending to her sister. Her sister was recently put in the hospital and just came home yesterday. I guess her sister coming home triggered his mother to remember something. The night before Mike was killed, apparently, the sister took a real turn for the worse. Cooper's mother had been up all night with her, and tensions between her and the sister's husband got tense. She wanted him to take her sister on to the hospital, but he wouldn't. What apparently happened was that she was threatening to come home.

"She called Cooper ranting about the sister's husband and also talking about how concerned she was for her sister. I guess he's about the only person she has, so they apparently talk some when she's there. She claims that she was talking to Cooper around the time that Mike was shot. The reason she remembers it is because it was soon after she got off the phone that the sister's husband agreed, and they took her in. Maybe the husband heard her on the phone with Cooper threatening to come home. Anyway, he may have an alibi."

"That's damn convenient. She suddenly remembers she was talking to Cooper at the same time Mike was getting shot?"

"That was my reaction too, but Derrick followed up with the phone company. He sent over copies of phone records that show there was someone talking from a phone at the sister's to someone talking to someone where Cooper lives. For thirty-four minutes starting at 12:42 p.m. What's the likelihood that someone other than Cooper was at his place during this time?"

"It's not out of the realm of possibility." Sean responded even though he was thinking: *Slim, from what I know about Cooper. He doesn't seem to have any friends or close ties.*

"Well, someone had to be there to answer, even if they laid the phone down and took off. But, Forensics puts the time of death around one o'clock. Could Cooper have made it from his place in time?"

When Sean didn't respond, Tyler continued, "I thought you should know. I'm going to do my own investigation into these phone records, but Sean, we don't want to take anything for granted. Derrick is just as thorough as Boone. He is going to turn over every stone. You know his reputation. I will need proof that the gun was Cooper's."

As Sean walked back to his office, he thought, *this could throw a wrench into the works. Maybe the timing of Mike's death is off?* He closed his office door and leaned back in his chair to consider the ramifications. If it wasn't Cooper, that meant that they didn't have Mike's killer. In honesty, although the gun that killed Mike was found on Cooper's property, a grain of doubt had continued to pester Sean. Now this. It would take planning on Cooper's part to have someone at his house talking to his mother at the same time he was shooting Mike, and why would she go along with something like that? Sean wasn't sure Cooper had it in him to think through those planning details.

Sean needed more information about where the gun came from. He also needed to look closer at the other suspects as well as focus in other directions. First, he needed to tie up any loose ends or Derrick would exploit those during the trial. On the other hand, if Cooper wasn't guilty, Sean wanted the killer. If someone planted the gun on Cooper, this was a breakthrough. It would eliminate Cooper at least in Mike's shooting. Anything they could learn about the gun would put them a step closer to the killer.

Sean called a meeting with Alex and Arlo. He told them that he had met with the prosecutor and they needed to lock down the evidence that the Remington belonged to Cooper. He also told them that they needed to be able to rule out the other suspects—Kyle and the Pinkstons. For now, Sean was moving Pawley to the bottom of the list, because Kyle and the Pinkstons appeared to have stronger motives.

"Arlo, I want you to see if there were any complaints about Ben when Kyle was present or complaints about Kyle, or any irregularities in the arrest reports involving Kyle, including if Ben was present. I want to get a better picture of the type of cop Kyle was."

"Got it. I'll get on it. How far back do you want me to look?"

"Let's look back ten years."

Alex thought it sounded like Kyle was still a suspect. "Are we looking to eliminate Kyle as a suspect, or are we looking to prove Cooper is guilty?"

Sean didn't want the other deputies to know just yet that Cooper might have an alibi. Tyler could find something in the phone records to refute Derrick's claim, but, if not, he needed them to investigate as if the case wasn't solved. "I want this kept quiet, but let's investigate as if the gun was planted."

They both looked surprised. "Is that a possibility, Chief?" asked Arlo.

"I don't want to speculate. Let's tear off the lid and give everything a fresh look. Alex, I need you to look into Kyle's shooting skills. Check the law enforcement shooting ranges. Also, see what you can find about those that live in that Pinkston compound. We need to know if there are other family members that we might have overlooked, such as sons-in-law, cousins, whoever lives in that compound. See if you can find out if any of them are marksmen. Start with that."

Arlo said, "There is something interesting I just learned about Rocky. Back when Rocky was in high school, an owner of a well-drilling service claimed that Zeke stiffed him on the fee for drilling a well on his property. Zeke claimed the man didn't dig the well deep enough. The owner's kid was in school with Rocky and said some derogatory things about Zeke and the Pinkston clan. Rocky caught him out one night and forced his car off the road. Rocky nearly beat him to death. Elmer Puckett, the sheriff, got involved. He put out an investigative report that said that the boy ran Rocky off the road and attacked him. In the end, nothing came of it, but the man dropped his claim that Zeke owed him money. It wasn't long after that when Rocky dropped out of high school."

"That's just like those Pinkstons. It's all about family honor and that eye-for-an-eye," said Alex.

"Yeah, but in this case, Rocky's action could be viewed as excessive," Arlo added.

"Couldn't agree more," said Alex, "which may be a family trademark."

Boone and a client were finishing up a lunch in Max's bistro when Sean entered to grab a cup of coffee. Boone walked over to Sean and greeted him. Boone said, "I'm glad I saw you. I've been meaning to call you. One of the attorneys in my firm is helping Suzy Pinkston on the land dispute with her grandfather. During one of their conversations,

Suzy mentioned that one of the deputies was working on the side for her father, Tony."

"What did she mean by that?"

"Morgan's impression was that he did favors and ran interference for Tony for money. Suzy didn't know the particulars."

"Did she say who it was?" asked Sean.

"Yes, it was Ben."

"Ben? Hell, he worked for the Thompsons."

"Well, he must have had his own side business."

"Ben's name keeps coming up. Thanks for telling me."

"Sure thing," replied Boone.

As Sean was walking back to the station, he thought about Ben working for the Pinkstons. *I bet the Thompsons didn't know that. Maybe he had a side business so long as it didn't cross the Thompsons. Hell, maybe the Thompsons did know. Maybe Ben was an inside source of information to the Thompsons about the Pinkstons.* Sean suddenly remembered two murders that were never solved. When he first joined the department after returning to Bekbourg, he was assigned to identify two men found dead in the woods by a hunter. They had been dead for quite some time when they were discovered. As it turned out, they were brothers who had moved from Indiana to start their own meth business. After the Pinkston deaths, Sean had wondered if they had killed Jed and Brody Todd to snuff out the competition, but there was no evidence. *Was it possible that Ben had something to do with their deaths as a "favor" to the Pinkstons?* Sean decided to ask Kyle about it the next time he talked to him. Kyle might know something. After all, Mack had seen Kyle and Rocky Pinkston together at Knucklepin's.

Chapter 39

C.P. was thorough in selecting attendees for the pre-filing meeting with the Federal Railroad and Surface Commission's Advisory Board. Bri and Tessa were present to address the city's issues. Grayson and one of his attorneys attended along with two representatives from the investment banker. Twelve members of the commission's advisory board were present, including Lester Sims.

Kicking off the meeting, C.P. introduced the representatives accompanying him. He explained the background, including the history of the WVB&C and the lease. He outlined the terms of his purchase and how he planned to expand the service to area businesses and plans for service provisions with connecting rail lines. He told the advisory board that businesses and the city would be filing in support of his request for approval.

Bri then described that the OMVX gave notice to terminate the lease and the terms of its proposal for a new arrangement. She discussed why the city viewed the offer as one-sided in favor of the OMVX. In contrast, C.P. had plans to keep the railroad operational with real economic benefits flowing back to the city and its residents, including the workers. She emphasized the unanimous approval by the Bekbourg City Council to sell the rail line to C.P.

Grayson briefly spoke to the planned application and its timing.

C.P. wrapped up by telling the committee that it was his home town. He wanted to help the area, and he thought he could make a go of successfully running the WVB&C.

The meeting was then opened to questions. Initially, the advisory board's questions were supportive, which C.P. took as a good sign. Lester had been biding his time but didn't want favorable momentum to grow before he had his say, so he decided it was time to shake things up. "You've not mentioned anything about the terms for the employees, C.P., but that shouldn't surprise me. You've never cared about that aspect of running a railroad. Exactly what are your proposed terms?"

A shock tsunami careened through the room. Except for Grayson, who pulled off his glasses and started cleaning them with his tie, the participants froze—not daring to react. What happened next was that C.P. and Lester became the star performers as the others faded to gray.

"They will be under the new hire provisions of the umbrella union agreement under which all class A railroad employees are covered." C.P. was self-assured. "That's the contractual terms governing them now, and those terms will apply to this railroad."

"In other word," huffed Lester, "the workers won't get squat. Why am I not surprised? Just to put all the cards on the table, I got a call from one of the

OMVX's executives. They heard about you planning to buy the line, and they are going to protest. The WVB&C line hasn't proved valuable in ten years, and to keep it running will only increase costs to consumers."

"That is why I'm proposing to buy it—to bring efficiencies to the line and expand its service territory, which will bring competition and lower costs to consumers."

"Which brings me to the next point," Lester smirked as he looked around the room. Having recovered from the initial shock, the others' eyes were moving between the two men like watching a tennis match. "You were in charge of the merger that created the OMVX system. You likely came across this lease during that time. During your term at the Department of Transportation, you were negotiating terms to shut down many rail lines. You were planning all along to purchase this rail line. Now, you plan to reap the benefits by taking over a rail line on the verge of being shut down and running it. We can't allow this kind of activity. This really smells! You were on the negotiating team to close this railroad and now you want to run it. How should we look at that?"

C.P. was calm, but stern. "When I worked for the DOT, I oversaw the negotiation that the railroads proposed and the terms the union agreed to. I was in no way a mastermind of any closures."

Lester scoffed, "According to you."

"This is about competition. I'm offering a competitive alternative to the OMVX but also competitive rates on through-hauls. This is good for consumers. The commission should see protests for what they are—keeping higher rates on the big boys, which is harmful to consumers."

"Huh. We cannot allow a railroad like this that runs on such a razor-thin budget that would compromise the safety of citizens and employees. Everyone knows that a proposal like yours will be detrimental to employees and adversely impact the other rail companies in this railroad company's orbit."

"That won't be the case here. I'll meet all the safety and regulatory standards. You were on the union team that negotiated the umbrella union agreement. It's disingenuous, Lester, to argue against those terms governing the employees. Also, if the railroad is shut down, the employees you purport to be so concerned about will have no jobs. Not only will the city and the region be left without rail service, the employees will be walking the streets."

The two long-time adversaries went back and forth, until one of the other department heads wedged in herself and asked C.P. a question about the financing. C.P. deferred to his investment banker representative. Gradually, the dialogue returned to the proposal, but a seismic shift in the mood was palpable. The tenor of the advisory board's questions was more probing—with some hinting of skepticism. One advisory board attendee asked, "How do we know you won't shut the line down after a year and get all the assets?"

"I'm taking a risk buying the railroad, and I wouldn't be proposing to do so if I didn't think I could make the line profitable. That means growing business opportunities. I'm willing to try and make a go of it, and I believe I can. If I wasn't stepping forward, the OMVX has given notice to terminate the lease. You heard the mayor say that the OMVX proposal for a new arrangement doesn't guarantee rail service beyond one year, and that their interest appears to be the salvage value, which means removing the tracks and everything else.

"You additionally heard Ms. Sanderson explain that the city neither has the expertise nor resources to operate a railroad and that it may be impossible for them to do so within the year's time period. The city wants the rail service. This is a win-win for the city and other customers in the region and up and down the line.

"I've been meeting with companies who are going to file in support because they see the value of a viable railroad. You heard from my investment banker about the plans to infuse substantial investment into the WVB&C. The WVB&C will provide a competitive alternative for customers on through-freight. That's what the OMVX is concerned about. They don't want the competition. They opted to reduce service on this line so they could charge higher rates on their parallel line."

The meeting was winding down. Perceiving that some of the advisory board had cooled on the proposal as the meeting progressed, Bri wanted to accentuate the importance to the city of the continued rail service. "The railroad has been a major part of our city since the 1840's. It's part of our history and culture. We really need the railroad to maintain a standard of living for our citizens. We are a vibrant city and growing. People are moving into the area. Our businesses depend on the service, and our town depends on the revenues. It employs our citizens. Our city council reviewed Mr. Traylor's proposal, and we think it's fair. It's more generous than the one that is terminating. We voted unanimously to approve it. I am requesting that you recognize our decision and likewise approve this acquisition. Our town relies on the rail service and needs it."

The advisory board members filed out after bidding farewell to C.P.'s team. Tessa and Bri watched as C.P. and Lester left the room. Grayson and his team were preparing to depart when Tessa asked for Grayson's feedback on the meeting.

"Let me start by addressing Mr. Sims's comments, because I assume that is the gist of your question." Tessa's slight head incline told Grayson his assumption was correct. "We appreciated Mr. Sims framing his positions."

Tessa thought, *I'm intrigued to hear this rationale.*

"As we are putting the final touches on our application, we can be proactive and address his issues in our filing. I always think it's better to play offense than defense."

Okay, I can see that, thought Tessa.

Grayson continued, "Mr. Sims's points, along with the advisory board's questions and comments, were informative. It is important that we address the advisory board's issues, and we are now prepared to do just that. Over the past year, C.P.'s team has identified a comprehensive list of topics and potential sticking points. Regulatory proceedings always give venue to numerous participants with varying interests. We are prepared for this proceeding. C.P. has assembled an all-star team. Take comfort that C.P. knows what he is doing and so do I."

"So, we need not take away from today's meeting that, after a year of litigating this in the regulatory arena, the commission could reject C.P.'s proposal?" Tessa pressed.

"It is in the best interest of the city, its residents and businesses to keep the rail service. Customers up and down the line will benefit. Even the interconnecting railroads will benefit by increased freight service coming from the WVB&C. I have no reason to doubt we will cross the goal."

After Grayson and the others had departed, Tessa and Bri waited for C.P. to return. Bri asked, "Do you agree with what Grayson just said?"

"I never count my chickens before they hatch, but until C.P. or Grayson gives me reason to believe otherwise, I accept Grayson's evaluation. C.P. doesn't strike me as someone who waves a white flag. I suspect he is already thinking about his next move. But, we always have the option to negotiate with the OMVX if this falls through. We have what they want, and that's the railroad assets."

In the short time they had known each other Bri had come to trust Tessa's legal advice and judgment. Tessa's respect for Bri was growing, "Mayor, you were a show-stopper in there. You have really gotten up to speed on this thing real quick."

Bri laughed, "Thank you, but the memo you wrote on the history of the WVB&C and the articles Cheryl's paper has published about the business needs helped prepare me. After I saw Lester Sims tear into C.P., I wanted to remind the advisory board that personalities shouldn't come between what is best for our city and its citizens. Speaking of C.P. and Lester, where do you think they are?"

Tessa smiled. "Probably discussing their differing opinions."

As they were packing up to leave the meeting room, Lester came up to C.P. and told him that he wanted to talk to him. They went to a small room. Lester spoke through gritted teeth, "C.P., you've always been a company man. I knew that from the first time I met you. You don't give a damn about the employees. You might bullshit those people from Bekbourg, but you're not going to win this. You're dirty, you've always been dirty, and I'm not going to let this go through. I don't believe you are for the workers. You've never been for them. You got something up your sleeve, and I'm not going to let it go."

C.P. looked at Lester and simply said, "We'll see," and turned and left the room. Lester stood there thinking, *Somehow, I don't feel triumphant.*

Chapter 40

Cheryl arranged to interview Stella Long, the business manager for Geisen Products, Inc., as part of her series. The large paper company had been a major employer in Bekbourg until it was briefly shut down nearly two years ago because of a large illegal drug operation. Fortunately, new leadership that included Stella had saved the company, and it was back to full production.

Stella guided Cheryl around the plant and explained the operational phases, from receiving the raw materials to the manufacturing functions to the packaging and boxing in preparation for shipping. When they arrived back at Stella's office, Cheryl shook her head. "I had no idea how complex manufacturing could be. It is amazing how many steps there are. I learned a lot, Stella, and I really appreciate the tour."

Stella smiled. "Oh. That's just part of it. We haven't even discussed what is involved in procuring supplies and the marketing functions."

Cheryl laughed. "Maybe another time. My head is swimming."

Stella nodded. "Well, as you can see, we depend on the train service for delivering the raw materials for our polystyrene products, and we've discussed with C.P. ways we would like to transport by rail our products to long-distance markets. We are going to intervene in support of C.P.'s plan in the D.C. regulatory proceeding. We have relied on rail service since our founding in 1909. Even though we have turned to trucking over the years, it still is an economical transportation means. We are keeping our fingers crossed it works out."

Cheryl said, "I've been curious. You went through a rough time keeping the factory afloat. What was it like?"

"The biggest challenge was keeping our customers. Aside from that, we were spread super thin to avoid going under. I knew the operational side of the business, but I quickly had to assume responsibility for things I had never handled. My biggest challenge was learning about personnel matters. I now have a human resource specialist who handles hiring, payroll, benefits, all those types of things, but for a while, we were operating on a shoe-string budget, so I took care of personnel issues."

"It must have been a challenge."

Stella grinned. "It was, but also a learning experience. I found some fascinating things in the personnel files. One thing was that the Thompsons had retained a deputy as a security consultant for years. We didn't need, and couldn't afford, those services. That was one of the first things I did—terminate that contract. God, I couldn't believe how much he was being paid."

Cheryl was surprised and assumed, because of their history, it was Ben. "Ben Clark was a security consultant?"

"No, it wasn't Ben. It was Mack Harris. I don't remember ever seeing Mack on guard duty or acting as security, but it didn't matter. That contract had to go."

Cheryl was putting the finishing touches on stringing Christmas lights across the handrail when Sean arrived home. He grinned as Buddy charged to greet him and Cheryl plugged in the lights. "I didn't expect this," he pulled her to him as Buddy raced in circles.

She tugged on his hand. "I've got another surprise." Joy lit up her face. "Ta da! I thought we'd decorate it tonight after dinner."

He chuckled at the scrawny Christmas tree standing in the corner of the small living room. "You don't think it's a little early?"

"Of course not." Her eyes twinkled. "I didn't want one too big, because Buddy might knock it over trying to get by the chair."

Buddy's tail wagged enthusiastically at the mention of his name.

During dinner, Cheryl told him about visiting the paper plant. "It was really great to see Stella. She gave me a tour of the plant. Sweetie, there is something that Stella told me that I found interesting. She said that when she took over the personnel files, she saw that Mack Harris was listed as a security consultant."

Sean jerked his eyes to Cheryl, "What?"

"Yeah, not only that, but he had been on their payroll for years."

"That's surprising. The Thompsons ran the plant. Wonder why they hired him?" He took a bite of food and thought about what that might mean.

"Stella wondered the same thing. She didn't remember ever seeing him on security detail, and he was generously compensated."

"Huh. He had to be doing something for Jeff to pay him. I wonder what it was?"

After dinner, Sean said, "Honey, let's go for a walk. I'll help you put up the dishes when we get back."

"What about decorating our tree?"

He grinned, "That too."

Cheryl smiled and glanced out the window, "Okay, but it's dark."

Buddy had heard "walk" and was now standing at the door, wagging his tail. Sean grabbed a flashlight and a jacket. The night was quiet. People were tucked in their homes with light beaming through the windows, and the smell of smoke from chimneys filled the air. They didn't really need a flashlight, because they could see the sidewalk from light cast in wide swaths from street lights that faintly illuminated the damp air and mist from their breaths. Buddy pranced ahead on his leash looking and sniffing and stopping at every fire hydrant.

Sean held Cheryl's hand. "There's something I wanted to talk about."

Cheryl looked up at his profile. "What's that, Sweetie?"

He looked at her face and then turned to look ahead. "I'm sorry for the way I've been,

Cheryl. I've been absorbed in finding Mike's killer and haven't stopped to think about you. If someone had shot at you, I'd be worried as hell. I haven't thought about what you must be feeling, not only with dealing with your own personal feelings with Mike's death and Geri's pain, but in worrying that someone might still be out there planning another attempt on me." He looked at her profile and grinned, "Unless, of course, that wasn't a worry."

She jerked toward him and gave him a mini slap in his arm with her free hand, "You know better than that."

They both laughed. He squeezed her hand. "When I was in the military, intensity was modus operandi for me. I've tried to be more chilled since returning here, but . . ."

"I understand, Sweetie. You're doing what you have to. I won't lie, though. I've been worried about you, but I didn't want to say anything, because you had enough on your plate, and also, I figured you've survived life-threatening situations many times over your career."

He grinned. "A few."

"You must be relieved though to have solved Mike's murder, but do you think it's the same person who made the attempt on you?"

They stood in silence for a few minutes watching Buddy intently checking out a large stump near the side walk. "I'm not sure I have."

"You're not what? Relieved or sure you have Mike's killer?" She was confused. "But you found the murder weapon."

"Yes, we did, but there is something that just doesn't feel right about Cooper being the suspect."

"What about the gun being found at his home?"

"If he didn't do it, then someone planted it. That would mean that someone felt we were getting too close and wanted the investigation to end."

"So, Cooper might not be guilty? Then, you may not even have the person who shot at you."

"That's right. You see the quagmire. It's damn frustrating. I can't seem to get my bearings on this."

Cheryl gazed into his eyes. "I love you, Sean. I know you will be careful. I also have all the confidence that you will solve this."

He lowered his head and gently kissed her, feeling the heat and desire run through his body. Buddy saw and didn't want to be left out as he loped forward and nudged between them. They broke apart laughing. "Let's go home and lock you-know-who out of the bedroom." Sean's mischievous grin lit up his smoky eyes. She loved the crinkles at his eyes' edges when he smiled.

Cheryl's laugh was contagious, "Let's!" deciding that decorating the tree could wait.

Chapter 41

While Suzy and Morgan were having dinner, Morgan asked her if she knew why Zeke had come to the property that day when they met there to go through the records.

"I don't know. I was surprised when he showed up. I think he was surprised to see me there."

"He didn't say?"

"No, he kinda acted like it was to talk to me. I asked Rose when I got home if she had told him, and she said he had not stopped by the house. She didn't know why he was there."

"Something I have a question about. I have scrubbed all the bank records and the other records we found. There was no indication of any money being transferred from Zeke to your parents. Zeke doesn't have a bank account, so there's no paper trail of money being given to your parents. What's odd is that when your dad made the first cash payment to Earl, your mother deposited enough in the bank for the payment. But, leading up to the final payment, which was a year later, there wasn't enough money in their account for that second payment. Then, your mother deposited cash to cover that payment. Do you know where that money came from?"

"No, I don't know. I knew they had a checking account. That's how Momma paid for things. Daddy didn't believe in credit cards. Sometimes, I'd hear Momma tell him that she needed some money put in the bank, but that's all I know."

"In their inventory of things they found on the property, the federal government never listed cash, except for a very small amount in your parents' wallets. Your dad must have had some money from the sale of the drugs. Do you think your father kept money hidden somewhere?"

Suzy paused, thinking to herself. *Daddy always had money when he needed it. It's possible he had a stash hidden on the property*. "You know, Morgan, that's an interesting idea. I need to think about that."

"Well, I've been wondering why Zeke is pushing so hard to get the property. With him showing up on the property like that, I wondered if he was looking for cash. That could be one reason he is trying so hard to get the property. Boone mentioned that there is some property out in the area that a fracking company was interested in, so that could be a possibility too."

Chapter 42

"Chief, I've found some things going back through the files," said Arlo. "There weren't many complaints about Ben." That didn't surprise Sean, because people were probably afraid to complain for fear of reprisals by Ben, or just didn't think it would do any good. "But there were some, and the reports show that Kyle was present for some of those incidents. For one, Ben arrested a woman for stealing a car. She claimed that Ben assaulted her and that Kyle didn't do anything to stop it."

"What happened?"

"Well, shortly after that, she withdrew the complaint, and it was never investigated. There were a few instances when Kyle and Ben were patrolling together, and they pulled over guys suspected of DUI. Ben got rough. The report shows when they were brought in they had physical signs of being beaten, but they never filed any complaints."

"Kyle was there?"

"Yes."

"Give me the woman's name, and Syd and I will go talk to her. I need for you to talk with the others and find out what happened."

"Okay, I'll do that. There's another thing. I went ahead and looked at Ben's records to make sure that there wasn't something about Kyle that may have been missing in Kyle's reports. There were six instances where Ben, working by himself—Kyle wasn't with him—arrested someone for a DUI and that person later filed a claim that his gun was missing after he got his vehicle back. Those guns were never found. I ran into Fred, and we got to talking about the guns and Ben. Fred said there was talk around town that you better hope Ben didn't pull you over with a gun in your car. It might disappear." Fred worked in the evidence room.

Sean remembered that Cooper claimed that his handgun went missing out of his vehicle after Ben arrested him on the drug possession claim.

"What types of guns?" Sean asked.

"There was one hand gun, but the rest were rifles. Here's the *big* thing, Chief. One of the rifles was a Remington 742. The report showed a serial number. I checked the serial number, and it matches the one that we found at Cooper's."

"Do you have the owner's name?"

"Yes—and his address."

Sean and Arlo visited the man whose Remington 742 had disappeared after Ben arrested him. He told them the gun had disappeared out of his truck, which was towed to the police lot. Although he suspected Ben, there was no way to prove he was the one who stole it. For one thing, there was another deputy that night.

Arlo asked, "Are you sure about that? The police report only listed Ben at the scene."

"Oh, yeah. I had been drinking, but I remember another deputy, because he stood toward the back of the truck, but he never said anything. He just watched that jerk—Ben—who arrested me. Ben had a reputation. I'd heard from some buddies how a few of the deputies would beat the hell out of people. Well, Ben was one. He definitely was trying to provoke me that night. I knew better. I kept my mouth shut."

"What was this other deputy doing during all of this?" asked Sean.

"Seems like I remember him opening the back door for me to get in, but I don't remember him doing much. I can't remember which one drove me to the station. One stayed with my truck waiting for the tow. At the time, I thought it may have been Ben, but I can't say for sure."

"At the time you filed the report about your missing rifle, you had the receipt which showed the serial number. Do you still have it?"

"I don't know, but I'll check. It's been several years since all this happened."

Brenda Lowe lived in an older brick four apartment building—near the university in Athens, Ohio. Syd called ahead and arranged a meeting time. Sean and Syd entered the small foyer area and walked up the steps to a landing. Her apartment was on the left. Brenda was a slender woman with brown layered hair hanging down her back.

Syd took the lead. "Ms. Lowe. We are investigating something that involved you a few years back. Going back through our files, we found a complaint you filed against Ben Clark, a deputy. It alleged he assaulted you. A short time later, you dropped the charge. Can you tell us about the incident?"

Sean noticed that Brenda started rubbing her hands together. Syd must have noticed her discomfort, because she hastily added, "Ben Clark died almost two years ago. Sheriff Neumann was just sworn in, and he's trying to get his arms around things that may have gone on in the past."

Sean followed up on Syd's point. "I will not tolerate any of my officers conducting themselves unprofessionally."

"I see. Okay. That's good to know. I don't really like to think about it. I was a rebellious teenager. I don't blame anyone but myself, but thankfully, I grew a brain," she smiled ruefully, "and got my life on track."

She told them what had happened. She left home when she was seventeen, moving in with a loser of a boyfriend. He worked at the car dealership washing cars, and she worked part time at one of the fast food places. They lived in a camper on his mother's property. For recreation, Brenda and her loser boyfriend drank and smoked pot. Brenda soon realized that this was not the way she wanted to live her life. When he came dragging in one morning, she confronted him, and he slapped her hard across the face. Brenda recoiled from him and turned to leave—when he grabbed her arm and pulled her into his arms promising to never strike her again. She believed him, but it happened two more times—each time worse than before. After the third time, she left in the only car they had, which was in his name. He called the police and reported it stolen.

She had gone to spend the night at her friend Lauren's home. Around midnight, the doorbell rang. When the deputy told her she was under arrest, she tried to explain the situation. Ben Clark wasn't interested in what she had to say. When he grabbed her arm and yanked her out the door and slammed her against his cruiser, she knew he was bad news. He wrenched her arms back—sending pain shooting through both arms as he cuffed her, causing her to scream out in agony. He yanked her head back by a fist full of her hair and hissed for her to be quiet. He then told her that he was going to have a little fun before taking her to jail. Suddenly, Lauren stepped out on the porch and yelled, "Brenda, what's happening?" Lauren started walking down her front steps, and Ben stepped back and yelled for her to go back into the house.

Lauren yelled, "I seen what you did to her when you put those cuffs on her. My uncle knows the sheriff. I'm going to tell him what you did."

Ben tried to get control of the situation. He turned to Lauren and ordered, "I'm taking her in. Stay out of this, or I'll arrest you, too."

Lauren held up her car keys and said, "I'm going to follow your car to make sure she is taken to jail. Then, I'm going to call my uncle."

"The report says that there was another deputy that night," Syd pointed out.

"There was. He was just going to stand there and let Ben do whatever."

"What was he doing during this?"

"He was just standing in back of the car. I don't know what he was doing, but when Lauren came out and started yelling, he walked up and said something like, "You best stop, Ben. Let's take her on in."

"What happened then?"

"Well, they put me in the back of the car. Ben was driving. I was crying, but I could see the lights shining through the back, so I knew Lauren was following. I heard the other deputy say, 'You 'bout got caught this time.' Ben yelled at him to 'shut his blanking mouth.' I always shudder to think what might have happened to me that night if Lauren hadn't intervened. Later, Lauren told me that her uncle didn't know the sheriff, but she saw Ben shove me up against the car and heard the scream, and so she had to do something."

"You filed a complaint?"

"Yes, when I got out, I was freaking mad. I filed the complaint."

"But it was soon dismissed."

Brenda looked down at her hands and slightly shook her head. "Yes. It was a case where money talked. My mom bailed me out, and I moved back in with her. Bless her heart, she told me it was time to straighten out. On that, I agreed. Well, a couple of days after I filed the complaint, I got off work and was waiting for my mother to come pick me up. This man walked up and told me that he wanted to talk to me. He told me that he was a commissioner and that he was aware of my complaint against Ben. He told me that he thought I'd be best to drop it. I told him that I wasn't going to let that creep get away with it. I had heard the other deputy in the car tell Ben that he had almost gotten caught this time, so I knew Ben had tried it with other women.

"He said that he was sure the other deputy wouldn't remember that. I knew he was implying that the other deputy would deny everything, but I just stood there. He finally said that he would be willing to resolve the matter if I was. He said that he'd be willing to give me some money if I dropped the case. He said he could arrange for the charges against me to be dropped. He told me that he'd talk to Ben, and if Ben did anything like that again, he'd be fired and possibly prosecuted.

"Nothing went too far, thanks to Lauren being there, and I didn't think I would win if the other deputy was going to lie. I didn't have money for an attorney, so I was glad the charges would be dropped. I didn't want to drag Lauren into it. I'd done pretty good in high school until I went off with that jerk-o boy. It was enough money to cover two years at Hillsrock Community College in Bekbourg. After that, I transferred here to finish my degree. I've been working my way through, and it's taken a while, but I will graduate this spring."

As they were returning to Bekbourg, Syd said, "That Ben Clark must have been a bad dude. It's too bad that you weren't the sheriff then. You wouldn't have tolerated the stuff he did."

"No, I wouldn't have, but he did have some powerful people backing him."

"Who was that commissioner she mentioned?"

"I'm pretty sure it was Jeff Thompson. His dad, Randall, was also a commissioner but would have been retired by then, but he still was often in the area on business matters. So, it could have been him. Unfortunately, either one was capable of doing what she said happened."

"Oh, those are the two men that were corrupt?"

"Right."

"What do you think about Kyle? He just seemed to stand around and let Ben do whatever he wanted to. He never reported Ben."

"I don't have a good understanding yet about Kyle. You're right. He never came forward about Ben's illegal activities. I haven't heard of Kyle himself actually engaging in anything like Ben, but in my mind, he is just as guilty because he knew it was happening and did nothing to stop it."

"Do you think Kyle did some things himself?"

"I don't know."

Kyle must have heard them pull up, because he opened the door before they got to the small concrete pad that served as a porch. "Hi, Sheriff, Syd. I heard you pull up."

"Mind if we come in?"

"Okay."

The place looked about the same. He hadn't done much packing from the look of the cardboard boxes sitting around. The kitchen chair was still in the small living room from the last time they were there.

"Kyle, we've been looking through the records. You were listed in some complaints, you and Ben, and in one case, a complaint listed you for not stopping Ben from a sexual assault. You led me to believe that you weren't involved, that Ben did things like that on his own, but that's not true."

Kyle wouldn't look at Sean or Syd and didn't say anything.

"There's another thing, Kyle. Ben is suspected of stealing people's guns when he pulled them over for DUI. What do you know about that?"

Kyle had started chewing on his fingernail. "Yeah, I guess Ben did that some. I never saw him take a gun, but I heard him talk 'bout it some."

"You knew he took people's guns and didn't report it?"

"Well, I nev'r knew for sure. You know'd how Ben was. He'd talk 'bout things, but I never knew when to believe him."

"What happened to the guns he took?"

"I don't know. He sold some."

"Who'd he sell them to?"

"I don't know."

"Did he sell any to you?"

"No."

"Did you ever steal a gun from someone being arrested?"

"No."

Early into the investigation, Sean asked Kim about who in the department had ever used the long SWAT rifle the department had. She told him that several years ago, Randall Thompson brought the gun to the precinct and gave it to Mike and told him that the county commission bought it for the county's use and that someone should get certified for a SWAT team. Mike put the gun in the cage and told the deputies that if any of them wanted to practice with it, he was fine with that, but he wanted her to maintain a log of anytime someone used it. She told Sean that, at first, some of the deputies took it out. The only deputy still with the department that practiced with it was Mack, but Kyle had used it, too. The last entry for Kyle was about two years ago, and Mack had used it about eight months ago. No one ever used it on a regular basis, and no one ever received their certification.

"You practiced with the department's SWAT rifle."

"Yeah. It was there, so I shot it some."

"Where did you practice?"

"I'd take it up to the old quarry and practice there. No one's ever 'round there and there's plenty of space."

"Who trained you on it?"

"Mack had learned during his Army days, so he showed me. After I got used to it, I took it out myself. Didn't do it much."

"What about the rifle you own? Where do you practice with that?"

Kyle didn't like Sean's probing questions. "I've said 'bout all I have to say, Sean."

Sean watched Kyle's expression with his next question. "Kyle, what do you know about Jed and Brody Todd?"

Kyle's mouth popped open. "Who?"

"You remember they were found murdered in a deserted area about two years ago?"

"Oh, yeah. I remember now. I don't remember you ever found out who killed them."

"No, but I was wondering if you might know something about it?"

Kyle knitted his brows. "No, Sean. I don't know nothin' 'bout that."

"You don't know anything about Ben being involved?"

The startled looked in Kyle's eyes told Sean that his next statement was a lie. "No, Sean. Don't know nothin' 'bout Ben and the Todds."

Sean narrowed his eyes—causing Kyle to look away. Sean thought that Kyle knew more about Ben than he ever let on and probably was a participant in more of Ben's schemes than anyone knew.

After they left, Kyle walked to the window and watched them drive away. *How in the hell did he connect Ben with those Todd boys? More importantly, why is he asking me? He can't possibly know. No one knew, did they? Did Ben tell someone?*

Kyle remembered the night. They each were sitting back in a pull-off. Ben's instructions to Kyle were to sit there after he pulled out to follow a pickup truck, which Kyle recognized as the Todds. There would be another truck soon following Ben, and Kyle was to make sure that no one else got through. After a while, Ben pulled up and told Kyle to leave—that they were done. Kyle tried to ask Ben about what happened, but Ben didn't want to talk about it other than for Kyle "to keep his mouth shut."

When they were identified much later, Kyle figured Ben was behind their deaths, but he didn't know exactly what part Ben had played, because the second truck that night belonged to Tony Pinkston. *Would Tony's daughter, Suzy, somehow have found out and told Sean? Maybe I should tell Zeke. Sean's a smart SOB. Those Pinkstons are smart too, but they better watch their asses around Sean.*

Kim reached Sean on his phone. "Boss, Irma Ritter called just now. She's complaining again about John Pawley."

Sean inwardly sighed. "Okay, Kim. I'll drive by and talk to her." *Now what?* Sean needed to mediate a solution between Irma and Pawley. Pawley was a reclusive mountain man with unusual quirks, and Sean didn't believe that Pawley each day set out to show Irma his goods. Pawley told him that he would try and hide behind a bush when he heard her car coming down the road, but apparently that wasn't happening. *There must be some way I can resolve this.*

Sean pulled into her driveway and knocked on the front door. He saw her peek out the front window and heard her remove a door chain. She opened the door. "Mrs. Ritter, I'm Sheriff Neumann. You called about Mr. Pawley. Can I come in and talk to you about it?"

"Come in, Sheriff. Have a seat. Would you like some coffee?"

"No, but thank you. Ma'am, you want to tell me what's going on."

"Well, he walks around naked on his property. When I drive by there, I never know if I'm going to see him naked."

"When was the last time you saw him?"

"Well, it's been a couple of weeks. I called in a complaint, and I thought maybe someone in the police department had been to see him, because every time I've driven by, I haven't seen him, except today."

"What happened today?"

"Well, I was driving slow down the road, and I saw him run to get behind a bush. Didn't get a good look, but I did see his backside before he got behind that bush."

"So, it looked like he was trying to hide?"

She thought for a minute, "Well, yes, that's right. He didn't come out until I got by. I looked in my rearview mirror, but he didn't come out while I was looking."

"I see. Has he ever said anything to you or done anything toward you?"

"Well, no. He hasn't ever said anything. When I drive by, he just keeps marching with that big gun. Like I said, I haven't seen him lately until today."

"I see. There are not many cars that come by here, are there?"

"No. I rarely see anyone come by here. That's probably why no one else ever calls. There's just not anyone else who sees him the way I do. I have to drive by there."

"Mmm."

"I don't ever see a police car up here. You're the first one to ever come up here to talk to me." John Pawley and Irma lived on the northern end of Mader Valley, with Irma's place just past Pawley's.

"It seems he's making an effort to stay out of your sight. Do you think maybe if you honk as you start getting near his property so that he has time to get out of your sight that might work?"

"Mmmm. Well the honking wouldn't bother anybody, because no one else lives around here. That would give him time to hide."

"Let's see if that works. He can hear the horn a long way, so give him a couple of long blows before you get to his property."

"Okay. Sheriff Neumann. Say, I really like the *Tribune* since Ms. Seton took over. She's had such interesting articles and new things. I thought about writing her and seeing if she would start a cooking section. I have some recipes that I could share."

"Good. I'll tell her you are going to make the suggestion."

Chapter 43

Grayson called C.P. "There's some trouble brewing on your planned filing."

"What's that?"

"I made a follow-up call to one of the advisory board members who attended our pre-filing meeting to see if there were any questions or if they needed us to provide any information before we made our filing. The OMVX people are coming in for a meeting with the advisory board. From what I gather, they want to try and poison the well before we file. She told me they plan to vigorously oppose your acquisition of the WVB&C."

"Well, we thought that would happen."

"Yes, but she told me something else. Lester carries a lot of clout with the advisory board. You and I both came away from the pre-filing meeting knowing he plans to oppose your application. If the advisory board is against you, it may be difficult to get the commission to overturn the advisory board's recommendation. This could get drawn out longer than a year; and if Lester undermines us, we could lose.

"One other thing to consider—even if the city wants continued rail service and even with us carrying the heavy water in the regulatory proceeding, at some point, the city could decide it's not worth the time and expense. The OMVX could sweeten its offer and convince the city to sign their deal."

"I hadn't considered that possibility, Gray."

Grayson laughed. "It's a big dog's game. Could get rough. Have you given any more thought to your Plan B?"

"I need to consider the best way to proceed. Let's see what happens over the next week or so, and then we'll decide on our next steps."

"Okay. I'll let you know if I hear anything else."

A couple of days later, the OMVX took out a full page in the *Bekbourg Tribune.* It told how the railroad industry had changed over time and that a substantial investment would have been needed in the WVB&C. Also, given its geographic location, its points of interconnection were no longer commercially viable. They planned to vehemently oppose the sale of the rail line and, given the overall dynamics, suggested it would be an uphill battle for the city in the regulatory proceeding, which would result in the city expending a tremendous amount of time and resources. "Over the one-hundred years, we have enjoyed the partnership we had with the city and its fine citizens, and our relationship has brought many benefits to the city. We don't want to see any hardship come to the city and the region, and as we go through the regulatory proceeding, we are hopeful that the city and the OMVX Railroad can come to an agreement that will be beneficial to Bekbourg and the great folks that we have long considered our friends."

The following day, there was a short article referencing the OMVX editorial.

> *The Tribune contacted Mr. Traylor and asked for his comments regarding the OMVX editorial. He said that he was "evaluating his options and was optimistic about keeping the railroad operational. The OMVX showed how little regard it has for the city and its businesses and employees when it submitted its termination notice. Its reduction of rail service on the WVB&C over time bears truth to its decision to shut down the rail line. This course of action will hurt businesses, employees and the city. I don't share its view that the WVB&C is uneconomical and unable to compete. I am from Bekbourg. I walk the streets here every day. I care about the businesses and the people*

here. I look forward to moving ahead with ensuring that the WVB&C Railroad remains a mainstay in the community and continues to be instrumental in its prosperity as well as to the stakeholders up and down the line."

The city spokesperson would only comment that the city will participate in the proceeding at the Federal Railroad and Surface Commission to ensure that the WVB&C remains operational.

Dusty, Chaw and Mule Head were quietly drinking their coffee when Anita walked up to take their orders, "Boy, you guys are gloom and doom. What's going on?"

"Well, it doesn't look like our railroad deal is going to happen," Dusty said as he held up his cup to be topped off.

"I thought the railroad was going to close," she glanced around at the men.

"That's what we all thought 'til the newspaper said that it might be sold, but now it looks like that's fallen though. It's a can of worms." Chaw grumbled before giving her his order.

Dusty ordered and turned to Chaw, "Well, aren't you quite the crepe-hanger sitting there with your payoff and retirement."

Mule Head added his gloom, "I knew it was too good to be true."

"C.P. is a good man, but I guess he just doesn't have the clout we thought he had," Dusty said after Anita left with their orders.

"I didn't understand what the OMVX article was saying, but did it sound to you like they might try and keep the train running?" asked Chaw.

"I didn't understand that double talk either, but I agree with C.P. that they showed their stripes when they sent the city that termination notice. Why would they now say they want to keep it running? They have been reducing service for several years," Dusty said.

"They clearly don't want C.P. to buy it," offered Chaw.

Mule Head asked, "What are you going to do, Dusty? You could still put in for the payoff."

"That's the problem. I just don't know what to do. What a lousy outfit to work for."

"Now look who's the crepe-hanger," Chaw ribbed.

Jules walked up to the table. "My, what a table of long faces."

"What are you so cheerful about?" grunted Mule Head.

"Every day is a great day, and I don't think today is as dark as you boys think it is."

He sat down, and Anita came up and smiled, "What a contrast, Jules. These boys look like they lost their best friend. Good to see a smiling face."

"Well, I've always lived by the principle, when things are the darkest, sunshine is around the corner." That was met by head shaking and eye rolling. Jules ignored them and tucked his napkin in his shirt collar.

After Anita left, Dusty asked, "But seriously, Jules. What do you think can be done about all this? It looks like the bureaucrats in Washington are going to block keeping our railroad open."

Jules pulled another napkin from the holder and as he wiped his silverware, he opined, "I think our good friend, C.P. Traylor, will have a trick up his sleeve. It's much too early to give up."

"Trick or no trick," said Dusty, "you never win when you go up against the big boys and the railroad."

"Be that as it may, you just never know." Jules closed his eyes as he savored the coffee's aroma.

Chapter 44

The Legend of Mader Valley:
Fact and Fiction – Part 4
By Cheryl Seton

In 1904—nearly nine years after Jarvis Mader went missing—a farmer was walking his property near the spur line looking for an errant cow. Something caught his dog's attention, and it started sniffing and digging. A deluge the night before forced the creek from its banks, and soil and debris were loosened and washing through the raging currents. Thinking it had found a dead animal, the farmer went to shoo the dog away. Having tended to livestock and hunted most of his life, the farmer quickly realized that the partially unearthed remains were not from an animal. He went to town and told the sheriff.

The sheriff found buried along with the human remains a belt buckle and an oil-skin rucksack. The doctor's examination revealed damage to the leg bone—the foot had been nearly severed, and the bone was crushed right above the ankle. A bullet, having entered at close range, was embedded in the skull.

Inside the rucksack was a piece of paper mostly undamaged despite the passage of time. The sheriff was surprised, but relieved, that it bore a name. As the sheriff was later to learn, Jarvis Mader was illiterate. So, before he embarked on his journey to reach the work camp in search of work, his brother Herman had written for him his name and where he lived so he could give that information to the lumber and mining camp for their records.

Seeing Jarvis's name on the paper, the sheriff mailed a letter to Herman, not sure if the letter would ever arrive.

About a month later, Herman received the letter, and two weeks later, he appeared at the sheriff's office. Herman confirmed that the belt buckle and oil-skin pouch belonged to Jarvis. Knowing its sentimental value to Jarvis, he inquired about his brother's hunting knife, but the sheriff didn't know anything about that. It had not been recovered. Herman asked him to watch for the knife, which had a unique red stripe on its guard. He felt that if someone had the knife, they could possibly be the killer. He also requested that the Tribune ask if anyone knew of such a knife to advise the sheriff. No one ever came forward with any information about Jarvis's prized hunting knife.

Fortunately, we have an historical accounting from the Bekbourg Tribune's archives of articles that were written when the remains were discovered and when Herman Mader identified his brother's body. Perhaps the gruesome discovery served to embolden speculation, because as time passed, rumors swirled around Bekbourg, and people began referring to the valley where Jarvis died as "Mader Valley." Sightings of his ghost have been reported off and on since then. The mystery of Jarvis Mader's demise may never be solved, but we know the man. From all accounts, he was a kind man, hardworking, who came to Bekbourg to get a job to provide for his young family.

Jarvis never made it to the work camp. But a piece of the mystery has been solved, albeit, over a hundred years later. A hunting knife believed to have belonged to Jarvis was discovered by the state police as they searched for evidence in the shooting of the former sheriff, Mike Adams. This was the same area where Jarvis's remains were discovered. The knife has a red circle around its guard as described by Herman. We can only surmise that while being chased away from the track by the railroad detectives his knife was lost.

It was growing dark, so he likely decided to stop for the night near the creek and planned to walk on to the camp the next day. Maybe he wanted to retrace his steps to locate his knife, his only prized material possession. It must have been that evening when he sustained the crippling injury. He didn't have a gun, so he couldn't shoot hoping to draw attention to his plight or protect himself from whoever fired that fatal shot. Whoever shot Jarvis in the head was never discovered.

The writer relied on historical sources to the extent available. Special gratitude to Jules Leroux and Martin Jackups, who contributed to the story based on tales passed on from their forefathers who worked on the railroad at the time of Jarvis Mader's death.

As a postscript, the sheriff's office is endeavoring to locate Jarvis's descendants to return his hunting knife.

Chapter 45

Alex reported back that he had talked with personnel at a law enforcement shooting range. According to their records, Kyle went to the range on a routine basis. He was above average with a hand gun as well as a rifle. His rifle of choice was a Remington. Alex talked to people who lived in the vicinity of Kyle's place. They reported hearing shooting from time-to-time, but they didn't know the location. According to those he talked to, the shooting sounded like target practice, but everyone in the area owned guns, so it could have been anyone. Some admitted that they took target practice on their properties.

There had never been anything about Kyle to suggest that he was interested in guns or that he was such a good marksman. Ben and Kyle worked together. Had they actually been friends? Was it possible, Sean wondered, that Kyle held a grudge against Mike for Ben's death? Kyle was an enigma who Sean needed to learn more about.

"Hi, Sean. Come in," Geri said as she and Sean hugged. "I was so glad when you called and said that you were stopping by."

They walked through the living room toward the kitchen following an aroma of freshly baked cookies. "I see you are decorated for Christmas. That's a nice Christmas tree."

Geri smiled as she indicated for him to have a seat. She put a freshly brewed cup of coffee and a decorated Christmas cookie in front of him. "Thank you," she said as she did the same for herself and sat at the kitchen table. "Miranda and her friends put up the decorations. Having Miranda here has been a godsend. Her friends visit almost every night and keep my spirits up." Geri chuckled, "They left me with the task of baking cookies while they went to Athens to do some Christmas shopping."

"I'm glad she's here, Geri. Matt is coming home for Christmas, isn't he?"

"Yes, and I'm really looking forward to that."

Geri's peppy spark had dimmed somewhat, but she was pushing forward. Sean felt the holidays were a two-sided sword. On the one hand, this would be her first Christmas without Mike in nearly thirty years, but on the other side, it was a joyous time of year that she could celebrate with her children and friends.

"How are you doing, Geri?"

"I guess as well as I can. I'm coping. Having Christmas coming and all the people stopping by is really helping. I've also started thinking about something."

"What's that?"

"It's going to be quiet here after the children are gone. This house is filled with memories. Other than the small place we rented when we first got married, it's the only place Mike and I ever lived. When we were thinking of moving to Montana, Mike and I went through a lot of clutter and downsized. We mailed all the things belonging to the kids to them. I don't need all this space and yard. I am thinking of selling the house. Without Mike, I don't want to move to Montana. The kids have their own lives. My life is here, and I can always visit them. I'm going to find a small house downtown. After the first of the year, I'm going to call Becky's brother, Jason. With Pauline Kaufmann no longer around, he has opened a real estate office. I'm going to ask him to help me find a place and sell this one."

"What do the kids think about that?"

"Miranda is all in favor. I'll tell Matt when he comes in, but I don't think he'll have a problem with it. I wouldn't be surprised if he doesn't get engaged soon. He is making a life in Montana."

"Well, let me know if you need any help with anything. Danny and I can help move you, and Cheryl and I will be glad to help pack or anything else we can do. By the way, these cookies are great."

She laughed. Geri got him another one. As she put it on his plate, he said, "Geri, I need to ask you about a deputy that worked for Mike."

"Okay," she said as she took a sip of coffee.

"What can you tell me about Kyle Ramsey?"

"Well, I know that Mike was never really happy with Kyle. He didn't think he did much, and he was always suspicious about Ben, and they mostly patrolled together."

"Did he think Kyle was part of Ben's corruption?"

"Well, I don't know. He didn't think Kyle was that smart."

"Do you know why he kept Kyle or Ben on?"

Geri thought about the question. "You know, Sean. I'm not sure how much control Mike had over naming his deputies. He never talked much about the job, but after he retired, he once said that 'at least Sean will be able to do with the department what he wants to.' One of the deputies he felt was forced on him was Mack Harris."

"Mack?"

"Yes. Sheriff Rhodes had an assistant, and Mike planned to keep him on as his assistant. However, shortly after Mike became sheriff, he took a job in another county. Mike planned to promote another deputy he really liked to be his assistant, but someone pressured Mike to appoint Mack. He didn't like doing so, but he did."

"Do you know who told him to appoint Mack as his assistant?" Sean thought it was interesting that Mike kept him as his assistant for so long. It must have been one of the Thompsons who insisted on Mack, but why?

Geri shrugged, "No, but Mike thought he was lazy."

Tyler Forquet, the prosecutor, called and wanted Sean to stop by his office to discuss Cooper

Townsend. "Sean, Derrick was over here earlier. You remember I told you about him talking to me about Cooper having an alibi talking to his mother. Well, Derrick's making noise about filing a motion to have the case thrown out against Cooper. First, there are the phone records, which he claims establish an alibi. Second, Cooper is claiming that either the police or someone is trying to frame him again. He's adamant that he didn't know anything about the rifle being on his property. You said that you all searched his property a few months ago and didn't find the rifle then, but did you—or one of your deputies—search the shed at that time?"

"Yes, we searched it. I personally climbed up the ladder and looked in the rafter."

"Derrick is raising questions about the scope and bullets. None of that was found at Cooper's."

Tyler was raising some of the same questions that had been rolling around in Sean's mind, but there were reasonable explanations. "Well, it's possible whoever had the gun before Cooper used the scope. Maybe Cooper never had a scope and maybe Cooper used the last of the bullets and threw the box away."

"Was the shed door locked when you got there?"

"No."

"Derrick is raising a question about why Cooper would wipe all the fingerprints if he was hiding the gun."

"It's possible he was planning to get rid of it and just hadn't followed up."

"Okay, okay. Those are plausible theories, but you see the potential weak links. We've got the proverbial smoking gun, but you can bet your bottom dollar Derrick will expose every one of these weaknesses. Aside from you finding the gun on his property, let's go back through why you considered him a suspect."

"Well, he had made a number of threatening statements. For one thing, Mike ran into Cooper, and he said that Mike and I were going to get what was coming to us because we couldn't clear the record for when he was sent to prison. He said a similar thing to me. Then, someone with whom he interviewed for a job called me after the interview. When he realized he wasn't going to be hired, he got angry and said that Mike and I 'just as well be dead' since we weren't helping him.

"The final straw was what Mack overheard Cooper saying at Knucklepin's, which was after Mike had been killed. He blamed Mike for him going to prison and said that he got what was coming to him. He also said that I was lucky I wasn't dead and that people like me and Mike can't run forever."

Tyler paused. "So far, we've only charged him in Mike's death, not in your shooting. You found the murder weapon on his premises, and there are witnesses who can corroborate his incriminating statements. Having said that, you know I'll need more evidence if I hope to get a conviction. Where did he get the gun? We don't have any forensic evidence that ties him to the crime scene. We need more, Sean."

Sean didn't want a conviction for the sake of a conviction. He wanted the person who killed Mike behind bars. But, the murder weapon was found on Cooper's property, so he wasn't willing to throw in the towel on Cooper. Until Derrick had mentioned the possible alibi, he thought they had Mike's killer and possibly the shooter in his case, although that had remained murky. "I hear you. We'll work it harder. I'll keep you posted on what we find."

"Sean, another thing," said Tyler. "You wondered where Cooper got the money to buy that old pickup truck."

"Yeah."

"Well, his mother has to drive back and forth to Chillicothe because her sister is sick with cancer. She has to drive her car, which left Cooper without any transportation. Her sister's husband came through with the money as a way to repay Cooper's mother for helping out."

"Interesting," Sean mumbled, now distracted.

"Okay, we'll see what Derrick does," said Tyler. "He may not want to present his case on a motion to get the chargers dropped and spill all his arguments. If he loses, he could hurt his case at trial. But if he files to get the charges dropped, I can't be hanging out there with just the gun being found on his property. Bergmann's bias is pro prosecutor, but he'd rake me over the coals if I don't have sufficient answers to Derrick's issues. Get me more evidence."

Chapter 46

Although finding the Remington at Cooper's initially seemed to be the linchpin in solving Mike's murder case, Sean acknowledged to himself that there were some unanswered questions. Those doubts nipped at Sean from shortly after he arrested Cooper. Tyler was right. He needed solid evidence to prosecute the case, and Sean needed to nail down the loose ends to satisfy himself that he had the killer. He decided to walk back over the crime scenes with Alex.

They drove to where the shooter was believed to have parked and walked to the perch where he had stood to take shots at Sean. They looked out over the area below. It was a long-range shot. "Alex, let's start with Cooper. Someone knew I would be parked down there. He would have had to have planned this—where to park, where to stand. What do you think?"

Alex thought for a minute. "Every time anyone from the department has been to Cooper's, if it's earlier in the day, he's still in bed. I find it hard to believe that he would be up early to do something that requires this much thought and focus."

"He was in town at Frau's early that morning. He initially told us he was in bed, but that wasn't the case," Sean said.

"Yeah, I know. Frankly, since he usually sleeps late, I don't think he intentionally lied. He may have just assumed he was in bed since that's what he usually is doing that time of day." Sean looked skeptical. Alex shook his head. "I agree that it's odd, but given we're talking about Cooper, I think it's plausible."

Sean wasn't convinced but didn't rule out Alex's theory. "Okay, let's shift gears. The shooter took time to find all the casings—except the one that rolled under the rock," Sean said as studied the ground.

"One other thing, Sheriff. This may be irrelevant, but you saw how he ran that day we found the rifle. He's not athletic. Syd could find nothing about him ever playing sports. He doesn't appear very coordinated. I know Syd found that he was a good shot in high school, but that's been nearly twenty years ago. Maybe he is a better shot than I know, but I don't see him being able to shoot four rapid shots that close to you."

"Forensics did find evidence of a scope having been mounted on the rifle that was used to shoot Mike."

Alex looked at Sean. "That's something that I have wondered about. Why would Cooper have taken the scope off of the rifle? If he was going to hide the rifle, why not just keep the scope on it?"

"Mmm. Maybe he sold the scope. It would certainly be worth quite a bit more than the rifle.

Maybe he needed some money. Let's get back to the shots taken at me. Those shots were rapid fire by someone who knew how to operate a firearm."

Alex turned to look at the long distance where Sean's truck would have been. "We haven't found any evidence of him going to area gun ranges to practice, and Syd said people who live near him didn't recall hearing many gun shots and never heard what they thought was practice shooting."

"Okay, let's go."

They drove to where Mike's truck had been parked the day he was killed. They walked toward the railroad spur, which was about a quarter of a mile off the road. "Alex, let's assume that we didn't find the gun on Cooper's property. What do you think about Cooper being the killer of Mike?"

Alex was surprised. "Well, this was a much shorter distance. Only one shot. A scope would make that possible, but not necessary if someone was a good shot. Again, where is the scope if Cooper used one?" Alex was quiet for a few minutes as they continued to walk toward the track. "It would have required a lot of planning if the shooter intended to kill Mike. Cooper just doesn't seem like a person who would put a lot of thought into planning something like this. Also, Syd hasn't found any evidence that Cooper was a hunter. So, if he wasn't a hunter, I can't see that he would be back here hunting and it being an accidental shooting."

"What about him planning the murder?"

"The Cooper I know just doesn't strike me as someone who would walk back in here and ambush Mike. That would not only require planning, but nerves. Cooper is a hothead, for sure, but . . . . I guess, Chief, I'm having a hard time seeing it, if we hadn't found the gun at his place."

Sean and Alex turned to walk back to the road. Alex asked, "Are you thinking he didn't shoot Mike?"

"Let's just assume for a minute that Cooper is telling the truth, that he was framed. Why do you think someone would frame him? Why not just keep the rifle."

"He must have thought we were getting close or wanted to send us down a rabbit trail thinking incorrectly that we had the murderer."

"Alex, I need for you and Arlo to look into some things. When we get back to the office, find Arlo and the two of you come to my office. Tell Arlo to keep this among us three for now."

"Sure thing, Sheriff."

Before he returned to the station Sean dropped by Cooper's attorney's office. Derrick Compton was one of a handful of men that Sean felt slight beside. A former professional football offensive tackle, he was 6'6" and weighed around three-hundred pounds. Being a former quarterback himself, Sean figured any quarterback would relish playing behind Derrick. He was injured after four years of pro ball and elected to pursue his second passion. While attending law school, he met Tessa, who was now the city attorney. He specialized in criminal defense but also handled civil litigation.

Derrick said, "I was surprised to see you penciled in for a meeting this afternoon. What can I do for you?"

"Tyler told me that you are thinking about asking the judge to dismiss the charges against Cooper. He told me that you believe that the phone call provides an alibi for Cooper. That he couldn't have possibly made it from his place in time to find Mike and kill him."

Derrick didn't respond. Sean continued. "There are explanations for that, and we found the murder weapon on Cooper's place."

Derrick started to object, but Sean held up his hand. "Hear me out." Derrick leaned back and crossed his hands with his fingers propping up his chin. "Let's assume for the sake of argument that Cooper is telling the truth, that someone tried to frame him. That person cast the dye to have Cooper take the fall. If Cooper gets out, will he try for another patsy, or will he double down on Cooper? I don't know, but if he decides to double down on Cooper, he might believe that if Cooper ended up dead by apparent suicide and with more incriminating evidence, the investigation would grind to a halt.

"Derrick, my job is to get to the bottom of this. If Cooper is the murderer, I'll nail his ass to the wall, but if he's not, I want the SOB that killed Mike, and I won't stop until I know I've got the right man." Sean paused. "One more thing, I'm working on this as hard as I can. I can't promise anything about the timing, but I'd hope that a few more days might do it."

Derrick and Sean eyed each other—message delivered and received. Sean finally said as he stood, "That's all I have to say." Derrick and Sean walked silently down the hall. Derrick said, "Thanks for stopping by, Sean. You take care of yourself. Whoever shot at you is still out there."

They shook hands, and Sean left.

Derrick walked back to his office, deep in thought. He had already started drafting a motion for dismissal, but perhaps he should review the evidence in more detail and spend more time researching his legal positions. After all, he wanted to put forth his best case if he was going before the "hanging judge" with a motion to drop charges against Cooper.

While Sean was waiting for Alex and Arlo to return, he was talking with Kim when Mack walked into the station. He nodded and was going to walk by when Sean spoke up, "Hey, Mack. This is perfect timing. Kim has put some files in the room next to the interrogation room on reports about building supplies disappearing from building sites around the county. I need for you to review them and see if you can see a pattern. Also, check with surrounding counties and see if they have had a similar problem."

"Sure, Sean. I'll grab some coffee and get on it," he said as he walked off.

"Thanks." About that time, Alex and Arlo walked in. Sean told them he needed to talk to them, and they followed him to his office. Through the open door, Mack saw them head toward Sean's office. He was looking at the stack of files and thought to himself, *Damnit, this is what getting a demotion is all about.* He opened a file.

Sean told Arlo and Alex that it looked like their case against Cooper was falling apart and explained what he and Tyler had discussed. "Tyler gave me a heads-up a few days ago about a possible alibi, but now it appears Cooper's attorney is going to file to dismiss the charges against Cooper. Keep investigating and keep this to yourselves, but I may have to move the investigation in another direction."

Alex and Arlo walked through the hall toward the deputies' stations, dispirited. Arlo grumbled to Alex, "Sounds like the case against Cooper is cratering."

Alex replied, "Yep, looks like we may be back to square one."

"Yeah. The state police might be coming in after all," Arlo said.

Chapter 47

Suzy and Morgan were standing in the hallway waiting for Boone when Zeke and Hiram walked in. Hiram headed into the courtroom, but Zeke stopped. He scowled at Morgan. Morgan picked up her briefcase and urged Suzy towards the courtroom. He turned his hard eyes on Suzy. "You know, Girl, this ain't done between us—no matter how the judge rules. I've got evidence you ain't fit to take care of that baby, and Rose, she's too old. That baby belongs ov'r there with her kin. Just remember who you're dealin' with."

He turned and meandered into the courtroom. Suzy's face had paled. Morgan came up close and touched her arm. "Suzy, he's just trying to intimidate you. Just ignore him. Boone and I aren't going to let him push you around."

Suzy looked frightened. "Morgan, you don't know him. I'm even scared for you. I wish I hadn't ever involved you."

"Don't you worry about me, Suzy. I don't let people like that push me around. I'm not worried about him.

Suzy whispered, "Maybe you should be."

"Nonsense. Let's go on in. I need to get the papers out. Boone will be here soon."

They walked in and sat down at the counsel's table. Hiram ignored them, but Zeke's glower was intended to unnerve them. Morgan paid no attention as she laid out the files and papers. Although she exuded calm, flutters churned in Morgan's stomach and her heart raced. Suzy was looking straight ahead. Morgan didn't know if the encounter with her grandfather or her concern about the hearing or both were weighing on her mind. Morgan was unsettled because she wanted to impress Boone. This was the first case that she had worked from start to finish. She consulted him, and he reviewed her filings, but he was going to let her set out their positions today. The main reason, though, was that she didn't want to let Suzy down. Morgan wasn't fond of Zeke and the way he treated Suzy.

A couple of minutes later, Boone sauntered in and bent close and spoke to Suzy. She smiled. He sat at the table beside Morgan, and they whispered for a couple of minutes. Zeke looked surprised and leaned toward Hiram, "Who's that?"

"That's Boone Carter. He's also one of her attorneys."

Zeke frowned. He didn't know another attorney would be there, especially one who wore confidence like a second skin.

Judge Bergmann entered and sat down behind the bench. After the preliminaries, he looked at the attorneys. "I've read the pleadings in this case. We'll have opening position statements, and then you can call your witnesses. Mr. Tysdale, since you filed claiming that your client is entitled to this property, you'll start."

"Thank you, Your Honor. Tony and Ruby Pinkston bought this land from Tony's uncle, Earl Pinkston. Earl and my client are brothers. This property has been in the Pinkston family for over a hundred years. That's why Earl called Mr. Pinkston here when he decided to sell it. He knew the importance of it staying in the family. There are several things here, Your Honor. The first is that Mr. Pinkston here loaned his son, Tony, the money to buy that property. He never got a chance to repay his father, because he died along with his wife, Ruby, and their son, Aaron. Since the loan hasn't been paid off, Mr. Pinkston has a claim to this property. His granddaughter doesn't have money to pay back the loaned amount, but that wouldn't matter anyway. Mr. Pinkston has an ownership interest, your Honor, and Mr. Pinkston is entitled to the property, not Ms. Pinkston here.

"Tony's bank statements show that leading up to the first payment on the property, he didn't have enough money to make that payment. But right before it was time to close on the sale when Tony needed the money, cash was deposited for the exact amount due. Now, we know money doesn't grow on trees. It doesn't magically appear out of hats. No, the reason the money showed up in Tony's checking account is that—according to my client's affidavit and the hand-written note attached to our filing—my client loaned him that amount. That didn't happen for just the first payment, it happened again for the second payment a year later.

Tony didn't have enough money in his checking account to make either payment. Where did he get it? There's only one logical conclusion, and that is what my client said. He loaned him the money. Not for just part of the payment; he gave him the full payment. Tony never repaid any of it. Not because he didn't intend to. He died. But, the bottom line is that my client paid the full amount for the property, he never received any repayment, so he is entitled to full ownership of the property.

"Another thing is that it was clearly Tony's intent that Zeke have this property. Tony Pinkston would never have wanted this property to pass outside the family. If this young woman here gets the property, who knows what she might do with it. Rather than Ms. Pinkston moving back over with her grandfather and the rest of her family, she's living here with her grandmother on her mother's side. She's got a young child and not even married. They don't understand the importance of keeping this property in the Pinkston family. That's what Tony Pinkston would want—for this property to stay in the family, and his wishes should be honored."

Hiram sat down, and the judge looked at Boone. "Okay, Counsel. I guess you have a response."

Boone stood up. "Your Honor. My co-counsel on this case is Morgan Ramirez. She is going to address this Court."

"Very well. Ms. Ramirez."

"Thank you, Your Honor. As she got wound up, Suzy thought she must have majored in theater.

Standing before the judge, Morgan had a presence about her. Boone seemed to be enjoying the show. "Yes, Your Honor. First, I want to apologize that I plan to use Mr. Tysdale's client's first name, Zeke, throughout my argument. There are several people who have the same last name, and I don't want to be confusing. If that is okay with Your Honor."

Judge Bergmann nodded, "Proceed, Counsel."

"From the outset, let the record reflect that the checking account that Mr. Tysdale kept referring to was a joint account held by my client's parents, Ruby and Tony. Now, let's take Mr. Tysdale's last point first. If Tony Pinkston felt as strongly about this land staying with Zeke as Mr. Tysdale claims, he could have written a will, but he didn't. Not only that, Tony didn't own that land alone. Ruby Pinkston, my client's mother, was also listed on the deed. Tony and Ruby owned it together. If something had happened to Tony before Ruby died, she would have owned the property and could have done with it whatever she wanted.

"Now, let's take Mr. Tysdale's second claim that his client loaned Tony money to buy that property and he hasn't been repaid, so he's entitled to it. There's no evidence whatsoever to support that claim. We've been through the bank records for Tony and Ruby. There is no record of a transaction that Zeke Pinkston gave them money. There are no checks from Zeke, there is no wire transfer from Zeke, there is no paper trail at all that shows Zeke gave them money to buy the property."

Hiram jumped up, "That's not true, Judge. If you look at Tony and Ruby's checking account, it shows sums deposited in their account right before they made the first and second payments to Earl Pinkston. That's why there is that handwritten note made by Zeke Pinkston that I attached to my initial pleading. It shows that he loaned them the money."

Morgan said, "Mr. Tysdale, I didn't interrupt you. I was getting ready to address that."

Hiram sat down. "I'm glad Mr. Tysdale raised that, Your Honor. There is no trail leading back to that money coming from Zeke. They haven't shown a withdrawal from Zeke's bank that matches that amount, because he doesn't have a bank account. During depositions, he refused to tell me where he kept his money."

Judge Bergmann turned to look at Hiram, who dodged the judge's keen eyes by looking down at his pad, "and that may be because there wasn't enough money. So, how can we possibly believe he gave Tony and Ruby money? Other than what he tells us, and we don't even know when he wrote that note. There's no record whatsoever. Not a notary or anything. It could have been right before they filed this claim."

Hiram jumped up. "I object to this. She's claiming that my client made up the whole thing and that this note isn't genuine."

"Counsel, let her finish, and then we'll sort this out."

The judge turned back to Morgan. "Anything else, Counsel?"

"Yes, I don't mean to impugn Tony's reputation, but it's no secret that he and his brother, Ray Pinkston, and cousin, Victor Shultz, sold illegal drugs—meth and marijuana. They had a large operation, and we have included the details of the scope of that illegal drug operation in our brief. Their operations were large enough to supply meth in the surrounding area, capable of raising more than the price paid for this property. We can all imagine that he wasn't going to put the funds from those illegal drug operations in the bank account! We don't know where he kept that money hidden, but he sure didn't deposit it in a bank account where it would raise questions with the authorities. I submit he used that cash that he had hidden away to pay for this property. There is no formal contract between Zeke and Tony and Ruby, no filed lien, nothing to support Zeke's claim."

Hiram lumbered out of his chair again, "Your Honor. Of course there was no lien. Zeke didn't need a lien. This was between family."

"Your Honor. Earl and Ruth filed a lien against the property when they signed to sell the property to Tony and Ruby. That lien wasn't removed until Tony and Ruby made the second payment, which was when the full purchase price was made. That transaction was between family members, Pinkston family members on both sides, and there was a lien. We have attached an affidavit to our brief, signed under oath by Earl and Ruth Pinkston. They were the property owners who sold it to Tony and Ruby. Earl is not in good health, and Ruth, his wife, doesn't like to leave him for long periods, or they would be here. In that affidavit, they say that they only dealt with Tony and Ruby in the transaction, that neither Tony nor Ruby ever mentioned getting money from anyone to buy this property. They specifically state that they had no knowledge or had any reason to believe that Zeke loaned or gave money to Tony or Ruby to buy this property."

Hiram jumped up again, "That's because it was strictly between Zeke and Tony. There was no reason for them to know that Zeke loaned them the money. It wasn't their business."

Morgan brushed him off. She knew he was attempting to break her concentration, but his disruptions did not sidetrack her. She continued, "But, Judge, more on point and more dispositive than all of that. Ms. Pinkston here is Tony and Ruby's sole remaining child. There is no will. By law, she is the sole heir and entitled to full ownership of this property."

Morgan sat, and Hiram rose. "The intent of Tony Pinkston was for this property to stay in the family. In fact, that was the intent of all the Pinkstons. That is why his uncle, Earl Pinkston, called Zeke when he was ready to sell it to see if he wanted to buy it. Tony stepped forward. If he was here today, he would tell you that my client is entitled to it because he loaned him the money, but more important, it is Pinkston land. It's been in the family for generations. This property rightfully belongs to Zeke. If his granddaughter wants to be part of it, she could move over there with the rest of her family. Zeke will see that she and her child are provided for, but Tony would want this property to stay in the family.

Judge Bergmann looked at Hiram. "Counsel, you say that Tony would have wanted the property to stay in the family. Is there something I'm missing?"

"What do you mean?" asked Hiram.

"Ms. Ramirez and Mr. Carter's client—isn't her last name, 'Pinkston'?"

Chapter 48

C.P. and Grayson had discussed a backup plan for C.P. taking control of the railroad in the event they ran into insurmountable headwinds at the agency in Washington. In some ways, the fallback plan had been C.P.'s preferred approach, but he wanted to test the waters on possibly purchasing the WVB&C to see who might oppose the deal as well as what issues might be raised. Had he felt that the situation was amendable for him to buy the railroad, he would have moved forward with doing so, but now, the writing was on the wall. He didn't want to waste nearly a year trying to get regulatory approvals that might not happen.

C.P. said, "I've decided to make the alternative proposal to the city. Because the number of issues will be fewer and less intrusive, the commission should approve the application quicker. We should have everything in place in plenty of time for when the lease lapses."

"Any reason to think the city will be opposed to leasing it to you?" Grayson asked.

"There shouldn't be. The major discussion with them will be the payment arrangement, which I think is fair to both parties. I don't want to take a chance that the OMVX will undercut me. I can show them why it is a fair proposal based on projections and other data. I will discuss my proposal with the city attorney and the council members themselves. I'm going to talk to Bri first though to make sure she is on board. I'll set up a corporation and enter into another one-hundred-year lease. If the corporation defaults, the railroad will revert back to the city. The city will have representation on the board of directors—one chosen by the mayor and one selected by the city council. That will give the city two seats on the board of directors. There will be full transparency to the city. An annual report will be submitted to the city by an independent CPA firm detailing the accounting and finances. One more thing—if the corporation ever decides to cease operations, the city has the option to take control and continue operations. If they don't exercise that option, I've proposed a fair sharing mechanism for the salvage value."

"What about the union agreement?"

"Well, it's the same as we discussed for the ownership proposal. We are going to streamline the operations and implement new technology. I won't need as many workers, but the buyout provisions are comparable to what other railroads have done. That will depend on the employee's status as a 'new hire.'"

"That guy was going to fight you every step of the way. I'm glad you had a Plan B. So, what's the timing?" asked Grayson.

"I'd like to get the city council approval before Christmas and then file with the Federal

Railroad and Surface Commission soon after New Year's. What do you think?"

"That works. I'll go ahead and get a junior attorney drafting this new application. Like you said, it will be easier to get through the Federal Railroad and Surface Commission, because it doesn't involve the transfer of ownership. OMVX will still file its protests, but our position is pro-competition where their position amounts to limiting competition. I like our odds on that one. Since a lease arrangement is replacing another lease, opposing parties will have fewer issues to attack."

"Okay, I'll let you know the terms once I get them worked out with the city. Let's plan for a filing in early January."

Cheryl had met Earl and Ruth Pinkston when she first returned to Bekbourg nearly two years ago during her investigation into the deaths of Earl's nephew, Tony Pinkston, and his family. Since that time, she had not seen either of them. For that reason, she was surprised when Ruth called her and asked if she would come by and talk with them. The anxiety in Ruth's voice signaled that the invite was intended to be more than a casual visit. She heard Earl coughing in the background. Cheryl said she could stop by the following day. After she hung up, Cheryl was curious as to the urgency she had detected during their short phone conversation.

Chapter 49

Arlo knocked on Sean's door, "Hey, Chief. Can I talk to you about something?"

"Sure, Arlo. Have a seat. What is it?"

"I was talking to some people. One of the men got to talking about the annual Turkey Shoot that Koot's sponsors every year. It's a big regional event for this area. It's been around for about a hundred years. They used to set loose a flock of turkeys for people to shoot at, but they stopped doing that a long time ago. Now, they set up targets. They have different levels of competition, starting with the teenage group. This year, the man who won the purse for winning the longest shot was Rocky Pinkston. That's the second year in a row that he has won it. According to the man I was talking to, it was two-hundred-fifty yards."

"So, he could have made the shot against me and easily against Mike."

"Sure could have. There's something else that I thought you'd find interesting. Kyle participates almost every year, too. This year, he came in third in the long distance competition."

"That means he also could have made both shots." Sean was silent for a couple of minutes. "There's something I've been trying to put my finger on. The final straw in me deciding to execute a warrant against Cooper was when Mack told me he heard Cooper sounding off at Knucklepin's one night about me and Mike. He said that everyone near the bar area would have heard him. Something else he told me was the Kyle and Rocky were sitting at the bar, so they would have heard Cooper.

"Mack was off the next day, so it was two days later that he told me about Cooper's ranting. That would have given either Kyle or Rocky enough time to plant that gun on Cooper's property. Hell, for all I know, they may be in on this together. Both the Pinkstons and Kyle have motives and the means to carry out the shootings." Sean paused. "It's time we see if we can find any evidence. Arlo, we need warrants for both Kyle and the Pinkstons. I may need to get the state police involved, but I'm going to call Tyler and ask him about getting a warrant in Tapsaw County. I'll also get one for Kyle's place. Find Alex and tell him that we need to be ready. We'll execute the search warrant at Kyle's place this afternoon. We may have to wait until tomorrow to search the Pinkston place since we don't have enough daylight. Get Syd lined up as well."

"Will do."

Sean had just laid down the phone's receiver after talking to Tyler about the warrants when Kim walked up to his door. "Boss, Irma Ritter just called. I've never heard her like this. She's in a real state and insisted on you coming out right away. Something about John Pawley, but I don't know what. She needs to talk to you as soon as possible. She insisted you come. She wouldn't even wait for you to get off the phone. She just hung up."

Since he had the background with Irma and Pawley and she was insisting that he personally come, he had time to drive out there and get back while the warrants and deputy assignments were being finalized.

"Okay. I better go see what's happened."

"I hope it is okay with you," Kim said. "I'd like to leave about an hour early. The custodian at our church died of a heart attack this morning. I'd like to get home and make some food for his family and go by and see them before it gets too late."

"Sure, Kim. That's fine. I'm sorry to hear about that."

"He's going to be missed. He was there a long time. He was so kind, and everyone in the church knew him. He was there whenever the church doors were open."

"Let me know if there is anything I can do."

As he drove toward Irma's, Sean was thinking that something was going to have to give between Pawley and Irma. He thought he had mediated a solution, but it obviously hadn't worked.

Sean got out of his cruiser and walked up the couple of steps to Irma's porch. He knocked, but she didn't answer. He knocked louder. When she didn't respond, he rapped harder and shouted, "Mrs. Ritter. It's Sheriff Neumann."

He felt a gun barrel press against the back of his head. “She’s not able to come to the door, Sheriff,” a voice behind him growled. “I’m going to take your gun. Don’t make any moves, or I’ll blow your damn head off.” The gun remained solidly thrust against his head as he felt his gun removed from his holster and tossed off the side of the porch. “Now, slowly. Off the porch. We’re going ’round back.”

Sean was surprised, “Mack, what are you doing?”

“Shut up. Don’t think of trying any tricks.”

As they slowly started to descend the steps, Sean asked, “What did you do to Mrs. Ritter?”

“None of your concern, Sean. You should worry about yourself.”

Mack still held the gun tight to his head. Sean knew his plan was to kill him once they got around back. If he could keep him talking, he might find a way to escape his control.

“Why are you doing this, Mack?”

“Ben used to talk about how you waltzed right back after being gone for twenty years and took over the department—even though you weren’t the sheriff. He was right. Then you got Mike to recommend you for interim sheriff when he decided to retire. You treat people like shit. You drove Ben to try to kill you, you fired Kyle, you got Mike pushed out. Now, you demote me. Well, I ain’t goin’ to let that happen. I should have been named sheriff. I could have finished out my time as sheriff and retired. Because of you, I’m about bankrupt, and my wife is probably goin’ to leave me.”

They were still standing in the front yard—Sean hoping to keep him distracted as long as he could. "I didn't fire you, Mack. I could have. I had lots of information, but I didn't."

"What information?"

"Well, for one. Your being on the payroll at the paper plant as a security consultant—what was that all about?"

Mack paused, wondering how Sean knew that. "That's none of your business."

"You were working for the Thompsons. It was the Thompsons that insisted Mike hire you as his assistant. Why was that, Mack? Were you giving them inside information from the department? Reporting on Mike? What was that all about?"

"Move." Mack shoved the gun barrel hard into Sean's head, but Sean didn't budge.

"Were you involved in Ben's scheme to steal guns from people he pulled over?" When Mack didn't answer, Sean continued, "You knew about it. You even bought some from him, didn't you?"

"Not all of them."

Sean took a gamble, "I know about the Remington that Ben stole several years ago on a DUI. That's one of the guns you bought from him."

Mack didn't respond. Sean couldn't see his face. Mack shoved the gun harder into the back of Sean's head causing Sean to wrench in pain. "If you don't move, I'm going to kill you right here."

"Okay, Mack, but why not tell me about the Remington? Why kill Mike?"

"That rotten SOB. He treated me like shit. I was his assistant, but he never included me in anything. Then, the 'Big Man'—you—come back, and he gives you all the cases. Sets you up to be in line for sheriff. He recommends you over me when he retires. Hell, if he'd recommended me instead of you for sheriff, I'd be the sheriff now! Not you! He had it coming. With you out of the way, I'll be the next sheriff, because I have more experience than all those punk deputies combined. Hell, when I told him I wanted to get certified for a SWAT team, he laughed and asked what we needed that for. This is the last time I'm saying it. Move!" as he rammed the gun into the back of Sean's head jerking it forward." Sean grunted as pain racked through his head.

"DROP THE GUN, DEPUTY! NOW!" someone yelled at the top of his voice—startling Mack.

When Mack flinched, Sean's military training kicked in. In a split second, he evaded the gun, turned and threw Mack to the ground, overpowering him. He looked up to see Pawley still with a gun pointing in their direction. "John, grab my gun. He threw it off the side of the porch."

John relaxed his gun stance and brought Sean's gun to him. Sean was in the process of securing Mack's hands.

"Where's the old biddy?" Pawley asked with concern.

As Sean continued to bind Mack, he shook his head, "I don't know. Go check inside."

Pawley hurried inside and found Irma tied to a kitchen chair with her mouth gagged. As he started to untie the gag, he asked, "Woman, are you okay?"

When he removed the gag, she exhaled, "At least you've got some clothes on today."

He continued to untie the rope, "It sounds like you're alright, Irma."

"How'd you know my name?"

"It's been all over those complaints over the years."

Sean hoped John's delay in coming outside didn't bode ill for Irma, but he figured if she was injured or dead, John would already have returned. He rushed to the cruiser and called the dispatcher.

After making the call, he saw John and Irma walk down the steps. "Mr. Pawley here rescued me, Sheriff. I'm sorry about calling like that asking you to come up here, but he forced me," she said pointing to Mack.

Sean didn't think Irma looked any worse for wear, but he was concerned about her. "Are you okay, Irma? I can have the medics take you to the hospital. I think you should be checked out."

"I'm fine, Sheriff. I don't need to be checked out. I can't wait to tell my Sunday school class about this."

"John, how did you happen to be here?"

"I was up on the hill and saw the deputy's car and then yours drive by. I was wondering if something had happened here and walked down to see."

"I'm sure glad you did."

Chapter 50

Mack's wife answered the door. "Ma'am, I'm Sheriff Neumann, and I have with me a warrant to search your premises. I'm asking you to please have a seat. Deputy Johnson here will sit with you while we search."

Her face reddened. "What in the world is this all about? Where is Mack? You don't have any right to search our place. Mack is a deputy."

"Ma'am, if you don't have a seat over there and let us in, I'll arrest you."

She huffed and stomped over to the sofa and sat down. "This is outrageous." She saw Arlo start to open the china cabinet doors. "Don't touch my things!" When Arlo ignored her and continued to look though the cabinet, she screeched, "Be careful! Those things will break! They're worth a lot of money!"

Finally, when Arlo moved into the kitchen where she couldn't see him, she stopped shrieking, but her protests continued.

Sean found the bedroom where Mack kept his guns. He found a half-filled box of 308 Winchester shells. The gun cabinet contained five rifles, and a mounted rack held two large hunting rifles. An expensive scope—complete with a laser—had been found in Mack's vehicle.

After the search was complete, the deputies, except for Syd, went to the front yard to wait on Sean. Arlo said to Alex, "Can you believe this? I never suspected Mack."

"Me neither."

"Why the hell do you think he tried to frame Cooper? I don't see how that did anything to help him."

"I've been thinking about that," Alex said. "Remember when the sheriff threatened to turn the investigation over to the state police?"

"Yeah."

"Well, he knew they had a lot more manpower and money so he may have thought they could turn up something, so he decided to get us distracted by framing Cooper. The sheriff said that Mack told him about overhearing Cooper making incriminating statements at Knucklepin's. The sheriff thinks he reported it, hoping to prompt us to search Cooper's place, which we did. Mack probably bought the Remington from Ben years ago when Ben stole it. Anyway, with Cooper charged with killing Mike, Mack planned to find the right time to kill the sheriff. If he somehow overheard that the case against Cooper was falling apart, he may have rushed things. You know how he was always lurking around the station."

"Why do you think Mack went to Mrs. Ritter's house and lured the sheriff there?" Arlo asked.

"Mack's not talking, but the sheriff thinks he was planning to set John Pawley up to take the fall. He was going to make it look like Pawley was the one that framed Cooper and killed Mike, Mrs. Ritter and Sean. He planned to frame Pawley by killing Mrs. Ritter because she was always complaining about him, and Mike and the sheriff because they were invading Mader Valley or they had harassed him about Mrs. Ritter or something. Who knows exactly what he was thinking, but that seems to have been his strategy."

"Do you think that's why we found the scope in Mack's vehicle?" asked Arlo.

"Yeah. I think after he killed Sean and Mrs. Ritter, he was going to plant the scope in Pawley's truck or somewhere."

"Jeez. How crazy. If it hadn't been for that mountain man, the sheriff might be dead."

"I know. It was a close call."

Sean returned to the living room, where Syd sat silently near Loretta. "Mrs. Harris. We've completed our search. Mack is being held in a cell at the station. He's been charged with several crimes including kidnapping and attempted murder on a police officer and murder of Mike Adams." Loretta sat mute and looked like she was dazed. He continued, "Do you want us to call someone—a friend or family member? We know this is a shock."

She looked at him. "I just don't believe all this is happening. I don't want my friends to see me."

"Who can we call? I don't want to leave you like this."

"My sister lives in Athens. I'll call her."

"Can she drive here to be with you?"

"I'm sure she can, but her husband or son could also come get me."

"Okay, then. Syd will stay here until they arrive."

"I'll call them right now. I want to leave here as soon as I can."

Despite Loretta going into the bedroom and closing the door, Syd could hear Loretta talking to her sister. After telling her that she needed someone to come pick her up as soon as possible, she responded, "It's terrible what's happened. This new sheriff is accusing Mack of killing the old sheriff."

Syd could hear that Loretta was crying. "I can't believe it either. There's no way that Mack would do something like that."

Responding again, "No, I've not talked to him. They've put him in jail. I just need to leave."

Responding after another question, her voice grew more shrill. "Yes, he needs a lawyer. He'll know that for God's sake. He's a policeman. I don't know what I'm going to do, but I can't face people here. I'll be the laughing stock!"

Loretta was near hysterics, which her sister comprehended, because Loretta's next words were, "Okay, I'll get my suitcase packed and be waiting. Hurry. I want to leave as soon as I can before people start calling."

One of the deputies escorted Mack's brother-in-law, Brad, to the visitor's room. Brad sat on one side of the partition, waiting for Mack to be brought in. After a few minutes, the same deputy ushered Mack in from the other side and then stepped right outside the door. Mack glanced at Brad as he sat down. Brad thought, *My God. He looks like an old man.* The transformation from the past summer was startling.

"You doing okay, Mack?"

Mack shrugged but didn't make eye contact.

"You need anything?"

"Naw."

"I drove over to get Loretta and take her to stay with us."

"Yeah, that makes sense."

"Have you talked to her yet?"

"Naw, but I didn't expect to."

"You got a lawyer?"

"Naw."

Brad was a retired police officer. "I'll call the union agent and have him send someone down. They have attorneys who will represent you."

Mack's despondency concerned Brad. "You sure I can't do anything for you? You don't need anything?"

"Naw."

"Okay, Mack. I'll call the police union and take Loretta to Athens. I'll check back in soon. Let me know if there is anything I can do."

When Mack didn't respond, Brad rose to leave. The deputy opened the door, which had been cracked, and said, "Okay, Mack."

Mack eased out of the chair and shuffled out of the room.

Brad asked to speak to Sean. He introduced himself and said, "Sheriff, I've never seen Mack like this. I think you should put him on suicide watch."

"Okay. We'll monitor him."

"Thank you. I'm a retired officer myself. I'm going to ask the union to send a lawyer to represent him."

Brad gave Sean his phone number. "Loretta's going to be in Athens for a while, so this will be the best number to reach someone if you need to."

Sean took the number and looked at it. When Sean didn't say anything, Brad left. Sean continued looking at the number, thinking about Mike and the senselessness of it all.

Chapter 51

Derrick knew Cooper's tendency to lash out and speak before thinking. The last thing he wanted was for the press to go to Cooper's place after he was released and start questioning him. There was no telling what Cooper might say. For that reason, Derrick called Saul Timmers with the local TV station and Cheryl. He informed them that Cooper was being released today, and that he was prepared to talk to the media with Cooper at his side. After this media event, he was instructing Cooper not to talk to the media.

Alex led Derrick to the cell where Cooper was being held. Alex unlocked the door and stepped aside. Derrick said, "Cooper, all charges have been dropped against you for the murder of Mike Adams. Let's go to the conference room here and talk about some things for a minute."

Cooper grabbed a paper grocery sack that contained his few belongings and followed Derrick down the hall. "I told them I was framed. I'm goin' to sue their asses off. They ain't heard the last."

By this time, they had reached the conference room. Alex closed the door, leaving them alone. Derrick asked Cooper to sit down.

"Listen, Cooper. I know that it's been difficult being held like this."

Cooper interrupted, "You're damn right it has been."

Derrick continued. "But, here is something to remember. First, the sheriff didn't stop investigating. He could have, and then instead of walking free, you might have gone to trial. Frankly, I had some things to defend you on, and you might have been acquitted, but you might not have with the gun having been found on your property."

"Yeah, but, it was a frame."

"Yes, it was, but we only know that because Sheriff Neumann didn't give up on the investigation. Now, when they found the gun on your property, and the ballistics came back as a match, he had no choice but to arrest you. This is the most important thing to take away from this, Cooper, and I hope you pay close attention. You need to be careful what you say. You wouldn't have been on Sean's suspect list if you hadn't been saying the things you were saying about Mike and Sean. Then, once the gun was found on your property, you looked guilty. Take this as a learning experience. Don't be saying threatening things against people. It just gets you in trouble."

Cooper didn't say anything, but then, "I'm ready to get out of this shit hole."

"Okay, Cooper. There's one more thing. The press is waiting out front to talk to us."

Cooper sat up straight, "Really?"

"Now, here's what's going to happen. I am going to talk. You are not to contradict anything I say, no matter what you feel. Is that clear?"

"Yeah, but what am I going to say?"

"When I ask you to speak, all you are to say is that you are glad the right person has been arrested; you are sorry for what happened to Mike Adams; and you are ready to go home now and move on with your life. You got that, Cooper?"

Cooper said, "But I want to say that I shouldn't have been arrested in the first place. That they tried to pin something on me like Ben Clark did."

Derrick couldn't allow this. This was exactly the type of talking that would eventually lead Cooper back into a hole again. Derrick came out of his seat like an offensive tackle coming off the scrimmage line on the count, causing Cooper to shrink back so fast his chair scooted backwards. Derrick did not need to shout, because his size made his words sound like a roar. "Absolutely not! You are not to say any of that. I'm trying to get things turned around for you, Cooper. You told me you wanted to find a job. Well, you start talking like that, no one will hire you. This is your chance to look good in the eyes of the community. This is important to your future, Cooper."

Derrick sat back down in his chair, but his stern look never left his face. Cooper was not about to defy the huge man. "So, I'm supposed to say that I'm glad they arrested the right man and that I am sorry the old sheriff was killed. That I'm glad this is behind me and I'm ready to go home?"

"Yes. That's it."

"Okay, but I'd sure like to say more."

"Don't! Let's go outside."

When Derrick and Cooper walked outside, Cheryl was there along with another *Tribune* reporter, and the TV reporter and cameraman moved toward them. Derrick had Cooper standing beside him. Cooper was restless and didn't know what to do with his arms so he put his hands in his pockets. His long hair and facial hair did little to hide his sour and uncomfortable expression. In his resonant voice, Derrick commanded the media's attention. "I'd like to thank the sheriff and his deputies for never giving up on this case."

Derrick heard a murmured groan from Cooper, but he kept speaking. "My client, Mr. Cooper Townsend, always maintained his innocence, and as the investigation results have shown, he *was* innocent. The murder weapon that was found on his property was planted there, we believe, by the man who has now been charged. All charges have been dropped against Mr. Townsend, and he is a free man. While this has most certainly been an inconvenience on Mr. Cooper and his family, justice prevailed. He is ready to return home and move on with his life. Now, Mr. Townsend has a statement to make."

Until that moment, Cooper hadn't thought about being in front of the media like this. People were watching him, waiting for him to say something. He looked at Derrick, who was looking at the minuscule crowd. He fought for his words, not remembering what Derrick told him to say.

People were expectedly looking at him. He finally found some words, "Uh. I agree with what Mr. Compton said. I'm uh sorry about what happened to Sheriff Adams. He was a good man. I'm glad I'm free, and I want to thank Sheriff Neumann."

Cooper looked at Derrick, who had been watching him. Derrick gave a slight nod and turned to address the media. "This is the only statement my client will be making on this matter. Please respect his privacy and do not contact him any further."

Alex was standing off to the side. Derrick steered Cooper toward him. "Mr. Townsend, I'll take you home," Alex said and opened the front passenger door.

Cooper looked surprised. "First time I've ever ridden in the front seat of a police car."

The morning's headline in the *Tribune*:

Cooper Townsend freed of
all chargers in Mike Adams'
murder

Under the headlines, a large photograph showed a smiling Cooper appearing alongside his attorney, Derrick Compton.

Chapter 52

The Legend of Mader Valley: Fact and Fiction – Conclusion
By Cheryl Seton

An elderly citizen in Bekbourg, who has been following my columns on the death of Javis Mader, reached out to me. He told me a story that brings closure to the mystery behind Jarvis Mader's death.

When he was seven years old, he never wanted to go with his grandfather to hunt in Mader Valley. He had heard the legend of the Mader ghost, and he didn't care if there were lots of deer or squirrels or rabbits—he was afraid. His grandfather had little patience for the young boy's unfounded fears, but he still couldn't get him to go to Mader Valley. Finally one day, his grandfather, intoxicated, lost his patience. "Boy, there ain't no damn ghost."

"But Mader died there. It's his ghost 'cause they ain't never found out who killed him. I heard from the boys that his ghost will be there 'cause he don't have no peace.'"

"I swear, boy. That's damn nonsense."

The young boy stood his ground, shaking his head.

His grandfather yanked him by the arm, shaking him. "I know'd who killed him."

"Huh?" He thought his grandfather was telling him a lie just to get him to go hunting in Mader Valley.

"Damnit, boy." He released his arm. "Don't you ev'r breathe a word, but it was me."

The young boy felt like a quake shook beneath his feet.

"You?" he whispered.

As it turns out, his grandfather had set a bear trap in Mader Valley near the creek. When he went to check it out, he discovered that a man had been caught in the trap, and he was nearly dead. His grandfather told him that he didn't recognize the man and that the man was not from around Bekbourg. His grandfather explained that he didn't think the man could be saved, and he didn't want anyone to know that he had set the trap, so he shot him in the head, killing him. He removed the bear trap and buried Jarvis the best he could.

This elderly citizen told me he has carried this insufferable secret with him since he was a young child. Over those years, he tried to ignore that he knew that his grandfather killed Jarvis. He didn't want to bring a taint to his family even though it happened over a hundred years ago. Now, however, his health is failing. As he read these Tribune articles, he knew that if he died before he told someone, the story of Jarvis Mader would go to the grave with him. He hopes that by coming forward, "it will ease his soul before he passes and that it will put to rest the rumors about a ghost. Such a fine man as Jarvis Mader deserves better. He deserves peace."

May Jarvis Mader rest in peace.

Chapter 53

Judge Bergmann was going to rule on her case this morning. As she and Boone and Morgan walked toward the courthouse, Suzy was so jittery, she became nauseous. As soon as they walked inside, she excused herself and rushed to the restroom. She leaned against the sink, telling herself she had to hold it together. She splashed water on her face and reached for a paper towel. As she was drying her face, she looked into the mirror. Her face was pale and her eyes red. She remembered the pep talk Rose gave her this morning before she left to meet her attorneys. "Suzy, it's out of your hands now. You had the best lawyers around. Just go in there and see what the judge has to say. It's not the end of the world if he rules against you. You still have Pete and Tootsie. It'll be okay."

Suzy wiped her face one more time and straightened. She still felt somewhat shaky, but her Ma Maw was right. It would be okay. She threw away the towel and walked into the hall. She looked up to see Zeke ambling toward the men's room. *Oh no, oh no. I don't know if I can handle this.* She braced herself.

"Well, well. I thought you might be back here. I saw that woman lawyer back there."

Suzy eked out, "Hi, Grandpa."

He frowned. "You know, Suzy Girl, it didn't have to be this way 'tween us. You're gettin' ready to learn that you don't go against family. That judge is goin' to rule that property belongs to me, and I don't want you to ever go there again. You hear me?"

Before Suzy could respond, Morgan came hustling up. "Come on, Suzy. Let's go. We need to go see if Boone has anything he wants to discuss." She gently took Suzy's arm and steered her away, leaving Zeke scowling as he watched them move away.

Morgan was reassuring as they walked into the courtroom. Suzy sat down at the table between Morgan and Boone and stared straight ahead. Rose's words kept trumping Zeke's as her mind raced.

Finally, Judge Bergmann entered the courtroom, and the call-to-order was issued. After the preliminaries, Judge Bergmann looked at both counsel tables. Suzy felt any remaining color drain from her face as she now knew why he was called the "hanging judge." His eyes were cold and his features severe. She grabbed hold of the table's edge for stability. Morgan glanced at her, but Suzy continued staring toward the judge.

"Mr. Pinkston, there is one thing that I don't like in my courtroom and that's a bully. From the minute you walked into this court—that is what I was looking at. The law doesn't support your claim in any way. You had no evidence to back up your claim of lending money to your son. It was a tragedy for your family, but especially for Ms.

Pinkston here, that her parents were killed like they were. You have compounded the tragedy with your insistence that you are entitled to this land. There are no liens on the property. There are no liens on Tony and Ruby Pinkston filed with this court. The law is very clear. Suzy Pinkston is the sole remaining heir and the sole owner of this property." He turned toward Boone and Morgan, "I assume you will handle filing the necessary paperwork to get the deed transferred into Ms. Pinkston's name and any other necessary filings and paperwork?"

Boone glanced toward Morgan, and she stood. "Yes, Your Honor."

"Case dismissed." He banged the gavel.

Chapter 54

Sean pulled up in Pawley's drive. Baby charged from around the back of the house growling and barking as he lunged from the other side of the chain-linked fence toward Sean's cruiser. Sean stepped out of his cruiser looking for Pawley. Sean noticed a set of empty plastic food containers sitting on a table on the porch. Pawley came from around the house and yelled a command. Baby stopped his aggression and sat down, but he eyed Sean with deep suspicion.

"Hi, Sheriff. What brings you up here?"

"Got something for you. You buy yourself a collection of plastic food storage containers?"

"Christmas has come early for me. The old biddy stopped by with some food. I guess she thinks I saved her. Best food I can ever remember eating. I cleaned her dishes so I can give them to her. She even brought Baby some dog bones. Baby thinks of her as his best friend."

Sean thought, *That's good news. Maybe Irma won't be calling about Pawley again.* "That's good. Hope you and she have put your differences behind you."

"Well, I'm not going to stop walking my perimeter, but I do try to hide when I hear her car coming. I'm glad it has a loud muffler."

"She's not honking before she drives by?"

Pawley looked confused. "No, why?"

"Just wondering," Sean said as he hid a grin. "I'm glad you were there the other day, John. I don't know if it would have turned out so good for me or Irma either."

John just looked at him.

Sean handed a brown paper bag to Pawley. "Take care, John. When you come into town, stop by and see me." Sean nodded toward the paper bag, "I enjoyed this. Semper Fi."

"Semper Fi, Sean."

After Sean drove away, Pawley opened the bag and pulled out a book authored by G. Keb. He looked at the book. "Let's go in, Baby." The dog bounded ahead and waited for him to open the door. Baby zipped in and flopped on his pile of quilts near the fireplace. Pawley walked over to a large wooden desk. Above the desk were shelves still supporting several empty spaces. He laid the book on the desk and looked up at the shelf of seventeen draft books authored by G. Keb. Five sat ready for publication, but despite the publisher's urgings, Pawley had never given his final approval. The publisher was unaware that twelve others had been completed.

When Lucky called Sean to tell him about Pawley's war record, he told Sean about Pawley being an author writing under the pen name, G. Keb. Sean recognized the name. Unknown to anyone around Bekbourg, the novel that many people around Bekbourg were reading, the novel that Cheryl had reviewed in her break-out column in the *Tribune* for book reviews, was authored by John Pawley.

Cooper opened the door of his mobile home and peered warily at Sean. "Now what?" he squawked as he looked past Sean to see if there were other deputies. "What are you here to blame me 'bout this time?"

"Cooper, put on a coat and step outside. I'm not here to accuse you of anything. I want to talk to you about a possible job."

Cooper was surprised. "I'll be right back."

Shortly, he came through the door and said as he was thrusting his arm through the sleeve, "What's this 'bout a job?"

"Cooper, I was talking with Father O'Brady at the small catholic church downtown. His custodian passed away of a heart attack. He had been there a long time. Now Father O'Brady needs a good man to replace him. It requires a lot of different skills. You would be kind of like his right hand man as far as the building goes. I thought you might try it out during the winter and see how it works out. He really wants to meet you. I have scheduled you a meeting tomorrow at 9:30 at the church to talk to him. He is familiar with your situation, and that is not a problem for him. He'd really like to talk to you."

Cooper didn't react. It was as if he didn't believe Sean.

"Here's his name and address and the time," Sean said as he handed him the paper.

"Okay, Sheriff." Cooper reverently stared at the slip of paper as Sean turned to leave.

The city council voted in favor of entering into a lease agreement with C.P. to keep the WVB&C running. Citizens and businesses were supportive. C.P. was quoted in the *Tribune* saying that he was optimistic that the lease arrangement would be approved by the regulatory agency in D.C., because it was similarly structured to the original lease and there were fewer issues for the commission to address since it was not an ownership transfer. He added that the city had a right to operate the railroad in a way that was in its best interest. The application would be filed in January.

Every year for as long as people remembered, many people throughout Bekbourg, regardless of their faith or affiliation, attended a Christmas Eve candlelight service at the downtown catholic church. As Sean looked out over those in attendance, he saw C.P. and Mary, the railroaders and their significant others, deputies, Danny, Sally and Drew Chambers, Milton and Martha, his parents and many others from the county and city offices. He and Cheryl stood beside Kye and Geri and her children. As he looked forward, he did a double take. Hustling around the sanctuary was a lanky man with hair cut short and no facial hair. He wore a pair of jeans with a worn plaid sports coat and tie. He was working to get the candleholders in place. Sean noticed that when Father O'Brady entered, he looked around the sanctuary and then turned a warm smile on the man who looked unsure about his work. When he saw the priest nod his approval, a smile brightened Cooper Townsend's face. Sean reached over and took Cheryl's hand and gently squeezed. They looked at each other and smiled.

ABOUT THE AUTHOR

Sherrie Rutherford lives on Florida's Gulf Coast and has ties to Ohio, East Tennessee and Houston. She and Larry love traveling, hiking (especially in the Great Smoky Mountains), and playing Bridge. She is a retired attorney. Her passion for Appalachia and railroad history inspired the Bekbourg County Series.

Sherrie's website
http://www.sherrierutherford.com

Follow Sherrie on Facebook
Sherrie Rutherford – "Author"

Made in the USA
Middletown, DE
05 February 2023

23978589R00229